PENGUIN BOOKS

LIVIA

Lawrence Durrell was born in the Himalayas in India in 1912 but grew up in England and Corfu. He has been a Foreign Service press officer in Athens, Cairo, Cyprus, and Belgrade, and he has worked at many things—once even performing as a nightclub pianist—in addition to the writing that has made him one of the most distinguished contemporary men of letters. His published works include poetry, essays, and novels. *Livia* is the second book in Mr. Durrell's "quincunx," a cluster of five novels, *The Avignon Quintet*. The first and third books, *Monsieur* and *Constance*, are also published by Penguin Books; the fourth, *Sebastian*, has recently been published by The Viking Press. Penguin Books also publishes Lawrence Durrell's *The Dark Labyrinth*, *The Greek Islands*, *Nunquam*, *Reflections on a Marine Venus*, *Sicilian Carousel*, and *Tunc*.

By Lawrence Durrell

NOVELS
Monsieur
Livia
Constance
Sebastian
The Alexandria Quartet:
Justine, Balthazar, Mountolive, Clea
The Revolt of Aphrodite:
Tunc, Nunquam
The Black Book
The Dark Labyrinth

TRAVEL
The Greek Islands
Sicilian Carousel
Bitter Lemons
Reflections on a Marine Venus
Prospero's Cell

POETRY
Collected Poems
Selected Poems
Vega
The Ikons

DRAMA
Sappho

LETTERS AND ESSAYS
Literary Lifelines: The Richard Aldington–
Lawrence Durrell Correspondence
Spirit of Place (edited by Alan G. Thomas)
Lawrence Durrell and Henry Miller:
A Private Correspondence

HUMOUR
Sauve Qui Peut
Stiff Upper Lip
Esprit de Corps
The Best of Antrobus

FOR YOUNG PEOPLE
White Eagles Over Serbia

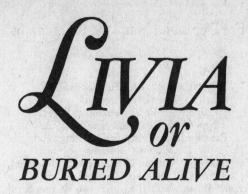

LIVIA
or
BURIED ALIVE

LAWRENCE DURRELL

PENGUIN BOOKS

For Denis and Nanik de Rougemont

Penguin Books Ltd, Harmondsworth,
Middlesex, England
Penguin Books, 40 West 23rd Street,
New York, New York 10010, U.S.A.
Penguin Books Australia Ltd, Ringwood,
Victoria, Australia
Penguin Books Canada Limited, 2801 John Street,
Markham, Ontario, Canada L3R 1B4
Penguin Books (N.Z.) Ltd, 182–190 Wairau Road,
Auckland 10, New Zealand

First published in Great Britain by
Faber & Faber Ltd 1978
First published in the United States of America by
The Viking Press 1979
Published in Penguin Books 1984
Reprinted 1984

LIBRARY OF CONGRESS CATALOGING IN PUBLICATION DATA
Durrell, Lawrence.
Livia, or, Buried alive.
I. Title.
[PR6007.U76L5   1984]   823'.912   83-23618
ISBN 0 14 00.7101 6

Printed in the United States of America by
R. R. Donnelley & Sons Company, Harrisonburg, Virginia
Set in Fournier

Contents

"In the name of the Dog the Father, Dog the Son, and Dog the Wholly Ghost, Amen. Here beginneth the second lesson."

"Between the completely arbitrary and the completely determined perhaps there is a way?"

"Five colours mixed make people blind."

Chinese Proverb

ONE

A Certain Silence

WHEN THE NEWS OF TU'S DEATH REACHED BLANFORD he was actually living in her house in Sussex, watching the first winter snow fall out of a dark sky, amidst darker woods, which had long since engulfed an ochre sunset. "Actually", because his own version of the event will be slightly different, both for the sake of posterity and also on stylistic grounds. A deep armchair sheltered his back from the draughts which, despite the rippling oak fire burning in the grate, played about the old-fashioned, high-ceilinged room with its tapering musicians' gallery. His crutches lay beside him on the carpet. As he put down the swan-necked telephone he felt the knowledge boom inside him, as if in some great tropical conch – the bang of surf upon white beaches on the other side of the world. She would miss reading (the selfishness of writers!) all the new material he had added to his book – a novel about another novelist called Sutcliffe, who had become almost as real to him and to Tu as he, Blanford, was to himself. He took the handkerchief from his sleeve and dabbed his dry lips – dry from the eternal cigar he needed to bite on when he worked. Then he went swaying to the looking-glass over the bookcase and stared at himself for a good moment. The telephone-bell gave a smart trill and a click – long-distance calls always did this: like the last spurt of blood from an artery. The writer stared on, imagining that he was Tu looking back at him. So this is what she saw, what she had always seen! Eye to eye and mind to mind – this is how it had been with them. He suddenly realised that he was surrounded by the dead woman's books. Underlinings, annotations. She was still here!

He felt his image suddenly refreshed and recreated by her death – the new information was so terrifying, so hard to assimilate. Goodness, there was still so much they had to tell each other – and now all that remained was a mass of severed threads, the loose ends of unfinished conversation. From now on there would be nobody to whom he could really talk. He made a grimace and sighed. Well then, he must lock up all this passionate and enriching conversation in his skull. All morning he had played on the old pipe-organ, glad to find that his memory and his fingers still worked. There is nothing like music in an empty house. Then the telephone-bell. Now the thought of Tu. It is no use really – for once you die you slide into the ground and simply melt. For a while a few personal scraps hang around – like shoes and clothes and unused notepaper with abandoned phone numbers. As if suddenly one had had a hunger for greater simplicity.

Outside children chirped as they skated on the frozen lake. Stones skidded and twanged on the ice. How would his hero Sutcliffe take the news, he wondered? Should he make him whimper in the novel like some ghastly dog? Last night in bed he had read some pages of the Latin poet Tu most loved; it was like sleeping beside her. The phrase came to him: "The steady thudding of the Latin line echoes the thud of her heart. I hear her calm voice uttering the words." There were flies in the room, hatched by the heating. They seemed to be reading Braille. The treble voices outside were marginal. What good were books except to hive off regrets? His back ached all of a sudden – his spine seemed as stiff as a flagpole. He was an ageing war-hero with a spine full of lead.

He wished his own turn would come soon. From now on they could label him "Not Wanted On Voyage" or just "Unaccompanied Luggage" – and sling him into the hold, into the grave. In his mind he gave a great cry of loneliness, but no sound came. It was a shrill galactic cry of a solitary planet whirling through space. Tu had loved walking naked about the house in Italy, she had no sense of misdemeanour, reciting aloud the 16th Psalm. She said once, "It is terrible, but life is on nobody's side."

So the Sutcliffe he invented for his novel *Monsieur* shot himself through the mirror in the early version? "I had to," he explained, pointing to Blanford. "It was him or me." The writer Blanford suddenly felt like an enormously condensed version of a minor epic. Buried alive! The crutches hurt him under the arms. He groaned and swore as he dragged himself about the room.

The consolations of art are precious few. He always had a sneaking fear that what he wrote was too private to reach a reader. Stilted and stunted, the modern product – meagre as spittle or sperm, the result of too rigorous pot-training by his mother who had a thirst for purity. The result was retention of faecal matter – a private prose and verse typical of the modern sphincterine artist. In ordinary life this basic refusal to co-operate with the universe, to surrender, to give, would in its final stage amount to catatonia! In the "acute" wards at Leatherhead they had one twilight catatonic who could be suspended by his coat-collar – suspended by a meat-hook and hung on a bar where he stayed, softly swinging in the foetal position. Like a bat, dreaming his amniotic dreams, lulled in the imaginary mother-fluid. It was all that was left of a once good poet. The whole of his life had been spent in creative constipation, a refusal to give, so now he went on living like this – a life in inverted comas, to coin a pun. Blanford reached out and touched the earlier manuscript of his book *Monsieur*. He had given it to Tu and she had had it bound. He wondered where in his imagination, which was his real life, Sutcliffe might be – he would have liked to talk to him. Last heard of in Oxford, famous for his work on his friend's study of the Templar heresy. Blanford's last communication from him had been a cryptic postcard which said: "An Oxford don can be distinguished among all others by the retractable foreskin."

He risked another thought of Tu again and suddenly felt as if he were running a temperature. Breathless, he rose and succeeded in unfastening the French window, to let in a cloud of snowflakes and a rush of cold air. Then, bending his head, he lurched out on to the lawn, watching his breath plume out before him. He rubbed a little snow on his temples with a theatrical gesture. Then he laboriously returned to his fireside seat and his thoughts.

Cade now sidled into the room with the tea things and set them down beside him without a word, his yellow puritanical face set in expressions of fervent concentration such as one only sees on the faces of very stupid but cunning people. He bore in his arms with a kind of meek pride the new orthopaedic waistcoat-brace which had at last arrived from the makers, tailored to size. There was a good hope that this contrivance might allow Blanford one day to throw away his crutches. He gave an exclamation of pleasure while Cade, expressionless as a mandarin, helped him off with the ancient tweed coat he so loved (with its leather-patched elbows) and locked him into the new garment of soft grey rubber and invisible steel. "Stand up, sir," he said at last, and the writer obeyed in smiling wonder; yes, he was free to walk slowly about, to navigate on his own two legs. It was miraculous. But at first he was only allowed to wear it for an hour a day to get his muscles used to its stresses. "A miracle," he said aloud. Cade watched him attentively for a few moments and then, with a nod, turned away to his domestic duties while Blanford, feeling newly born, leaned against the chimney-piece, staring down at his fallen crutches. Cade would never know how much this new invention meant. The valet looked like the lower-class ferret he was. Blanford watched him curiously as he went over the room, emptying the ashtrays and refilling the saucer of water on the radiator, refilling the vase with its hothouse blooms. "Cade," he said, "Constance is dead." Cade nodded expressionlessly. "I know, sir. I was listening on the extension in the hall." That was all. That was Cade all over. His work done, he took himself off with his customary silence and stealth.

> Carbon into diamond
> Sand into pearl.

All process causes pain, and we are part of process. How chimerical the consolations of art against the central horror of death; being sucked down the great sink like an insect, into the *cloaca maxima* of death, the *anus mundi*! Sutcliffe, in writing about him, or rather, he writing about himself in the character of Sutcliffe, under the satirical name of Bloshford in the novel *Monsieur* had said somewhere: "Women to him were simply a commodity. He was not a fool about them; O no! He knew them inside out, or so he thought. That is to say he was worse than a fool."

Was this true of Constance or of Livia her sister, the writer wondered. The blonde girl and the dark. The girl with the velvet conundrum and the girl with beak of the swan?

> Grind grain, press wine,
> Break bread, yours mine,
> Take breath, face death.

Where had he seen these lines underlined by Constance in a book? At that moment the telephone seemed to thrill again, and he knew at once who it was – it could only be his invention Sutcliffe. He must have heard by telepathy the news about Constance (Tu). He realised now that he had been expecting this call all day.

He did not bother to utter the usual Hullo but immediately said to his *confrère*, his *semblable* and *frère:* "You have heard about Tu," and the voice of Sutcliffe, speaking through a heavy cold, and nervous with regret, replied: "My God, Blanford, what is to become of us?"

"We shall go on sitting about regretting our lack of talent; we shall go on trying to convince people. I am as grieved as you are, Robin, and I never thought I would be. I had so often thought of dying that I thought I had the hippogriff under control; yes, but of course like everyone I cheated in my mind by being the first to die. I suppose Constance did the same."

"You made my own life come to a halt when Pia died," said Sutcliffe both reproachfully and gravely, and then blew his nose loudly. "So I set up shop here for a while to completely rewrite Toby's book about the Templars – to apply a bit of gold leaf here and there, to give it such orotundity as befits a fuddled don. But now he is famous and I feel the need for a change, for a new landscape. Tobias has the Chair in History which he coveted. Why not the Sofa? He will live on in a conical dismay, lecturing loudly on the plasticity of pork to the new generation of druggie-thuggies." He chuckled, but mirthlessly. "What about me?" he said. "Have you nothing I could do short of entering the Trappe?" "You are dead, Robin," said Blanford. "Remember the end of *Monsieur?*" "Bring me back then," said Sutcliffe on a heroic note, "and we shall see."

"What happened to the great poem and the *Tu Quoque*

book?" asked Blanford sharply, and Sutcliffe answered: "I was waiting to get over Pia a bit before finishing it. It was cunning of you to make Pia a composite of Constance and Livia, but I never felt I could really achieve the portrait of her simply because I was blinded by love. I wasn't cruel enough. And I wondered about Trash, her black lover. I think your story is better than mine, probably sadder. I don't know. But the death of Tu, of poor Constance, should be celebrated in verse by an Elizabethan."

For some reason this irritated Blanford and he said with asperity, "Well, why not a poem called 'Sutcliffe's Salte Teares upon the tombe of Tu'?"

"Why not?" said his fellow writer, his bondsman, "or perhaps in seventeenth-century style, 'Sutcliffe's Big Boo-Hoo'."

"Poetry," said Blanford on a lower key, talking almost to himself, "which always comes with sadness; poetry, in the jumbo version of the supermarket, enough for a whole family. The economy size. Robby, you can't go on being cheerful in Oxford. Shall I send you to Italy?"

"Another book? Why not?" But Sutcliffe did not sound too sure. "I really think it's your turn to write one – and this time the true story of your love, our love, for Constance and indeed for Livia despite what she did to you, to us, to me. Would it hurt too much if you tried?" Of course it would. Good grief!

Blanford did not answer for a long moment. Then Sutcliffe said, in his old flippant vein: "Last spring I went to Paris with a girl somewhat like Pia-Constance-Livia. The word *archi* had come into vogue as a prefix to almost everything. Our own translation would be *super*, I suppose. Well, everything was *archi* this and *archi* that. I realised that one might describe me as *archicocu*, what? Indeed I went so far as to think of myself as absolutely *archicocuphosphorescent*."

"In a way I did tell the truth about us," said Blanford haltingly. "Livia carried me out of my depth. I had always needed a feather-simple girl; but Livia was only fit to have her tail spliced by a female octoroon. Damn!"

"Aha! but you loved her. We both did. But where you lied was to graft onto her some of the femininity of her sister. You made her a female quaire not a male." After a pause, during which both writers thought furiously about the book which Blanford had called *Monsieur* and Sutcliffe *The Prince of Darkness*, their faltering conversation was resumed. If lonely people have a right to talk to themselves couldn't a lonely author argue with one of his own creations – a fellow-writer, Blanford asked himself.

"A hunt for the larval forms of personality! Livia was, as far as I am concerned – " Sutcliffe gave a groan.

"A powder-monkey in Hell," said Blanford almost shouting with pain, because her beauty had really wounded him, driven him indeed mad with vexation.

"A dry water-hole," agreed Sutcliffe. "Who is Livia, what is she?"

> All our swains commend her.
>
> Perfection's ape, clad in a toga
> And beefed up by the shorter yoga
> A Cuvier of the sexual ploy
> You forged a girl out of a boy.
> You wielded flesh and bones and mind,
> She was attentive, tough but kind,
> Yet unbeknown, behind your back
> She sought the member that you lack.

"Enough, Robin," cried Blanford in a wave of regret and mind-sickness as he thought of the dark head of Livia on the pillow beside him. Sutcliffe laughed sardonically and tormented him with yet another improvisation.

I am loving beyond my means
I am living behind my moans!
O!
Tra la la! Tra la la!
Toi et moi et le chef de gare
Quel baȥar, mais quel baȥar!

Blanford supposed him to be right; for the story for him
could have begun in Geneva – on a sad Sunday in Geneva. It
was cold; and ill-assorted, straggly and over-gummy were the
bifurcated Swiss under a snow-moon. He closed his eyes the
better to hear the tumultuous chatter of stars, or dining
later at the Bavaria with her face occupying the centre of
his mind, he engulfed the victorious jujubes of mandatory
oysters. Ouf! What prose! *Nabokov, à moi!* In hotels their
lives were wallpapered with sighs. Then tomorrow on the
lake, the white stairways to heaven splashed with a wrinkled
sunshine. "My sister Livia arrives tomorrow from Venice.
She is anxious to meet you."

That was Constance, made for deep attachments as a
cello is made for music – the viol's deepness on certain notes,
in certain moods. It was ages before they had both realised
that the words which passed between them had a certain
specific density; they were registered and understood at a level
somewhere below that of just ordinary speech. The sisters
had just inherited the tumbledown chateau of Tu Duc (hence
the nickname for Constance). It was near the village of
Tubain in the Vaucluse. Not too far from the one city which,
above all others, held for him the greatest number of historic
memories.

Here, Sutcliffe interposed his clumsy presence on
Blanford's train of thought; sniffing and adjusting those
much repaired spectacles of his. "But Livia had what excited
you most – the sexual trigger in the blood; she deserved to be
commemorated in a style which we might call metarealism –

in her aspect of Osiris whose scattered limbs were distributed all over the Mediterranean. Enough of the pornocratic-whimsical, Blanford. For my part I was hunting for a prose line with more body – not paunch, mark you, but body, my boy."

"Remember, Rob," Blanford retorted, "that everything you write about me is deeply suspect – at the best highly arguable. I invented you, after all."

"Or I you, which? The chicken or the egg?"

"The truth of the matter is that we did not really know much about ourselves in those old days; how happy it made one just to squander our youth, lying about in the deep grass eating cherries. The velvet English summers of youth, deep grass, and the clock of cricket balls marking the slow hours of leisure between classes. The distant clapping when some-one struck a ball to the boundary merged with but did not drown the steady drizzle of crickets. We slept in the bosom of an eternal summer.

"Tu once said that nature cured her own fertility imbalances by forcing sterile loves up on – illicit in the biological sense. Of what avail our belief in freewill? For her we were sleepwalkers caught in the current of an irresistible sexuality." He said aloud: "Poor enough consolation for the cowardly Robin Sutcliffe, sitting in that sordid house, drinking his way towards his goal – the leap from the bridge. His Charon was the twisted black woman with the crow's beak, who could procure something for every taste."

"I suppose so," said Rob with a sigh. "The bandages, the whip, the handcuffs – I should have put more of that into the book, instead of leaving it for you. She let her dirty rooms out by the hour. I came there hunting for Pia, just as you came in your turn hunting for Livia and found her in bed with that little hunchback with the pistachio eyes."

Blanford winced; he remembered the cracked bronchial

laugh, gushing out amidst cigarette smoke and coughing. She had said of Livia: "*Une fille qui drague les hommes et saut les gouines.*" He had struck her across the face with his string gloves. He said to Sutcliffe sternly: "It is your duty to demonstrate how Livia was tailored down to the sad size of Pia."

"Pia dolorosa," said Sutcliffe. "It would be more than one book, then?"

"Well, squinting round the curves of futurity I saw something like a quincunx of novels set out in a good classical order. Five Q novels written in a highly elliptical quincunxial style invented for the occasion. Though only dependent on one another as echoes might be, they would not be laid end to end in serial order, like dominoes – but simply belong to the same blood group, five panels for which your creaky old *Monsieur* would provide simply a cluster of themes to be reworked in the others. Get busy, Robin!"

"And the relation of form to content?"

"The books would be roped together like climbers on a rockface, but they would all be independent. The relation of the caterpillar to the butterfly, the tadpole to the frog. An organic relation."

Sutcliffe groaned and said: "The old danger is there – a work weighed down with theoretical considerations."

"No. Never. Not on your life. Just a *roman-gigogne.*"

"The more desperate the writer the more truthful the music – or so I believed then. Now I don't know. I wonder a great deal about wrongdoing in art, in a way I never did before."

"My dear old Rob, crime gives a wonderful sheen to the skin. The sap rises, the sex blooms in secrecy like some tropical plant. Take an example from me."

All that snowy day Blanford went on talking to his creation, trying to explain himself, to justify his feelings and his thoughts. He was trying to sum it all up – from the point of view of death.

———◆———

"From the ambush of my disability I watched and noted, hungry for disbelief. I watched my Livia coming and going in the mirror. I watched her walking about Venice from my high balcony, and I saw the woman who was spying on her at my request – for rather a stiff price. Livia was always looking back over her shoulder to see if she was being followed – clever, slender, nervous, and very caryatid, she had won my heart by her effortless sensuality. What a marvellous death-mask that dark face would make – ascetic, heart-shaped and pale. The way the lips and hands trembled when she became passionate.

"My God, what a muddle – it was Constance I really loved. She could have been my second skin. What a strange phrase, 'The rest of my life'. What does it mean? Surely that little rest – the steady diminishing of time – begins at birth? When you discovered you had married a homosexual what did you do, Robin?"

"The foolish fellow put a pistol to his brow."

"Even a writer must be truthful to decay. You burst out laughing first – the predicament was so foolish."

"But worse still, I really loved her, Pia," said Sutcliffe. "It was an unlucky dishonour forced upon me. But have you lived with one? They burn up your oxygen, being maladapted and out of true. They remove the classical pity which love engenders. The sadness which amends. And their beauty is like a spear, Blanford."

"Like a spear, my boy, like a spear."

"In Regent Street, in a sordid pub, a woman I had never regarded as being in any way intuitive listened attentively to my moans and said, 'Someone has wounded you very deeply and for utterly frivolous reasons. You should try to laugh and tell yourself that one is always punished for insincerity.' Damn her eyes!"

"She was right. But she had never seen Livia at bay, with flashing eyes, lying for dear life – you see, she could not bear it really, her inversion. She wouldn't admit it to anyone. With her back to the wall she fenced desperately. Tied to the wheel in the sinking vessel of her self-esteem – as who is not? – she foundered in my arms. I had had her closely watched for a little while when one day . . . my servant Cade had to return to England for his mother's funeral and during his absence I moved into the Lutèce on a narrow street; there I sat at evening watching the dusk fall, and the lights spring up over the canals. The street was so narrow that the balconies opposite were almost touching ours, or so it seemed. Three floors up, Lord Galen sat reading the *Financial Times*, full of the sense of his oneliness. I joined him for a cocktail and there, standing on his balcony, I looked across the street and saw the light snap on in a dark room opposite. Two women were just waking from their siesta – yawning and stretching. One rose and came to the balcony to thrust the shutters wide. As she did so the mouse raised her face and her eyes met mine. It was my spy, naked, and behind her in the rumpled bed Livia was drowsing, her fingers on her sex, dreaming – as if fingering a violin one is about to play. Her eyes half-closed, she was presumably riffling through the portfolio of her phantasy life. She had evidently seduced my spy! It was all over in a second. The girl retired, and so did I. Furious and thunderstruck, I said nothing to the old banker, who was particularly worried about the state of copper that day – he had once looked after some of my mother's modest investments for her and was never free from the delicious anal gnawing of money."

Sutcliffe: "So you were crushed with fury, and went

down to the bar; the porter gave you a fat envelope full of marvellous press cuttings, fulsome ones, interviews and pictures. I have always wanted to question you a little about them. For example, you are reported as saying 'I have never sought fame and fortune in my work. I sought happiness.' "

"Yes, I did say that. I thought that."

"And happiness, have you found it?" Sutcliffe put on the adenoidal voice of an interviewer.

"You find it only when you stop looking, Rob."

"And have you?"

"No."

"Why not?"

"Now that would be worth answering but I don't for the life of me know how to."

"I thought not. When you got back to the flat later you played on the little harmonium a whole grisly toccata."

"Yes, the background music for a nervous breakdown. And I reflected on all the psychoanalytic twaddle about our oceanic sexual drives. And in my manly agony I cried out, 'O God, my God, why didst Thou let me marry a Principal Boy?' When Livia slept with me who was she really loving in her imagination, in her phantasy? Who was my rival, the dark lady of the sonnets? And how could I find out? She had carefully masked her batteries. Once set off by the hair-trigger of a simple kiss she turned her face to this veiled form and used me as the *machine à plaisir*."

"And yet she was full of ideals, Livia."

"All ideals are unattainable – that is what makes them worth having. You have to reach for the apple. If you wait until it falls you will be disappointed – you will realise that it is imaginary."

"The apple of gravity, Newton's wish?"

"Exactly. And besides, never forget how much in the dark we all were about our selves, our predilections, our ruling passions. It took a trip to Vienna with Constance to teach us just a very little."

"It resolved nothing, it only unsettled you to know the truth about your sexual predispositions."

"Perhaps; yet knowledge is a sort of exorcism. I am very grateful to Constance, who was the only one among us to read German and thus have direct access to what was being written in Vienna and Zurich; moreover despite the abandoned studies she was already a fine doctor. She explained Livia to me satisfactorily."

"To what avail?"

"To no avail; of course it wasn't enough, it never is, but it enabled me to sympathise with her, to understand many things, like, for example, her deliberate grubbiness at times – the revolt against her femininity, the desire to insult the male. Then always restless, always wanting to be on the move. Several times a day she had to walk down to the village because she had forgotten to buy this or that. It used to puzzle me, it seemed almost deliberate, and of course it was. As Constance said, she was simply a man-at-arms on the look-out for a pick-up! Surely this was valuable, all this information? Eh?"

Sutcliffe deliberated for a moment, and Blanford lit a cigar, saying: "Soon there will be nobody to talk to except you. It is extremely sad – what shall I do for company? You bore me so! It will probably lead to madness."

"We will write a book."

"Of what will it treat?"

"Of the perennity of despair, intractability of language, impenetrability of art, insipidity of human love."

"Livia and Constance, the two faces? Transposed heads!"

"The two faces. You see, Aubrey, the male invert loves his mother, the female hates hers implacably. That is why she won't bear children, or if she does, makes changelings or witches. What we thought we found was that Livia really loved her sister Constance – that is why she set out to marry you, to cut Constance out. She could not bear to think of you coming together."

"But Livia slept with many men."

"Of course, but it was with brave contempt, to prove her own maleness, her masculine superiority. A talented Chartreuse. She would run with her bleeding male scalps and show them to her girl friends. This was a way of advertising her wares. 'Look, this is all men are worth, so easily scalped!' "

"Alas, it was only too true." Sutcliffe fingered the little tonsured part of his own huge cranium where recently the baldness had begun to show through. "After Pia I had to buy a hairpiece," he admitted. "And specially after all this psychoanalytic gibberish. All I learned was that male lesbians are notoriously kind to dogs – but I am not a dog and don't qualify. Another question – was Jesus a lesbian?"

"Cut it out," said Blanford, "I can't bear idle blasphemy."

At this point Sutcliffe sang the little psychoanalytic song he had once made up to celebrate the great men of the science; it went

> Joy, Young and Frenzy,
> Frenzy, Groddeck and Joy.

He broke off and said suddenly: "*Et le bonheur?*"

"Exactly."

"It cannot be impossible to find. It must be knocking about somewhere, just out of sight. Why don't we write a big autobiography? Come on, punish everyone!"

"The last defence! All aboard for the last alibi!"

"What does a man say when his wife leaves him? He cries out in an agony of fury: 'Thrice-tritrurated gasometers!

Who will burn sugar to this tonsil-snipping tart?' "

"Or seek the consolations of art: the little choking yelp of Desdemona is pleasant to dwell upon."

"Or he will become a widow and in desperation take up with some furry housemaid who will in due course be delivered of some rhubarb-coloured mite."

"The Kismet for novelists with cook-housekeepers. But I have only Cade, and he can't cook. . . ."

The snow went on falling out in the park with its resigned elms full of rooks' nests. Blanford pondered heavily upon human nature and its uncapturable variety while Sutcliffe in his Oxford rooms turned and put a log on the fire. Toby was coming to lunch with a young girl undergraduate. Then he took up the phone once more and said, "The relationship between our books will be incestuous, then, I take it? They will be encysted in each other, not complementary. There would be room for everything, poem, autobiography, short story and so on."

"Yes," said his creator softly. "I suppose you have heard of that peculiar medical phenomenon called the teratoma? It is literally a bag full of unfinished spare parts – nails and hair and half-grown teeth – which is lodged like a benign growth somewhere in a human body. It is removed by surgery. It appears to be part of a twin which at some stage decided to stop growing. . . ."

"A short story lodged in a book?"

"Yes. Do you know at what point Pia began to love you? I bet you don't. It was when you behaved so outrageously at Unesco and fell into the big drum."

"You mean Shakespeare's birthday? They should never have asked me."

"You should never have gone. And then to arrive dead drunk and take your place on the rostrum among the greatest modern poets, all prepared to render homage to the Bard.

And with Toby in the audience cheering and waving a British flag. It was obscene."

"Not entirely," said Sutcliffe, slightly huffed, "it had its moment of truth. Besides, nobody could contravert my twelve commandments*– the indispensable prerequisites for those who wish to make works of art. They were particularly impressive when shouted through a megaphone in a hoarse tormented tone. Why didn't you use them?"

"I will one day when I write the ridiculous scene. You made Ungaretti faint. And then having recited the whole iniquitous catalogue of drivel you fell into the Elizabethan madrigal society's big bassoon, festooned with wires and microphones."

"Rather like Ophelia," said Sutcliffe. "But I stand by my commandments whatever the French say. Let me repeat them to you lest you have forgotten or mislaid them." He cleared his throat energetically and recited them for the benefit of Blanford, who wrote them down in shorthand on the pad at his elbow.

He left a long pause for admiration or applause and then said: "Alas, it ended badly, but it was none of my fault."

There was another longish silence during which Sutcliffe blew his nose in a plaintive sort of way, feeling that he was disapproved of by his mate and pawn. Then he said: "Where will Tu be buried and when?"

"Tonight," said Blanford coolly, with a reserve he was far from feeling. "In the chateau vault, by dispensation, and no ceremony, no flowers. Some lanterns, I suppose, perhaps some torches."

"Will you go down to Tu Duc?"

"Later, when everything is settled and the chateau boarded up for the winter. I love the rain falling over Avignon with all its memories. There is a certain melancholy luxury in

* See Appendix for full text of 12 Commandments.

feeling that everyone has gone, one is completely alone. The place to experience this best of all is on deserted railway stations at night, empty airport lounges, all-night cafés in the town."

Sutcliffe said: "And Livia, who in my own personal life and book turned into Sylvie and went mad? What about her in this context?"

"Livia disappeared, was last heard of on the road to Spain with the old negro pianist. My last news of her was some years ago now, from a girl who had known her; it was in one of those houses which cater to special inclinations – indeed the identical house where you lodged with the old crone. From time to time I passed by just in order to check, because once I had found Livia there, shaking with fatigue or drugs, trembling from head to foot. She said, in a bleary tearful way: "Unless someone takes care of me I am finished." I realised then that I loved her and would never desert her; and all the while a voice inside me was raging and shouting 'Fool!' "

"That was where I hunted for Pia."

"We took her to the kitchen, tottering, and set her down on a stool, imploring her to eat something. The hag buttered some bread. Livia suddenly burst into tears and said, '*J'ai failli t'aimer*,' and the tears ran down her long sweet nose into the plate. Still crying, she began to eat, looking so like a small child in her tearful hunger that I was overwhelmed. I sat there biting my lips and remembering so much that she had told me.

"One day in a dark cinema a woman placed her hand lightly upon her thigh and she felt her whole nature tilt like a galleon in a wind, to run seething through fresh seas. She did not move. She did not speak. She offered no response. Then she got up and walked out of the cinema without looking round. In the vestibule she felt so ill she had to lean her head against the cold tiled wall. A hand touched her sleeve and a voice said, 'Come, let me help you.' And so it began. And as she diminished in my life I started to reinvent her on paper as accurately as I could. Once when she had gone and I was lonely I took another girl from the same establishment to a hotel – purely for the comfort of sleeping with someone who knew her and could talk about her, even though what she had to tell me was wounding. Cynically and with a strong twang to her French this poor creature told me about Livia's exploits in great detail, adding as she did so: 'She gives good value, that one. Among the girls who like it she is known as Moustache.' My dear Rob, my beloved was known as Moustache to her ingles!"

"Perhaps you were wise to make Pia passive rather than active – it gave her a dimension Livia lacked, a pathos."

"But Livia was magnetic, and much harder to paint. I was forever trying to push a bit of femininity back into the lady, like trying to fill a dolly with sawdust, trying to fill an eye with a drip, trying to fill a mind with a prayer. Then she would disappear for a few days, to be brought back by the police dead drunk or else be run to earth in a bar, guttering down, guttering out. You, know, her health was a worry, she was never very strong, and she persistently brutalised it. But her charm! She was irresistible, she smelt of perils and disenchantments. Men could not resist her, and she longed to be able to respond. Yes, she gave herself, but it was only a smear of a woman who responded to the kiss. Affectively she was anaesthetic, her soul was rubberised."

"How funny," said Sutcliffe. "I suppose you discovered the real truth once the wedding-ring was on her finger. It was just like that with Pia, I had all sorts of vague notions that even though she was wild and unstable she was redeemable – a little bit of settled ways and stylised married life . . . I should have known by then how to detect the quaire (feminine version of queer). After all she could neither swim nor dance, and in love she went all anaesthetic but kindly – her kisses were one-dimensional and softer than moths.''

"That was not Livia. Her favourite nail varnish was called Sadist Red, and she operated with a violence and zeal of a piglet at dug. A real predator, she liked to wear the fur of wild animals. Lean tomboy of the sexthrust, it was she who impregnated me with her despairing, anodyne, phantasy sensuality.''

"Why were you so annoyed about the ring? In my case I felt that Pia had taken an unfair advantage, and wanted to continue in her old style under cover of the status and the stability I offered her. I felt swizzed.''

"In my case it was the ring itself – it had belonged to my mother. I had all the tortured and confused impulses of only children, sickly in youth and consequently spoiled. School was torture, other people were torture. She was my only girl, mama, and I remained a *vieux garcon*, a bachelor, until she died when I thought that my loneliness might be less unendurable with a woman about the house. Of course I had had this long love-affair with Constance in between; but she never wished to remarry. Anyway Livia had disappeared somewhere in Asia and in those days it took years before a presumption of death permitted one to dream of divorce. You deformed her a bit in Pia.''

"But you are to blame, for making her passive instead of active. Pia, looking so lovely in her white night-dress, obligingly put herself into a state of abstraction to pump out her husband (tenderly, dutifully) but like a collector 'blows' a bird's egg. For the rest, lying warm in bed she played with a masturbatory little curl, and I suppose dreamed about her *fouetteuse*, or her *frotteuse*. Why not? What is cheaper than dreaming? But infantile dreams which recover an early sex life are as feverish as the dreams of an anchorite. Great

Amputator of Egg Bags, save us! The lady was a *station de pompage* merely."

"Childhood, with its gross sexual and psychological damage to the psyche – what a terrible thing to be forced to undergo. No really, Rob, one does not stand a chance!"

"They believed in God. Jesus on pedals! How could they?"

Blanford threw his cigar into the fire and thought with a sudden wave of nostalgic passion of Tu. She rose before his inner eye walking by the lake where they had once and for all staked a claim in each other's minds and bodies; he heard her low voice reading from the book about Nietzsche, whom they had come there to seek.

"What happens," said Sutcliffe thoughtfully, "according to the wiseacres you consulted with so little profit – what happens to the penis is coronation followed by decapitation – the king bowing so low before the ladies that the crown falls off on to the red carpet. Isn't that right?"

Blanford agreed and amplified the statement with a voice full of distaste. "The head lends itself particularly well to the expression of bisexual conflicts, and can cunningly represent both male and female genitalia. Both girls were highly specialised in migraines of great intensity. There are vaginal haemorrhages which can be stopped by the cocaine pad to the inside of the nose. The guillotine, remember, was called *La Vierge*."

"A fig for all this folklore," cried Sutcliffe. "All will end in munch and you know it. The black flag of pure cannibalism will be unfurled. If narcissists (artists) cannot love, what right have they to kick up such a row?"

"You're right."

"*Si on est Dieu pourquoi cochonner?*"

"You're dead right, as they say. What a useful phrase."

Blanford could hear his creation tearing open a bag of potato chips and starting to champ them as he reflected furiously upon these all too alembicated ideas. Blanford thought of his childhood. "An only child is doomed to nostalgia and uncertainty. Nobody will ever guess what it cost me against all my fears and despairs, to teach myself the profession of letters. Solo, solitude, solace ... everything beginning with Sol the father, Sol the Son and Sol the Holy Ghost. She lingered for many years, did my mother, bedridden, suffering from an ill-identified malady which purported to be a heart condition. I think now that it was some grave glandular disturbance – the thymus perhaps. It gave her languor, it gave her a skin like a magnolia; her breasts remained firm and her teeth good to the very end. We lived, she and I, without a father in number twenty-seven Ruskin Road, South Norwood – a gloomy house called The Larches, with arch statuary on the lawn and a fountain which had rusted and would not play. We shared everything, even sleeping – as one might share careers of common silence. Yet I hear her sighs in my dreams now. What a torture it was to pack up my little tuck-box, count my money and set off to school, having assembled my books and kissed mama goodbye. Sterling, the old butler, drove me shakily down to the country – my school was near Arundel – in the ancient Morris. He was a randy old Cockney and he used to say: 'Next week, d'you know what, Master Aubrey? Why, I'm going on a right bender – don't tell your mother because she thinks I'm respectable. In a way she's right, I am. But not on my holidays. I've got a couple of birds right over the pocket in Brixton, and I'm simply thirsting for a bit of knuckle, Master Aubrey, really thirsting.'

"My father had been a scientific don in a minor university; the photographs depicted a large, discordant-looking man with black lace-up boots. I stared and stared at the vague memory-bank of his face but it radiated nothing. 'Come, hand me my pins, my net and my killing bottle, and leave me in peace.' He said that to my mother once who found it inconsiderate. It upset her. The house was full of badly stuffed geese and wildfowl, and in his study was a cabinet containing shelves and shelves of brilliant butterflies all mounted expertly on slabs of cork. I would have to do without all this until the end of term when Christmas came round. Again! The smart toy of the crib, and sex awoken in some little old mistletoe-man with a red peak, at night, in the snow, driving his tinkling harim of reindeer across the snowy roofs.

"Sometimes at night, walking across London, to see scores of silent frozen girls offering their bodies for sale under the blobs of yellow gaslight. Hurrying home to mother with castdown eyes, dying of smothered desires and the all too real fear of syphilis. So my whole life took its direction from there – my mother had rendered me a lamb, ripe for the slaughter; Livia supplied the shears. Cause and effect, my lad, that is why I had to encourage you to have a richer and more robust childhood. Your people were millers, say, from the north country, with a firm fortune and coming of authentic peasant stock. I saw your prototype once, dining beside me in Avignon, and I jotted down in my notebook: 'She is rather frail, but he huge with an egg-shaped cranium and a face which had funny and rather unworldly expressions on it. They smelt of industrious love-making and yawned all through dinner.' "

"Thank you. Was I at school with you?"

"We were both at different schools together."

Sutcliffe answered a ring at the doorbell and then came back to the phone to say briefly: "Toby has arrived. For my part I told everybody that I lived in Ireland in a fairy's armpit. They gave the impression of believing me, I never had trouble like you. Your laughter was a private strategy, mine was whole-hearted."

"I am not so sure," said Blanford thoughtfully, "though it is true that I was loved by a mummy without margins. Result: I wrote tonsured poems in the style of Morris. But I soon came to my senses. The result was not vastly different – we both ran into Livia, but in my case I presented a very simple target, and the motive of course was my unrecognised love for Tu. By the time your turn came you were less vulnerable because of your tough youth and were able to surmount the catastrophe with commendable humour. You at least were able to stand on the Bridge of Sighs and, waving your stick, exclaim aloud: 'Help me, Pia, help me! I am going down by the stern like Laurel and Hardy!' I could never have done that. I was after something else – a cumulus of thought subsumed in one bold metaphor. I had realised something concrete, namely that small art creates a throb, big art a wholesome vertigo. I tried to teach you this in your dealings with the people around you, so that your writing might have pith and irony. But since human consciousness distorts in the act of observing, you and I, seen by a third person, are perverted images of one another. We exchange highly diversified memoranda about the state of our attachment, just like real lovers entering that state which probably never existed. Poets exchanging cowrie shells, not real coin. Unless the images sting you awake. Robin, before you obediently killed yourself, you scribbled in the margins of your unfinished manuscript poem – the *Tu Quoque* – the words, 'Of course like Tiresias I have breasts which see all, and a forked tail in the shape of a lightning conductor. And yes, hooves.' "

Sutcliffe roared with laughter and crunched away at his chips, while in the background Blanford could hear the bearish sounds of Toby clearing his throat and the voice of a girl. He could not imagine her face as he had not yet invented her. That would come, he supposed. O God! Writers! Sutcliffe said: "Toby has been making up an imaginary obituary for you for *The Times* – you know he makes a little cash from working in the graveyard bringing obits up to date. Here's a passage which will please you: 'It is said that when rich he twice refused the thistle.' "

"But the money gave me books and travel and secrecy. And anyway one can't do better than one's best. What more would you like to hear from me if I bring you back to life?"

"About Tu; about Livia; about Hilary the brother and Sam. About the lake, and about Tu Duc and the Avignon of those early days. About us, the real ones."

"Then let me ask you one question," said Blanford sternly. "Just how real do you feel to yourself, Robin Sutcliffe?"

"I have never stopped to think," said his only friend after a pause. "Have you?"

"And you want to know about your own youth? Of course I endowed you with mine, for we are about the same age."

"But different milieux nourished us."

"Yes, but the age was the same, and an age is a state of mind. The twenties – that was purely a state of mind."

"Tell me the details, it will help me to act."

"Very well."

Blanford closed his eyes and let his memory draw him back to the very beginning of the story.

"It was to be their last term at Oxford and Hilary had invited them both to journey with him to Provence for the long vac. Neither he nor Sam had then met his two sisters, Constance and Livia. Indeed, they knew nothing of them at all. But recently, with the death of an old aunt, young

Constance had inherited the little chateau of Tu Duc in the southern Vaucluse, not far from Avignon. The Duchess of Tu, then, was the obvious nickname for her. The children had spent many holidays there once upon a time in their extreme youth; but in her old age the aunt became first eccentric, and then mentally unstable; she turned recluse, locked herself up, and allowed the whole place to fall into ruins around her. The rain and the wind settled down to finish what negligence had begun; the weight of winter snow cracked the black tiles of the roofs and entered the rooms, with their strange scrolled bull's-eye windows. In the rambling, disorderly park, old trees had fallen everywhere, blocking the paths, crushing the summer-house under their weight. The once-tended green plots were now a mass of molehills, while everywhere hares skirmished. They were to live largely on jugged hare that summer!

"Hilary, to do him justice, did not minimise the hardships they might have to face; but the prospect of southern sunlight and good wine was enough to offset any qualms they might have had. And then there was another capital factor – they had both youth and good health. Constance would meet them in Lyon, while Livia would come on later to join them, in her own time. Hilary mentioned Livia's name and frowned affectionately as he did so – as if he found the fact of her existence somehow troubling. His deep family affection for her had a sort of qualified, formalised air, as if he did not wholeheartedly understand her as did Constance. His way of talking gave one the notion that Livia was the wild and unpredictable one, while Constance was the stable and utterly dependable one. This proved to be more or less the case later when they got to know the truth about them – whatever that might mean. But Livia now spent all her time in Germany.

"It was this promise of a wild and somewhat primitive holiday which explained all the heavy camping impedimenta they found stacked up against their arrival in Lyon – they had sent it on in advance. Massive camp-beds and sun-helmets, sleeping-bags, mosquito nets – perfectly ridiculous items which had been invented for safaris in lion-country or for scaling the Indian Himalayas. But none of them knew old Provence at first hand, so perhaps these precautions were excusable.

"Today the world which fathered them is a remote and forgotten one; it was a world wallowing in the wake of one war, trying to gather itself together before plunging irrevo-cably into a second. Their youth had enabled them to escape the trenches – in 1918 they were still just under military age, though Sam nearly managed to join up by a subterfuge; but he was found out and sent back to school; whence, to Oxford where the three, though so different, became inseparable. Hilary was the ringmaster of the little group, for he had more experience than either of the others, and he always led the dance. As a boy he was blond and tall and had ice-blue eyes like a Teuton. Sam was tow-haired and rather massive in his awkward gentle way. I was ... how was I, Aubrey Blanford? Let me see.

"A bit of a slowcoach, I suppose. Sam boxed and Hilary rowed, while all three of us hacked a bit and when possible rode to hounds in a post-Surtees manner.

"I was the least mercuric, the most sedentary of the three, and my poor eyesight made me an indifferent athlete, though I fenced well and even got my blue for it. The post-Wildean twilight of Oxford was no longer a place to cool the mind – the stresses and strains of the war years still weighed on us by proxy, for many of the men who had seen blood and action in 1918 had come back to university to finish studies interrupted by the war. A disturbed and wild crew they were, like foreign barbarians.

"Yes, it is difficult to describe that world, now so

forgotten; its values and habits seem to have retreated into the remotest recesses of time. Do you remember it – a world in awkward transition? The new thing was violent and brash, the old had ankylosed. All that the war had not killed outright lived on in a kind of limbo. Intellectually, let us say, Anatole France and Shaw were at the height of their fame; Proust despite his prizes had not yet won the general public. Henry James versus Wells.

"Was I born old? I never seem to have had a proper youth – mine began at Oxford when I met Hilary. If he was by far the most sophisticated of the three of us it was due to chance. His father had been a diplomat and the children had always travelled with him to his various posts. This stiff old gentleman was something of a stickler for ancient forms, and wherever they went they had tutors and learned the language of the place. Thus Hilary and his sisters became good linguists and thoroughly at home in places which were, to me, semi-mythical – Middle Europe, for example, or the Balkans: Rumania, Russia, Greece, Arabia. . . . It is true that Sam and I spoke laborious French and Italian, with a smidgen of German. But in the case of Hilary he 'possessed' three languages in the French sense of the word, and smattered in four others. All this he turned to good account and took excellent degrees at Oxford. His objective then was archaeology, his hero Evans, and his heart he had set upon exploring the labyrinth at Gortymna which remains unmapped to this day because of its great extent.

"And Sam? I have a picture of him in the back of my mind, lying in the deep grass at the edge of a green cricket-field crunching an apple and chuckling over Wodehouse or Dornford Yates. You must remember that we were overgrown schoolboys then to whom even dull, but raucous London was an excitement, a dream. While Paris was Babylon. Sam's ambitions were simple – all he wanted to do was to climb

Everest single-handed, and on his return rescue a beautiful blonde maiden from a tower where she had been imprisoned by an enchanter, and marry her. Later on he would like to set off on his travels with her disguised as his page and join the Knights of the Round Table. You will see the disastrous effects of Malory on a guileless mind. In my case, I wanted to be a historian – at that time I had really no inclination towards this hollow servitude to ink and paper. I pictured myself doing a definitive book on some aspect of medieval history and winning an Exhibition to Wadham, or something of that nature. As you see the bright one was Hilary, with what he called his 'Minoan tilt' – for his plans and projects opened windows on the world of Europe. Am I right?"

"I suppose so, but it's a bit pedestrian your exposé – it proves that the dull historian is not quite dead in my poor Aubrey. I would have gone about it differently myself."

"Tell me how."

"I should have enumerated other things like school ties, huge woollen scarves, Oxford bags, college blazers, Brough Superiors à la T. E. Lawrence, racing cars with strapped-down bonnets, Lagonda, Bentley, Amilcar. . . . The flappers had come and gone but the vamp was present in force with her cloche hat and cigarette holder."

"I had forgotten all that."

"It is the small things which build the picture."

"London."

"Yes, and the places we frequented in London most of which have disappeared – wiped out one supposes by the bombings?"

"Like the Café de Paris?"

"Yes, and Ciro's and The Blue Peter, The Criterion Bar, Quaglino's, Stone's Chop House, Mannering's Grill, Paton's, The Swan. . . ."

"Good, Robin, and then the night-clubs like The Old

Bag O' Nails, The Blue Lantern, The Black Hole, and Kiki's Place. . . . We simply never slept."

"The music of shows like Funny Face ('Who stole my heart away?'), Charlot, and the divine Hutch smoothing down the big grand piano and singing in his stern unemphatic way 'Life is just a bowl of cherries'."

"Just before dawn Lyons' Corner House, everyone with yellow exhausted faces, whores, undergraduates, all-night watchmen and workers setting off on early jobs. The first newspapers appearing on the icy street. Walking back in the pale nervous rinsed-out dawn, the whole way back across London – over Westminster Bridge and into the baleful suburbs of the capital; perhaps with the memory of some whore in mind, and the ever present worry of a dose. Marry or burn, my boy, marry or burn."

"I did both."

"So did I. So did I."

"And so we come to the misty slip at Lyon where we waited impatiently for Constance and filled in the time by loading all our ludicrous equipment aboard the *Mistral*, a huge flat motor-barge with a capacious hold and enough deck space to take a few passengers. The hold was already battened down and covered with a tarpaulin which gave us a large flat area for lounging and eating; it was not envisaged that we should spend the night on her, but ashore. And then, amidst all these foolish deliberations, the stacking of our gear – you would have thought we were setting off for the Pole – the girl arrived; and with her, suddenly the whole summer too took place – I mean the consciousness of it, the density of its weight. As yet we were only in the mulberry-tree belt of dishevelled Lyon and its sprawling green surroundings. Far from the dustry garrigues as yet, the olive oil, and the

anisette. But with Tu one saw what it was: it was sunlight
filtered through a summer hat of fine straw onto bronzed
shoulders and neck, creating a shadow that was of the darkness of ripe plums. It was ash-blonde hair made rough but
silky by too much sun and salt water. It was a neck set
perfectly on slender but strong shoulders, it was an eye of
periwinkle-blue, which could turn green with the light, an
eye full of curiosity and humour. She had cut her foot bathing,
and her limp was explained by a bandage. She looked at us
without much ardour or interest, I think, but with friendliness
because we were her brother's friends. I felt at once that she
shared some of his superiority over us – some of what I
would call nowadays sophistication. 'Sorry I'm late; it was the
train as usual.'

"Our skipper was a grave rotund man, who had the air
of a great character actor out of work. His old sea-wolf
yachting cap was cocked at a jaunty angle, and his liberality
was not in question, for he produced frequent glasses of
strong wine and urged them on us as a protection against the
inclemency of the weather. What inclemency? The weather
was perfectly fine, the old man obviously raving. Nevertheless
the full beakers of Côtes du Rhône put us all into a great good
humour; Constance sipped from her brother's glass and asked
permission to put on shorts which he gravely granted. We
winked at one another. The skipper's wife allowed her to
make this transformation in the little cabin below which
contained a cage bird and some old prints of the days of
water haulage on the Rhône – really not so far away in time.

"We were fully loaded for Arles but were waiting for
two more passengers who had been delayed. But they were
not to detain us for long, and they were profuse in their
apologies. One was a lanky, raffish-looking individual with a
yellowish complexion and hair all in tufts about his greatcoat
collar. He had a kind of shabby air of majesty, but it was only

much later, when he advanced to the prow and let fly with an aria from Verdi, of tremendous volume, that we realised we were in the presence of a star from the opera of Marseille. The other was a humble, elderly man with a crown of white hair and the venerable appearance of a beadle. He had a brown old face which was full of character, and he regarded the world around him with an air of slightly impudent amusement. He seemed, however, a man of some real cultivation, not only from his manner but also because he carried under his arm a volume of poems, and actually sported (it is only now in retrospect that I recognise the fact) in his lapel the golden cicada which betokens a member of that famous poetic society the Félibre. Everything about our skipper – his rotundity, his accent, his gestures – seemed to fill this old gentleman with delight. I realise now why, they were both from Avignon, which was also our landfall and from where we hoped to find a carriage to take us to Tubain, if Felix was not at the rendezvous with his spluttering little consular car.

"The hooter gave a hiss and a boom, while drops of steam dribbled down the funnel; we had cast off and were away almost before we knew or felt it. Lying at ease on the spacious deck we saw the sunlit world turn slowly about us, spin faster and faster, and begin to slide away to stern. We swept under a great bridge where the silhouettes of a few onlookers were set against the arc of a sky of utter blue. Constance settled herself among the cushions thoughtfully provided by the gallant old skipper and apparently fell asleep, which gave me a chance to observe her and be struck once again by her beauty, and her resemblance to her brother. The fine blonde hair at her temples was, I thought, finer than the work of silkworms; her sleep was light, she smiled at some happy dream or thought. I would never have dreamed that she was as shy as Hilary, so formidable did her self-possession seem to us poor Englanders, bursting with conventions and the need to worship. Many years later when in a letter I made a reference to this first meeting she wrote on a postcard the one word: 'Shyness'.

"There was no sign of all this in the pose of the calm sleeping girl on the deck. Hilary, if my memory serves, rapidly got on good terms with the old poet and fired questions at him about the places through which we glode so smoothly, over a river suddenly widened by the green junction with the Saône. What I did remember was the droning voice of my geography teacher as he told us its history, softly touching the big wall-map with the black malacca cane which also, in certain contexts, served him to give us the brutal thrashings which were then the order of the day in most schools. They did no harm, I might add, and indeed were really useful as a rough and ready absolution – for one expiated one's sins this way and forgot about them once the blue weals had gone. While those hundred lines or hundred Hail Marys never really did the trick.

"But this first enticing venture towards the south, towards the Mediterranean, has got itself mixed up and superposed upon the many other times when I returned to Tu Duc to spend the summers there. 'The Rhône rises in Lac Léman,' said the droning voice of my geography teacher."

At this point in Blanford's recital Robin Sutcliffe cleared his throat and chuckled and made a noise like someone snuffing. "I bet I can tell what you think of now in that context."

"Carry on. Tell me," said Blanford.

Sutcliffe said: "The Chambre Froide of the central abattoir at Geneva. Of all the extraordinary places to sit and watch the Rhône rise. It was there that Pia took me to tell me that she had met poor Trash. It was a singular place to choose, perhaps more apt than it appears at first sight. The great factory that is the abattoir is built over the lake, remember, and at the back of it there is a little glassed-in restaurant built right over the water, where the personnel of the place take their meals. They call it the birdcage, if I recall right, and it is certainly small. Naturally the prime food is the meat. Trash had found it one day on her wanderings – she had been sent to order a carcase for the old American lady's birthday-party – one which would unite all the queers and queens and quaires of the town. Here among the swinging carcases on their big hooks the butchers in their bloody aprons had a festive air. They found Trash very much to their taste, and after several of the younger ones had refreshed themselves with her they invited her to the canteen for a glass of wine.

"Without this invitation it would have been impossible to find, for the entrance was actually through a huge meat-safe which was usually kept closed. Naturally the place was not open to the general public, it was reserved for the butchers and their friends. But a few people had discovered it and the supervision was lax. Well, I remember sitting over the water listening to this sad recital of Pia's fears and regrets; and all about her love for me which made me blow my nose rather loudly because I was touched, and I felt awfully as if my heart had been broken with a sledge hammer. To be hugged by a boy in a bloodstained apron – Ugh! Of course it was Trash who had been hugged, but now Pia was going to try the same thing under the tuition of the negress. It upset me so much this recital (the foolish girl was asking for my encouragement, for my absolution, repeating that she could not live without me and that I must understand). . . . I got so damned livid with her stupidity in succumbing to the lures of that male succubus with a slit that I rushed out of the place and took a taxi to Trash's hotel with the intention of thrashing her. Luckily she was out and I cooled down as I walked by the lake."

"Lucky is the word," said Blanford, "when I took a dogwhip to Livia for one of her misdemeanours I put her into a transport of sexual delight. Bathed in tears of pain and gratitude she fell to her knees and started licking my shoes. She was my slave now, she told me, utterly my slave. And she kept repeating, 'O why didn't you do it before?' I was disgusted."

"And the abattoir restaurant?"

"If I must disinter Livia's thoughts – it was she, the original of Pia, who took me there – I must record that she adored the smell of blood and fresh water. Indeed everything about new blood delighted her. It reminded her of her first period – she had been so poorly instructed, and was so innocent, that she thought she was bleeding to death like Petronius. And then, of course, the sorrow because it was the first physical proof of the lack of manhood she so coveted inside herself. The tremendous sadness of realising, as she said in her own picturesque phraseology, that she was a boy scout with a vagina. My dear Robin, she did not actually suffer the embrace of bloodstained boys, but she dreamed about it; only in her case the butcher was an elderly man who looked like her father. While we sat over the water and I saw her face suddenly go dead and transform itself into the resolute face of a tough little sailor, something guttered out like a spent candle. My love, like a sick fish, rose to the surface belly upwards. Under the floor of our birdcage the lake-water, narrowed and sluiced by the two banks, gathers speed, as if it could smell Arles already.

"The driving channel was a dark shade of amethyst verging on ultramarine; but right in the middle there was a portion raised like a muscle in a forearm, a green muscle of water which seemed to have more thrust than the great body in which it was embedded. Following the direction of my gaze Livia said: 'You see the green ribbon there? It's the

Rhône setting off on its race for the sea.' I hear her voice, I see the water, and a thousand thoughts throng in my mind. The great rivers of the human sensibility threading the jungles and swamps and forests of lost continents. The big rivers like Nile or Mississippi ferrying their human freight from one world to another. Though short in length our Rhône was one with them as was its cousin the Rhine. . . .

"Livia told me that one night she had been taken by her lover to La Villette where an old kind butcher with the face of her father had, on request, hobbled a cow which was about to be destroyed, and made a swift incision in its throat, like slitting an envelope. He held it by the horns, though the animal felt nothing. But the jet of blood spurted out into the tall wineglasses they proffered. They drank copiously while the old man watched in kindly fashion. Later they had trouble with a policeman for they were both splashed with blood, and it was difficult to explain how they had acquired these smears. But you, Robin, above all will have easily explained Livia's aberrations satisfactorily to yourself by now – didn't you take a degree in Philosophy and Psychology?

"What always bothered me was the question of a stable ego – did such a thing exist? The old notion of such an animal was rather primitive, particularly for novelists with an itch to explain this action or that. Myself, I could hardly write down the name of a character without suddenly being swamped by an ocean of possible attributes, each as valid and as truthful as any other. The human psyche is almost infinitely various – so various that it can afford to be contradictory even as regards itself. How poor is the pathetic little typology of our modern psychology – why, even astrology, however suspect as a science, makes some attempt to encompass the vast multiplicity of purely human attributes. That is why our novels, yours and mine, Robin, are also poor. There were many Livias, some whom I love and will love until my dying day; others fell off me and dried up like dead leeches. Others were just larval forms in the sense of Paracelsus, umbratiles, vampires, ghosts. When she had definitely gone she sent me the taunting telegram which seemed to amuse you.

A little bit of addled Freud
Won't take you far towards the void.

"But the letter to which the thought belonged was written from Gantok and she had headed it, 'On the road to Tibet'. It was long, rambling and inconsequential, and it upset me so much that I destroyed it. But I remember one part in which she wrote: 'You cannot imagine what it is like to find myself in a land where beautiful six-armed Tsungtorma raises her lotus-soft palms.' It was a fair enough criticism of my literary method – why not six-armed psyches? Would it be possible, I wondered, to deal fairly with a multiplicity of attributes and still preserve a semblance of figurative unity in the personage described? I was dreaming of a book which, though multiple, embodied an organic unity. The limbs of Osiris, scattered as they were round the whole known world, were one day united. Out of the egg of futurity stepped that dark and serious girl who was to say one day, with a confident contempt, 'Anyone can see which one of us he loves.' One discovers these things years afterwards, in another context, perhaps even in another country, lying on the beach, pressing warm pebbles against one's cheek. 'What did you do?' I asked Constance. She replied, 'I suddenly realised that I must get free of her, she would always block my light, my growth. I embraced her so hard it drove all the breath from her body.'

"The Livia of that epoch was dark and on the thin side – a contrast to the fairness of her sister. She had beautifully cut cheekbones and eyes of green, while her black soft hair seemed to fly out of the crown of her head and flow down the sides in ringlets reminiscent of Medusa – the snake is quite an appropriate metaphor. Her beauty was not obvious, it came in a sudden kind of revelation. But of course, she slouched, and always had her hands in her pockets, and a cigarette between her lips. We were conventional enough to be shocked by this. But I was dazzled by her brains and her abrasive and articulate way of speech. The voice was deep, and from time to time an expression came into her eyes, a tense fierce expression, and one suddenly saw a man-at-arms peering at one out of a helm. I was too inexperienced to recognise the carapace of her defensive masculinity. But whenever she looked in the direction of Constance, whenever she found us laughing or talking with animation, another more calculating look came into those clever eyes. She could not stand the complicity of our obvious friendship whose warmth at that time was innocent of all ulterior purpose.

"Livia set herself quite deliberately to work upon my obvious inexperience. An easy target. Later when I came to wonder about the shape which events took in the lives of us all I thought that perhaps Livia's role had been less conscious than I had thought; she also was just an instrument registering the electrical impulses set up by a suppressed childhood jealousy. Being wise after the event is one of the specialities of elderly novelists. Quack! Quack! Of course she had no choice, none of us did. It was the peerless beauty and brilliance of the elder sister which magnetised the younger; and I must go on to add, the brother as well. For Hilary, too, formed part of this constellation, and I think that he also found the easy rapport between Tu and myself disquieting, to say the least. But whenever a brother and sister are very close together they naturally fear that marriage, on either side, will wantonly separate them. But Livia was a born conspirator, and once she had decided to prevent anything maturing between Constance and myself she set to work to undermine us – with what success you know only too well; I was captivated by this lizard-swift girl who flattered me in ways which now I would find grossly obvious. But, inhibited as I was then, her praise was manna.

"At that time Tu was taking the first distasteful steps in general medicine, and already had decided not to continue it to the end. The coarse jokes of the students as they handled the fragments of human bodies disgusted her. They betrayed their fear of death thus, the internal shrinking from having to carve up the bodies of drowned, unidentified people, tramps, suicides and the like. Flesh bloated, disfigured, or smashed beyond recognition. And then the smell of formaldehyde following one about the draughty schools! It got into one's clothes, aprons, skirts, white skirts. The loathing was impossible to overcome wholly, though for the present she persevered. Her only inspiration was her anatomy tutor; he was so mad on his subject that his enthusiasm fired her. Once after a particularly bad street accident in Gower Street she saw him pick up a severed arm, wrap it furtively in an evening paper and hurry off to the laboratory which was hard by. Perhaps there was a hope that some less taxing science like chemistry might answer where general medicine and surgery had failed her? She was waiting to see.

"With Livia, alone, swimming in one of the numerous rock pools of the Pont du Gard while the others climbed to the top of the great aqueduct, I discovered another person – not less touching and appealing than her sister, but made of harder and more consistent material. It was very attractive, this down-to-earthness, and even later when I kissed her the lips that met mine seemed deliberately cool and questing and self-possessed. But her fingers were always cold – now I would tend to associate the fact with guilt over treachery; not then. Livia was a dream, impossible to regret, even today."

Sutcliffe cleared his throat and said: "Pia had little of Livia's forthrightness, nor her deep voice. Her own voice was melodious contralto, a fitting instrument on which to play the passive score you wrote for her – and with which I myself don't really agree. I cannot really imagine a Livia in tears. She was always seen walking alone or sitting alone in the middle of the night in deserted cafés, just sitting, staring into her coffee. Her lips were thin when pursed – you forgot to say that; and her eyes had a bitter glimmer. I like that. You fused her uncomfortably with her sister to make Pia, or rather I did, but I was following the hints left by you in the black notebook or the green. Livia had a special little look of smiling contempt when she saw a kitchen; but Constance's face lit up with joy – as if a musician had suddenly come upon a concert-grand in perfect tune."

"I think the trouble is that you are thinking one-dimensionally all the time, like an old-fashioned novelist. You do not seem to be able to envisage a series of books through which the same characters move for all the world as if to illustrate the notion of reincarnation. After all, men and women are polyphonic beings. They know they had previous lives, but they are not sure what they were; all they feel is the weight of their karma, the poetry of previous existences registered in the penumbra of past time."

"How sick I am of the time notions."

"So am I, but the obsession is the age's. We have at any rate come to terms with it, we know that calendar time is a convenience and not a truth. Time is all one sheet – and just as the germs of an illness, say tuberculosis, are there inside one, ready and waiting to be called out by circumstance, so from a temporal point of view are the maggots already in the flesh waiting patiently for the temporal circumstance of death to set them free. Pia into Livia, Livia into Pia, what does it matter? – somewhere in that recess of time they are conscious of each other, of their origins."

"You could go further back still, then?"

"Exactly."

"What are we, then, if not simultaneous artists, 'perishing symmetrically', to borrow the phrase of Madame de Staël?"

"But Livia – even Livia could cry, though you wouldn't believe it. The first time we made love as children was among the rhododendrons at the Pont du Gard, when she was starting to wean me away from my admiration for Tu. Even then she was the expert, the ringmaster, the instigator – and I followed her suit in a sort of daze. It took me dozens of love affairs afterwards to recognise when a lover is sleeping with an imagined phantasy shape, or even with herself. Now I would not be so easily deluded. But then? Yet afterwards she went and laid her head against a tree and gave a small dry sob. It seemed quite private, and was most striking – for even in an exhibition of weakness her self-possession shone through. Before I could place a loving arm over her shoulders the spasm was over and done with. Nor would I have recognised at the time what was an obvious act of contrition – for after all she loved Tu, and hated to do her down. Indeed she loved her all too much to surrender her to me. I only saw all this years afterwards. And reflecting on it, and the possible pity of it, I wondered whether perhaps she had not done me a service in imprisoning me – in preventing me from contracting a love for Tu which could prove premature, ephemeral? If I wasn't experienced enough for Livia surely I was even less so for Tu? Perhaps it is as well to learn to drive on an old, or at least used, car before investing in an expensive new one? I don't really know. But I think it was salutary to have the experience of Livia at that time – though the displacement was at once responsible for other changes, notably in the attitude of Tu herself. I asked her once if she had been in love with me at that early time and she wrote back, 'Yes, I suppose, though I did not know what the word meant then. I was suffering from a sort of undiagnosed pain which was connected with your existence. It took time to master it. It was a case of third-degree burns. But look, I am still alive, happy and breathing.'

"Later, much later, in the flush of her new Viennese science Tu was able to pronounce upon her sister with greater self-confidence – though of course it changed nothing. 'You must treat her with great compassion, for she belongs to the great army of walking wounded in the battle of life. Our mother deserted us, and died far away in another country, never showing the slightest interest in our well-being or even safety during the war. We have a right to a grievance, and a sense of insecurity. Livia was forced to grow a masculine carapace in order to defend herself against life. It is a great nervous strain to keep on subsidising the man in herself. Perhaps she realises it. At any rate nothing can be changed now – she is fixed, like a badly set fracture. It would have to be broken and re-set, and in terms of the human personality this would not be possible. Indeed it would be dangerous to try, specially by analysis. You might overturn her reason.'

"And of course, when I reflected upon Tu herself, I wondered why she did not manifest the same characteristics of a disturbing environmental inheritance. And finally, this is the point at which her new baby science of Freudianism fell apart. If two people share the same environment and circumstances, why would one fall ill and the other not? It is one of the major puzzles and annoyances – for who can doubt the basic accuracy of the diagnosis? I reflected for a long time on the matter without reaching any real conclusion; but the facts were plain, in that Tu was a woman and had the fearlessness of a woman fully conscious of herself. In some strange way she had overcome the hatred for her mother's shade which had had such a crippling effect upon Livia.

"But all this comes long after that sunlit slide under the bridges of Lyon, gathering momentum as the river thickened out and began its headlong descent through a limestone country of such prolix variety that there was not a moment when something new did not catch and fire our attention – it was not only the rosy baked little towns with their castles and battlements which excited one. They were like punctuation marks in a noble poem – a Pindaric Ode, say. It was the consciousness that we were passing out of the north into the Mediterranean; the rich mulberries which had made the silk of Lyon world famous were soon to give place to the more austere decoration of olives, shivering and turning silver in the mistral which followed us down river; a wind of such pure force that if one opened one's mouth it was instantly filled with wind. We were moving from a cuisine based on cream and butter to one more meagre, more austere, based on olive oil and the other fruits of the Athenian tree. We were moving towards the sea – blue bodies of swimmers in the gulf, blue waves drumming the coves and *calenques* of Cassis. We were moving from liqueurs towards the ubiquitous anisette of the south.

"One after another the Rhône bestowed upon us its historic sites and little drunken towns, snuggled among vines, bathed in the insouciance of drowsy days and drowsy silences broken only by the snip-snop of the secateurs among the vines – the holy circumcision which ends the elegiac summers of Provence. The very names were a spur to what imagination and instruction we had – between us we assembled a few shreds of knowledge based on old guide books. Yes, Vienne succeeded desolate Mornas whose very name seemed to echo the sadness of old wars and ruined husbandry; then Vienne with its funny spur – but no trace of the classical splendour recorded in the histories. It must have been the Bournemouth of the ancient world – diplomats retired there from service; the most celebrated among them was Pontius Pilate who spent his quiet retirement there after leaving the Middle East with all its tedious and vexatious problems and stupid agitators. We saluted him in a glass of rosy wine. The river ran through a number of locks and barrages, each with its watchful guardian in his glassed-in perch who took our details before expelling us out of the lock-gates at an altered level, to speed on once more southward.

"As Vienne disappeared round one of the broad curves of the river Hilary looked back at it thoughtfully and said, 'It was there that the Templars were officially abolished.' He spoke as if the event were of momentous significance, but at that time I did not know very much about the Templars – just the broad details of the ancient scandal perpetrated by a King of France and executed by the hooded monsters of the Inquisition. Hilary stood there, gazing back along the water, lost in thought. But now Constance was awake and had succeeded in charming the old Félibre – the Avignon poet; fired by her beauty, and delighted that she knew some French, he proceeded to recite to us, his face creased up like a fine soft handkerchief. It was the first time I had heard Provençal spoken – there seemed to be moss packed between every syllable. Its soft lilt made one think of Gaelic; it echoed the meanderings of the great river with its sudden little tributaries and the occasional mysterious islands of sedge and weeping willow which came up at us out of the distant hazy blue and vine-green. From time to time the lean wolf-like man at the prow practised a trill or a series of sky-shattering head notes, looking round him after each paroxysm, as if for admiration. It was some little time before we were suddenly aware that we were in the presence of a master-alcoholic, an amateur of *pastis*. What matter? He was in tremendous form.

"At one our hampers were unstrapped on the deck and the two French passengers were happy to join us; Hilary had made the purchases in the town before our departure, and with the skill that comes of experience. Never had the delicacies of the French table tasted like this, before or since, washed down as they were with the simple sunlight of a great wine. Never had fresh bread tasted like this. So this was Provence! Cloudless sky, tall planes with their freckled outer skin glimmering like trout in a stream – reflected in the flowing green current. Then weeping willows, like great character actors entangled in their own foliage, and later as we climbed down, lock by lock, towards Valence, the smell of dust, honeysuckle, convolvulus. Objects occupied a place all to themselves; one little donkey – the only donkey in the whole universe, the essence of all donkeys – trotted along a path with its panniers full, raising a plume of dense dust. At Tournon our poet launched into a history of wine – while on the opposite bank glowed like jewels the vines from which came the senior wines like Côte Rôti, St Joseph and so on. We tasted some, we trinked, we came back aboard in fighting form, ready almost to take part in the opera, snatches from which our fellow-passenger continued to sing. The sun burned like a brazier. The skipper's wife opened an umbrella – the mistral had offered us a respite – and settled to her knitting. Round the massive curves of the Rhône we soared, doing almost twenty knots I judged with the current at our backs. At Condrieu an old bent man in a sea captain's hat waved a paper flag at us, evidently recognising one of our number. We all waved back.

"That evening we came up with Valence as dusk fell – our skipper appeared to hate hurrying and we had lost a great deal of time at Tournon. We tramped dazedly ashore, full of the fatigue of sunlight and wine, and found ourselves a grubby billet in a small hotel – Valence was disappointing in spite of its Napoleonic associations, and we turned in very early as the skipper had warned us that the voyage would be resumed very early the next morning.

"But in the cool pearly light of dawn, when we made our way back to the ship we found that the skipper, amidst violent expletives, was trying to counter a mysterious form of engine-trouble which prevented the motors from firing. And here to everyone's astonishment Sam came into his own and after a short and intense examination of their intestines, proffered a diagnosis and a remedy which, being acted upon, set the whole matter to rights in a twinkling. So once more we were sailing down the Rhône spattering the sky with snatches of Verdi, half bemused by the rich verses of Mistral. But we had lost time, we had lost quite a bit of time, and it was late evening before we suddenly rounded a curve of the great river and were treated to a spectacle made more remarkable by a suddenly visible full moon rising in rhetorical splendour over the ramparts of Avignon. High above the city perched the Rocher de Doms – the hanging gardens of this deserted Babylon. It was as if fate had chosen to delay us in order to repay us with its inspiring entry into the city which was later to come to mean so much to us – we did not know any of this then. Now, as I think back, I try to disinter that first impression – the marvellous silhouette of the town magnetically lit by moonlight pouring over it from the direction of the Alpilles. It is still the best way to see it – by water and from afar; and with the historic broken bridge pointing its finger across the river. And the little shrine to St. Nicholas with its bright lamps of benediction for seafaring folk. We had been gliding for nearly an hour among silent islands and deserted channels, watching the bare spars of the Cevennes rise on the night sky. And now suddenly this severe magic. It took much more experience of the town to come to the astonishing conclusion that it was only beautiful

in profile – the actual Palaces of the Popes are hideous
packing-cases of an uncouth ugliness. Nothing here was built
for charm or beauty – everything was sacrificed to the safety of
the treasures which these buildings housed. But you must
walk about the town to find this out. It is a cathedral to
Mammon. It was here our Judeo-Christian culture finally
wiped out the rich paganism of the Mediterranean! Here the
great god Pan was sent to the gas-chambers of the Popes.
Yet seen from a long way off the profile and the promise of
the town – they are heartbreaking in their sweetness of line;
and by the light of the moon marmoreal in their splendour.

"We had arrived. With a roar we started reversing
engines now in order to brake our descent and enable us to
moor firm to the shore in that racing river. The boat drummed
and throbbed. A small group of gentlemen, all suitably
decorated, were waiting for our fellow-passenger on the
quay – his name, by the way, he said, was Brunel. They
seemed if anything somewhat subdued – they had an air of
affectionate sadness as they waited for their friend. Then, as
the distance shortened, one of them, a tall and distinguished-
looking man in a topcoat, and sporting a beard (much later
I was to recognise the poet Peyre from photographs),
stepped forward to the gang plank and in a low voice uttered
the words: 'He is dead.'

"A mysterious scene to me then – yet I scented that
there was something momentous about it, though I could not
tell what. Much later I read a modern history of the Félibre,
the poets who have been the lifeblood of the region's literature, and discovered the names of that little sad group waiting
under the ramparts of the city for Brunel. Their welcoming
embraces were long and loving – one felt in them a sort of
valedictory quality, perhaps for their dead fellow.

"But behind them in the shadows lurked Felix Chatto
with the clumsy old car which would ferry us over the river

to the tumbledown mansion which Constance had inherited. Felix, too, had just come down from Oxford and despite his passionate desire to become a banker had succumbed to family pressure and entered the consular service. His uncle, the great Lord Galen, owned a vast property quite near Tubain, while Felix himself was the recently appointed acting consul in Avignon. The two of them were to prove extremely valuable to us in many ways during the period – nearly the whole summer – it took to settle Tu Duc into some semblance of a habitation. No, I exaggerate. The old place was still very sound structurally, though showing signs of neglect which rendered it barely habitable. Water, for example: the pump on the artesian well lacked an essential spare part which (Sam again) had to be more or less re-invented. In the far depths of the grounds was a lily pool full of carp; the tall flukes of the artesian formed a most decorative shape on the evening sky – but though there was plenty of wind, and though the sails turned loyally, no water flowed into the tower, and thence into the kitchen of the old house. We were forced for a few days to resort to buckets drawn from the lily pond, which incidentally afforded us delicious icy swims when these activities made us too hot. The keys fitted the doors, yes, but very approximately: Felix had brought them with him. And it took a while to discover that there was not a lock on the house which had not been put on upside down, and which consequently had to be opened anti-clockwise. Later on we got so used to this factor that one always tried the anti-clockwise turn first in dealing with locks in Provence.

"The first few nights we slept on the terrace by the light of the moon – and began by setting the kitchen to rights in order to cook our meals. A little pony-trap secured our lines of communication with Tubain where we found enough shops to satisfy our modest needs. Here again the resourceful

Sam shamed us all by actually doing some respectable cooking with Constance. The tall shadowy rooms were full of heavy, spiritless furniture, dust-impregnated, and we had to move all this old stuff into the patio to beat the dust out of it and polish it up. The wood floors creaked agreeably but were full of fleas, and called for paraffin-rag treatment. The wallpaper was shredding. On the steep terraces large green lizards, insatiably curious, came out to watch us at work; they were obviously used to being fed and seemed perfectly tame. The cupboards in the bedrooms were full of linen, white with dust, while the big central dining table with its scarlet cloth still had plates and glasses on it – as if a formal party had been suddenly interrupted and the whole company carried off by the devil. In effect the old lady had been taken ill very suddenly, and fortunately for her, during the visit of a friend who was able to find a doctor. She had been taken to a clinic in Avignon, never to return.

"'How atavistic the sense of possession is,' said Constance. 'I am mad about this house merely because it is mine. Yet it's hideous. I would never have dreamed of buying it. And anyway, I don't believe in possessions. I am ashamed of loving it so much already.'

"We lay in the pond with the cool water up to our necks, chatting among the lilies. She wore her straw hat tilted back. Her hair was wet. Every evening it was like this as long as the moonlight held. Hilary and Sam played chess on the terrace with a little pocket set – Hilary was watching the dinner. We had discovered the local anisette – the *pastis* of the region; surely the most singular of drinks for it coats the palate and utterly alters the taste of a good wine and good food.

"There were owls in the tower, there were swerving, twittering bats in the trees, but as long as the heat of the long grass sent up insects into the evening sky the swallows and martins worked close overhead, swerving in and out like darts, to take the spiring insects in open beaks with a startling judgment and accuracy. One could hear their little beaks click from time to time as they snapped at an insect. And then of course the steady drench, the steady drizzle of cicadas in the great planes and chestnuts of the park. All succumbing and sliding into the silence of the full moon which only the dogs celebrated, together with an occasional nightjar and the plaintive little Athenian owl called the Skops. Coming from the cold north we were continually amazed by the beauty and richness of this land. There was only one old man who worked on the property and he lived far away in the valley; but after the first week he brought up a venerable blind horse and set it to turning about a water wheel, fixed to one of the shallower wells. Mathieu, he was called, and he was very deaf."

Poor Blanford! His reveries had carried him so far afield in the past that he did not notice that the telephone had gone dead. He curtly replaced the receiver, having rung for Cade to clear up the tea things. Then he moved with the stiff precariousness of a doll to the library which they had shared over the years; he had housed his own books here during his travels – Tu had set aside two large bookcases for him to which only he had the key. It was a very long time since he had taken to binding up her letters, unwilling to part with such a testimony of friendship and love so central to his inner life, his develop-ment. By now there were a number of slim volumes with brilliant Venetian leather bindings, stamped and tooled with emblems suitable to such an intimate correspondence; the little books were housed in pretty slipcases of expensive leather. He unlocked the bookcase and took out one or two to ruffle in that silent room. She would be, he felt, almost his only reading now that she had "gone". He could grimly follow the vicissitudes of his career through her letters from the first success to the time of the Q novels. Tu had been his oldest and most ardent friend; reading some kindly, ironic passages, he recovered the very timbre of that ever-living voice.

And his own replies? They too were there in her part of the library – an extensive collection of books and manuscripts for he had not been her only friend among the artists. One way and another Constance had known some of the great men of the day. A small pang of jealousy stirred in him with the thought. But it had never occurred to her to bind up his letters, they were in ordinary office folders, as if awaiting a final sorting. Nor were her own somewhat disorderly bookcases locked. He reached down a folder and, opening it, came upon a recent letter addressed to her from the city – sometime last year, it must have been. He had the bad habit of seldom dating his letters. He poked up the fire and sat down with the folder on his knee, trying to read the letter freshly, as if he were Tu, and as if it had just arrived.

"Once again I am here alone in Avignon, walking the deserted streets, full of reminiscences of our many visits, full of thoughts of Tu Duc and yourself. Yes, here I am again in the place where, according to cards set out by my horrible valet Cade, I am due to die by my own hand, sometime during my fifty-ninth year. That still gives me a year or two of clock time; but what Cade speaks of has surely been going on for a long time?

"How shall I explain it to you? For the writer at any rate everything that one might call creatively wrought, brought off, completed aesthetically, comes to you, his reader and his Muse, from the other side of a curtain. From the other side of a hypothetical suicide – ask Sutcliffe! Indeed this is the work of art's point of departure. It need not happen in the flesh to the performer. But it is indispensable to art, if there be any art in the commodity he fathers. Bang!

"Constance, the poet does not choose. The poet does not think of renown, for even the voices which carry the furthest are only the echoes of an anterior, half-forgotten past. The poetic reality of which I speak, and which Sutcliffe might have deployed in his unwritten books, is rather like the schoolchild's definition of a fishing-net as 'a lot of holes tied together with string'. Just as impalpable, yet just as true of our work. Art is only to remind.

"I think, if Cade is right, I shall have enough time to send this project down the slips; afterwards Sutcliffe can flesh it out and fill in the details. Come, let us buy some time for our clocks – a nice juicy slice of time. I must add in all honesty that Sutcliffe is somewhat scared of the idea. When I outlined it he said: 'But Aubrey, this could lead anywhere.' I said: 'Of course. I have freed us both.' The notion of an absolute freedom in the non-deterministic sense alarmed him. As usual he became flippant, to give himself time to reflect. Then he said, 'What would you give me if I wrote a book to prove that the great Blanford is simply the fiction of one of his fictions? Eh?' You know the answer as well as I do, but I could not resist saying it out loud. 'The top prize, Robin Sutcliffe, immortality in the here and now. How would that suit you?' This left him very thoughtful in a somewhat rueful way. He is lazy, he doesn't want to co-operate one little bit. He lacks my driving ambition.

"No, Constance my dear, ours shall be a classical quincunx – a Q; perhaps a *Tu Quoque* will echo throughout it. We will try to refresh poetry and move it more towards the centre of ordinary life.

"Then later, when the blow falls, and I disappear from the scene, it will have to do duty, such as it is, for my *star y-pointed pyramid*. Ever your devoted A."

TWO

Humble Beginnings

BLANFORD NAVIGATED FRETFULLY ABOUT THE HOUSE, talking to himself a little with Constance in mind – there seemed so much still to say to her. His fingers crept along the shelf of her Latin and Greek poets towards the volumes which contained their correspondence. "I know that poets make more boom and slither, but novelists can create personae you loathe or adore." He riffled the coloured pages and then read aloud: "Your notion of Sutcliffe intrigues me. Some detail please. I hope he won't become a provincial Heathcliff."

He had replied, "You ask about Sutcliffe? I cannot tell you for how many years he lay silent, living a larval life in the cocoon of my old black notebook. I did not know what to do with him – though I kept jotting away as directed. It was essential that he should differ greatly from me – so that I could stand off and look at him with a friendly objectivity. He represented my quiddity I suppose – the part which, thanks to you, has converted a black pessimism about life into a belief in cosmic absurdity. He was the me who is sane to the point of outrage. Often I kissed you with his mouth just to see how it felt. He never thanked me."

He sat down with the volume on his knee and stared into the fire once more – into its coiling shapes he read snakes and ladders of fire, a crusader burning on a pyre, a scorpion, a crucifixion.

Yes, a different background. Sutcliffe might get born somewhere north of Loughborough, say, to decent Quaker parents. Millers of grain? He was a scholarship boy who had won an Exhibition to Oxford, and then, like so many others, had found himself thrown upon the slave market of pedagogy. He had edited a few cribs which were badly reviewed by a tiresome clanging professor – and thus lost the chance of a post as a translator. Poverty intervened, and since he had nothing special for which to starve, he accepted the first opening which presented itself. He found himself teaching French and music to schoolgirls at Hymendale, a clergy orphans' establishment, where half the staff was ecclesiastical and half lay. Whence his downfall. For nuns called to dons, dons to nuns, deep to deep, dope to dope. . . . It was really not his fault.

Hymendale was a suburb of Bournemouth, that salubrious south coast resort, which even then was geared to the retirement requirements of professional men and colonial civil servants. Privet hedges, eyes peering from behind curtains, a draughty gentility; silent streets awoken only to the clip clop of the milkman's little van. It was a fine place to develop inner resources – so he told himself grimly as he grimly did his daily walks, twice round the sewage plant and once there and back along the cliffs in the rain. Ah! the eternal rain! Eight hours a week spent with his sallow, skewer-shaped girls with lank hair and torpid intelligences. *Que cosa fare?* He saw himself even then as a rather tragic figure, trapped by fate in this religious treadmill. He played the role to himself for all it was worth, sometimes being overheard laughing aloud – a harsh sardonic bark directed at the greasy teeming sky. The pubs in the place shut early and were full of tobacco smoke, at once acrid and throat-drying. There was one reasonable bookshop, Commin's, as well as a lending library, and of course two cinemas. He buried himself in books, thanking God that he could read enough French to amuse himself. We must imagine a rather large, short-sighted man clad in shapeless tweeds perforated with many a nameless cigarette and pipe hole. He had a stalking walk whose buoyancy suggested an inner exuberance which he was far from feeling. No; he was guilty of over-compensating.

Loneliness led to this passionate self-communing, which in turn led to somewhat eccentric behaviour – at least by the standards of such an establishment. For instance, on Sunday morning, when the class formed up in the quad to draggle to chapel in its desultory Indian file, Sutcliffe (who led the procession in gown and tippet) liked to imagine that he was engaged in other, more romantic activities. Thus one Sunday he would be leading his cricketers out into the field to win the Ashes back from Australia; he snuffled the wind, gazed at the light, sucked his finger boy scout fashion and held it up to determine the direction (before sending in his bowlers). He cleared his throat and made a number of finger signs to invisible umpires, directing the position of the screens ... and so on. On other days he was the leader of an African tribe, clad in nothing but a tiger-skin, and waving a knobkerrie as he walked, chanting under his breath to the rhythm of inaudible drums. He was head of the young hunters and they were going out for lion – nothing less! On other occasions he enacted a priest leading victims of the Terror towards the guillotine. The clatter of the tumbril on the paving stones of Paris were practically audible to the listener. It goes without saying that this intense miming and the strange postures were looked upon by his superiors with misgivings. But they were simply the outward and visible signs of an intense inner life.

There was nobody he could talk to, so he had developed the habit of talking to himself – interminable low monologue of the inner mind. People saw only the outward expression suited to these thoughts which passed in him like shoals of fish. A popping eye, lips pursing, eyebrows going up and down. His nose twitched. Often (he blamed this on the diet of spotted dog and treacle tart) he had piles which divided into three categories, namely Itchers, Bleeders and plain Shouting piles. For his walks he used a shabby old golfing umbrella and vast boots with hooks and eyes. "I was formed by Doctor Arnold," he was wont to tell himself, "whose wife much enjoyed his melancholy long-withdrawing roar." When he was overcome by depression he sometimes went down into the town and for ten shillings and a Devonshire Tea gave Effie a furtive caress, which only increased his sense of despondency and alienation. Effie was a barmaid at The Feathers and a good enough little soul, very modest in her demands upon life. She was indeed sweet but O the cold apple tart between her pale, frog-like legs. He bought her presents because he felt guilty at leading her astray — she was really a good girl and not a whore. She had a marked tendency towards cystitis. But the town, the monotony, the rain and the people can drive you to do anything. One thing about her intrigued him – the way she cocked her little finger over a teacup with such an affectation of gentility. . . . She did the same in bed as if to confer some of the same sort of gentility upon the love act. He adored this. For some reason not known to science Sutcliffe had the habit of carrying two french letters in the turnups of his broadly cut trousers. They were very expensive these things, and he kept them only for Effie; after use, he washed them out and pegged them up to dry on the mantelpiece of his little room for an hour. They had the word EVERSAFE printed on them. Effie insisted on protection and was affectionately responsive to such little attentions. She liked this man who suffered so often from chilblains and who walked about on his toes with rather a mystified air. She would have dreamed of marrying him perhaps, but he was a gentleman and it would not have done.

His duties entitled him to a little room with a fireplace, with a separate entrance onto the quadrangle – and he always dreamed of enticing some secret woman to visit him. But who? He had a small harmonium of the wheezy sort and a copy of the Forty-eight of Bach, which he played for his own amusement, but not too loud. For the rest he read opera-scores at night, eating an apple the while; occasionally he moved his eyebrows and let out a roar to correspond to a full orchestra unleashing top sound. Vaguely in the back of his mind a project was forming itself; to write a new life of Wagner.

Why not? Sometimes on his walks he saw a point of darkness move indistinctly upon the horizon repeatedly expunged and dimmed and recreated. A ship, forsooth! He waved his umbrella and cheered. All this monotony might be a good aliment for a poet but what if one had no gifts? Sometimes he got so lonely that he could have set his bed on fire.

Sister Rosa must have also suffered from it, perhaps more acutely, for she had come to England from some dusky clime. She was pretty, with a mischievous face, and an octoroon as to complexion. He caught her examining him in chapel, and she gave a dark rosy blush. He smiled at her and she smiled back in a way that suddenly made him feel that for her spring was not far behind. There had been some trouble that day with the Sixth; he had been summoned to the head and asked if he was really "doing" Mallarmé? "Just giving an account of the period," he had replied. The Mother Superior raised a white finger and said, "Mr. Sutcliffe, I know I can count on you not to let anything too French or too suggestive pass. It is a great trust we have put in you in giving you the Sixth. Please guide them in the paths of blamelessness, even if it means *stealing through* the classics rather than doing them in detail."

"Do you mean censoring them?"

"Well, yes, I suppose I do."

"Very well," said Sutcliffe grimly and withdrew. He had already planned a bowdlerised Mallarmé to meet the case. "*Le chien est triste. Hélàs! Il a lu tous les livres,*" he wrote on the blackboard in the classroom. It would have to do for today. Surely the English with their love of animals could not complain of *that*? But as he sniffed the air he felt that trouble lay ahead. The pieties of the place argued ill for free thinkers. He was thinking this over when. . . . But this needs a new paragraph.

Poor Sister Rosa, too, was bored to death. Her English was very bad, and it was in the hope of finding someone to speak to her in Congo Pidgin that she had appraised Sutcliffe whom she knew to be teaching French; almost inhaling him with her mind as she raised her neat little muzzle and tip-tilted nose. The inside of her lips were blackish purple, her teeth were small and regular, her smile delicious – or so thought the quivering Master of Arts. Boredom makes strange bedfellows, he could not help remarking, for he knew that all this frantic emotion was a little bit invented. When he closed his eyes he saw her naked on his shabby cot in the alcove, lying back with her eyes closed. Her dark skin tinted like rum, molasses, ginger . . . and so on.

For her part she found it vastly dispiriting to spend hours arranging waxed fruit on the High Altar of the chapel. Nevertheless it gave her access to Sutcliffe's pew which was convenient. At the next service he found a flower on his hassock and a highly suggestive Catholic bookmarker tucked into his hymn-book. The ingenuity of women! Sutcliffe blushed all over with pleasure. It was the work of a second to scribble on the endpapers of the hymn-book the magic words, "How? When? Where?" in French. If he did not add "How much?" it was because he did not want to hurt her feelings by being *too* French. After all, she *was* a bloody nun. Now a short pause supervened, for what reason he could not tell – the designs of nature perhaps, or the feeling that she had gone too far, or something of an administrative order? Hard to tell. Anyway he left another message inviting closer co-operation and tried to fire her by singing very loudly when interpreting hymns whose words ("Nearer My God to Thee", for example) could be taken in more than one way.

At last she yielded – though her handwriting was so inchoate that he had difficulty in making out the words "Tonight. Room 5". Sutcliffe swelled up with desire and pride. That evening he played Bach remorselessly and with keen impatience. He had never been into the nunnery side of the establishment, and while he supposed that they shuffled to bed fairly early he thought it wise to let them get to sleep before starting his own invasion of the premises, EVERSAFE in hand, so to speak. To tell the truth the prospect rather quailed him – wandering about in the gloomy corridors of a nunnery. He waited until midnight before embarking.

He crossed the quad and entered the silent building which showed not a spark of light anywhere. He made brief use of his pocket torch and mounted to the first floor. The numbers were not only battered and almost effaced, they were not in serial order – or so it seemed. But at last he hit upon a room which he took to be numbered correctly, pressed the handle of the door and felt the warm air flow out into the corridor. He stepped into the blackness and stood for a moment to let his eyes accustom themselves to the dark. A figure in a bed stirred and he heard what he took to be a welcoming sigh. "Sister Rosa," he breathed and switched on his little torch.

The Mother Superior gazed at him in terrified silence, with starting eyes; if she had had her teeth in they would have been chattering – but they lay and grinned in a tooth mug beside the bed. Sutcliffe let out an incoherent exclamation of utter panic. Her wig was on a stand by the bed and she wore a nightcap. He was about to turn and run for it when she turned on the light and exclaimed, "Mr. Sutcliffe, what are you doing here?"

It was difficult to explain. He spread his arms and pretended to be sleepwalking; then he awoke with a theatrical start and said, "Where am I?"

It carried no conviction.

As time went on the story changed shape almost as often as it changed hands or tongues; some of this was due to Sutcliffe himself who had the ingrown novelist's habit of embroidering on behalf of novels as yet to be. Thus in one version she produced a pearl-handled revolver and fired a shot through his coat-tails – in fact, he was not wearing a coat. In another equally implausible version she opened wide her arms and legs and cried, "At last you have come to claim me!" thus forcing upon him a distasteful and unholy conjunction of souls and bodies. It was the only way to keep his job.

But what really happened? She cried, "Mr. Sutcliffe, will you leave this room at once!" and this he did with some alacrity. In the morning he was summoned before the board of governors and dismissed with effect from lunchtime – hardly leaving him time to pack before catching the London train. He felt bad about having betrayed Rosa too, for on his way to the station he had a glimpse of her sitting upright between two granite-faced Carthusians in the little black bus of the school which could be converted into a hearse in times of need. Her cheeks were very flushed and her eyes cast down.

Once back in London he returned to the seedy agency which had found him the job and described the circumstances of dismissal to the little Cockney manager whose catarrh and adenoids took turns at interfering with his articulation. He heard Sutcliffe out, shaking his head sadly. "Not very clever," he said more than once. "You know what I should have done? Bicycled to the doctor's and asked for a prescription against sleepwalking." He spread his hands. "Then when the board called me up I would have a watertight excuse." Sutcliffe whistled. "I never thought of that," he said.

"Next time be more wily," said the little man.

"Or less susceptible to female charms."

"Quite."

He turned once more to his sordid register and went through a list of vacancies tracing them with a broken thumbnail.

So the long cultural calvary continued for our hero until (after many humiliations) he rose to glory and affluence by his superior merits. Yet looking back on these episodes in later years he was not displeased with some of his handiwork. When the class, for example, asked him what the last words of Verlaine were he had replied: "Happiness is a little scented pig."

But leaving Sutcliffe to his picaresque early adventures, the thoughts of Aubrey Blanford once more returned to those earliest memories of France, and of Provence. They were wonderfully pristine always – as if only yesterday:

There they were, for example, lying in the pond among the open lilies with the cool lapping water up to their throats, breathing in the silences of the abandoned garden, which, like the house itself, was full of presences which would have been real ghosts if only they had been visible. Doors which opened and shut of their own accord, footsteps on the main staircase at midnight. Voices which whispered names so softly that it was always possible to attribute the noise to the rustle of ivy in the changing wind. With shifts of temperature –

when the heat from the kitchen rose to the first floor – all the cupboards creaked and burst open as if to embrace one. In the dense foliage of the garden there was always a flickering of things just seen out of the corner of the eye. When one turned and looked directly there was nothing. And there was one loose tile on the footpath by the *potager* where every night at dusk one heard a footfall: someone passed and made it click.

Sometimes if you opened the cellar door a black cat flowed out which answered to no name, no blandishment, no caress. It made its way softly through the hall, to disappear by a side door. An animal? Or the ghost of one? It was like a portfolio of sketches of suave postures – something to grace a fashion plate.

A long time later Hilary said that he had once seen a girl in a white evening dress walking by the lily pond reading a letter; what struck him was that the blackbirds gave no sign of seeing a human being and were actually flying through her – or so it appeared. She passed into the trees and took the path to the house; he waited uneasily for her on the balcony but she never appeared. In the afternoons by the little coach-house someone beat the dust out of an invisible carpet. All the silences of the place seemed dense with things just waiting to materialise. A sense of immanence. Constance loved this; at night she was always blowing out the light and sitting in the dark trying to "see". But Livia could not stand it, and after a few days would find an excuse to set off on a camping-trip or spend a few days in neighbouring Avignon where Felix gave her his tiny spare room.

And then the portrait gallery, the three heads! This long gallery was an extension to the house with broad windows running the whole length of it and lit with white panes of toplight; the trees sheltered it from the direct rays of the sun. Now it was empty, for the old lady had sold all her portraits long since – an unremarkable collection by all accounts – and kept only three smoky heads printed in the typical ancestor-style of safe academicians of the last century. And now almost obliterated by corruptions in the pigment. The names too were hardly readable, though one could make out the word Piers on the portrait of the pale young man with a frail and consumptive expression, and the word Sylvie below that of the dark intense girl, who might well have been his sister. The third picture had fared worse and it was literally not possible to tell whether the subject was a man or a woman – only that its colouring was blonde and not dark, its eyes as blue and lucid as Hilary's. All three portraits were draped with black velvet, which created a singular impression on the beholder, who could not help wondering why. Was someone in mourning for them? Did it betoken some special religious gesture – a consecration? Who were they? We were unable to find out. On the back of one picture, written in yellow faded ink was the phrase, "Chateau de Bravedent". To study them one had to draw back their velvet covers with a gold cord.

Felix Chatto, no less intrigued than we, had spent a lot of time and energy trying to find out the meaning of this laconic inscription and the location, if possible, of such a chateau; in vain. "I swear there is no such place in Provence," he added with a sigh, "though of course one day it might surface again as the lost medieval name for a place." We were sitting downstairs then at the oaken kitchen table, having lunch. "And perhaps it is better that way – not to know, I mean, and to go on wondering about them. It would be difficult to invent a romantic enough story to suit that strange trio. And in my view you are wrong about the third person – it is really a woman, not a man. The fingernails are not painted." But of course this proved nothing and he knew it. But then: why the dusty velvet coverings? Were they dead?

Nevertheless the existence of the three and the name of

the apparently non-existent chateau exercised a great influence over the musings of Blanford; they existed as obstinate symbols of something to which the key had been lost. He said to himself sadly, "If only I believed in the novel as a *device* I would incorporate their story in a book which had nothing to do with real life. Bravedent!"

Livia turned her face to him; she had been sucking a coloured sweet they had bought at the village shop. With a swift motion of her tongue she passed it into his mouth and sealed it with a bitter-sweet kiss on the lips. He was lost, Blanford. He found such effortless happiness almost painful.

It was only now, in this backwash of time, and from these heterogeneous documents that he could follow out the slow curve of this *amor fati* – this classic attachment to Livia. When he asked her what her mother was like, for example, it was Constance who replied to him: but at some other time, in another context, for Livia simply looked at him with those dark eyes gone like dead snails and licked her lips as if about to speak, but nothing came. Constance wrote in a letter: "I remember an old, old lady with a piercing blue eye, whose cheeks had subsided for want of teeth and whose ill-fitting false ones did not fulfil the role completely. She had been a poor actress before she married. Now she was mad with regret and forever dwelling on ancient pleasures which had fed that sick vanity. The world of diplomacy – a world of kindly lampreys – provided a delusive background for her needs. Underneath the surface excitements the demon of accidie had her by the hair. She had always been avid for the meretricious, and when her shallow beauty faded everything turned to hate – but chiefly against her children because of their own youthful beauty. Not for her the Great Inkling! Here she was, subsiding into ashes day by day, while we were flowering. Soon she felt herself swelling with pure malevolence, a loathing strong enough to carry, she hoped, even beyond the grave, to blight our lives, to maim our spirits! She complained that her breasts were flaccid because she had nursed us too long, and tried everything then available to plump them out, except surgery. Even that absurd *ventouse* which was supposed to make them firm by suction. We have had to wade though all this powerfully projected hate without quite understanding it – except now, retrospectively. Forgiving it is another thing. Look at Livia!"

He was looking at Livia, at that face which for him spelt an invincible happiness; he was not so much wounded as astonished when the youthful Sam described her eyes like dead fish-eyes and her hair as dandruffy, adding that he could never care for a girl like that. The angle of vision is everything. The poetic vision is manufactured to meet desire. This experience was forming him, and would give him his first short story, which in the long run was what really mattered. But without her and the frightful jolt she gave him he might never have entered the immortality stakes with his first study of the circle she frequented in Paris where she was at this time a professing painter, prone to cubism. His inexperience shielded him from recognising the group of charming if effete personages for what they were – and they were careful not to enlighten him. She lived thus, in happy ambiguity, within this kindly group of homosexual friends whose charm and sensibility were undeniable. As a little band of outlaws they had grouped themselves into postures of social consequence; it was a wise precaution for they were for the most part rather insipid people and they knew it. Their social commerce betrayed a certain fragile uncertainty ... they felt somehow one-dimensional; almost opaque. They telephoned each other several times a day, as if to reassure themselves of each other's existence. They issued bulletins about their health and the state of their art which were like certificates of identity.

Later, when Constance was full (a little too full) of her knowledge, she expressed the cruel paradox of Livia's case more clearly; indeed the total narcissism which is expressed in inversion derives from the sense of abandon by the mother. But crueller still, the sexual drive which alone satisfies it consists of a mock incest precisely with her abandoner. But such a proposition would only have made Livia swear – and the oaths she used turned ugly in her mouth, accompanied as they were by expressions as distasteful as those of a sick bird. A phrase came to mind from the black notebook, where he was trying to lay down a few guide-lines towards a sketch of her character. Looking at Constance with remorse, regret and hate, Livia thought, "There is nothing more enraging than the sight of someone who is unwaveringly, naturally and helplessly good." After all, Constance had her own deceptions to live through, though she was at last able to swallow their absurdity and pretentiousness and write, "Love is the banana-peel that laughter-loving reality leaves on the pavements for men and women to skid on." The thing was that she comprehended and pardoned her sister because she loved her, and for her sake she always hoped against hope that our relations would survive despite the drawbacks. Blanford could not remember just when he made a note in his diary which said, "I fear she lives on tittle-tattle and smoke; I have married a rattle and a snob." But even that was not the worst of the matter; the central feeling of loss was to get denser and richer as bit by bit Livia grew more sure of herself, more careless about hiding matters.

The mind has limits, the body limits; the equation is easily made, the limits quickly reached. It was all my fault, thought Blanford, leaning forward to poke the fire. It was a case of transposed heads. Constance and I were slow to recognise each other. In all this amateur bliss I one day overheard a telephone conversation with Thrush, the little Martinique lover, which made me prick up my ears. In a different voice, one that I had never heard before, she said: "I simply made up my mind to make him marry me." Turning, she saw me at the door, and replaced the receiver. I said nothing and after a while her obvious anxiety died down – I suppose since I offered no comment on this remark. "It was just Thrush," she said, "we are going to the Opera tonight." She knew that I could never stand opera. But just for once I had taken the number of their tickets and had bought myself one in the Gods. I went that evening and easily located the stalls she had reserved; but the seats were occupied by other people whose faces I did not know.

It is only the context which renders such things painful or pleasurable – all that was basically wrong was Blanford's gruesome lack of experience. He knew that now. It was the pliant and lovely Livia's destiny to initiate him – and of course those we initiate we mark for life. "Nature's lay Idiot, I taught thee to f**k," she could have exclaimed as Sutcliffe did on another such occasion; nor would the glancing echo of Donne have been out of keeping. No. But the period of ardour and illusion led on and on for more than a summer – could it perhaps have gone on for a lifetime? – until by an unlucky accident he came upon the letter she had forgotten to hide or destroy and in which everything was made clear. His heart sank with sorrow and disgust; it was not the reaction of a moralist – it was simply that he found the deception cruel and unnecessary. From it all he suddenly developed an exaggerated hate for the little group of neuters – *les handi-cappés* – and by extension for the Paris he had always found grotesque, but vividly alive and nourishing. How would he stand August now, swollen with the knowledge that he was being run in tandem with some black-hearted Parisienne? He started to write her letters, and to leave them everywhere in the flat. He had moved to a furnished room but still had the key of the flat and used his bookfilled study to work in. He was still raw from the pleasures of her beauty and the excellence of her love-making; there was a poem of that period in which he described her with felicity as "a constellation of fervours". It was published in the *Critic* but he did not show it to her. Thrush, then, was the ringmaster? It was suddenly like being dropped on one's head out of a tree, or diving into an empty swimming pool. With one hand he did some automatic writing in his black notebook. ("The new sexual model will incorporate death somehow as the central experience. The lovers will float to the surface belly upwards, dead from exhaustion.") He wrote an indignant description of his discovery to Constance but did not post it. And years afterwards, in discussing this period of time, he felt glad that he had not, for Constance was busy with profounder matters, and still much hampered by her sexual inexperience. It was this same summer perhaps that she decided to marry Sam – which also called for long and elaborate reflections later on. But in one sense the shock was most salutary for Blanford; he was suddenly able to see all round himself; it was as if he had been living in a dense fog and suddenly it had lifted. It was a real initiation, a real awakening. He suddenly saw, for example, what the two lovers had done to Thrush's husband. He was a pious and swarthy little man, pleasantly coon-coloured and with dense ringlets. It is doubtful that he actually was conscious of what was going on – the notion rested on the edge of his mind like an ominous premonition. He began to feel first an overwhelming lethargy – the affect had started to bleed; the two vampires knew their stuff all right!

But first of all they made him rich and fashionable, a consultant for film stars and bankers, and that sort of animal. They lobbied him decorations of one sort or another, and made sure that he went to all the first nights and cocktail parties. It was about six years since he had last slept with Thrush, though they lived in tender amity; but he began to retire earlier and earlier, gripped by fatigue and the shadow of something like diabetes; until he took to having dinner with the children in the nursery and going straight to bed with them; he yawned more and more and looked vague. Retiring thus from the fray every evening he left the *champs d'honneur* free for the lovers and their doings. Once or twice they talked of finding him a substitute woman – a pretty *repoussoir* like Livia – but he had no energy left for such a project. So thoroughly had they done the work of affect castration that he had gone all anaesthetic. As for Thrush, *animatrice de petit espace* that she was, she kept him soothed and tranquil in his striped pyjamas. In her he had an impresario who had guided him to wealth and social success – should a man ask more? But Blanford could see that this same gloomy fate of Zagreus was going to be his unless he watched out. What to do? As he wrote in one of his letters to Livia, "Of course marriage is an impossible state with all its ups and downs, lapses, temptations, renewals. But the only thing the tattered old contract sets out is that you accord the primacy of your affections to someone, this side idolatry. The cheat was that yours were not free to bestow. It is all that sours me."

He was left with a mountain of scribbled exercise books – an attempted exorcism. But it did little good. It was as futile as founding a society for the abolition of bad weather. Yet the loneliness taught him discipline. There is nothing more beautiful than Method.

About Blanford; before writing the first words of a novel in his Q series he would close his eyes, breathe serenely through his nose, and think of the Pleiades. To him they symbolised the highest form of art – its quiddity of stillness and purity. Nothing could compare with them for noble rigour, for elegance. It was in order to cure this rather dangerous proclivity that he had invented that mass of conflicting and contradictory predispositions called Sutcliffe – a writer who recited the Lord's Prayer, putting a Damn between every word, before addressing *his* novel.

Blanford took an overdose of sleeping pills and had horrible dreams in which he was forever helping two nymphs on with wings they rejected. He imagined them lying together in the sand – Livia's face like an empty playground waiting for children, her large vague pale brow . . . The long middle finger which betokened bliss in secret.

Nor was it any solace to think hard thoughts about Thrush; apart from this unhappy situation he found her delightful. But he told himself that she opened her mouth so wide that she resembled a hippo, folding her food into it. As a matter of fact, even when she laughed her eyes cried "Help!" He could dimly intuit the terrible jealous insecurity that ravaged the two quaires – the negative of his own, so to speak. Once in the rue St.-Honoré when he was waiting for a massive American businessman (they had the simple authority of trolleys, comforting), the dentist came up to him in a bar and got into conversation. They only knew each other by sight then, and Blanford felt a kind of clinging, pleading quality in the encounter – as if he were hoping to find some solution to his case in a talk with Blanford. But they were ill matched for an exchange of consolations. He told himself that Thrush had a vicious, thirsty little French face; but it wasn't true and he knew it. He felt as if his brains had cooled and dripped into his socks. He could have written an ode called "A Castrate's Tears beneath the Shears" – but the tone was wrong and he delegated this to Sutcliffe who would come along in good time with his own brand of snivel. And then, on top of it all, to be unfair to poor Paris which all of a sudden became loathsome to him. He noticed now the dirty hair, cheaply dyed, and never kept up from meanness – so many brassy blondes with black partings. And in August the refusal to shave armpits. . . . The town smelt like one large smoking armpit. Acrid as the lather of dancers. And then the selection of sexual provender – perversions worthy of wood-lice. Well, he had come there for infamy in the first place, so what the hell had he got to complain about? He would die, like Sutcliffe, in the arms of some lesbian drum-major, dreaming nostalgically of hot buttered toast between normal thigh and thigh. Indeed he would go further and become a Catholic and enact the funky deathbed scene – the spider on the ceiling and the shadow of a priest and a notary. . . . It wouldn't do, said the voice of Constance, and he knew that it wouldn't. Eheu!

Under the shock of this misadventure Blanford suddenly found that he could read people's minds, and a sudden shyness assailed him; he found now that he lowered his eyes when faced with newcomers – the better to listen to the sound of their voices. It was the voice he was reading so unerringly. People thought that he had become unusually shy of a sudden. (In some lower-middle-class bedroom Sutcliffe heard his tinny wife say, *"Chéri, as tu apporté ton Cadeau Universel?"* And he replied, *"Oui chérie, le-voilà."*

THREE

The Consul Awake

THE PRO-CONSUL WAS RULED BY THE DEMON OF INSOMNIA, the royal illness; lying with his eyes fast shut in his little cage of a villa with its creaky bed, old chest of drawers and flawed mirror – lying there suspended in his own anxiety as if in a cloudy solution of some acid – he saw the sombre thoughts passing in flights across the screens of his consciousness. The hours weighed like centuries on his heart. Memories rose up from different periods of his life, crowding the foreground of his mind, contending for attention. They had no shape, no order, but they were vivid and exhausting – at once silky and prickly as thistles. Each night provided an anthology of sensations betokening only hopelessness and helplessness; this handsome and quite cultivated young man who dreamed of nothing so much as a post in the Bank of England (the excellence of his degrees justified such a hope) had been unwittingly sold into slavery by a mother who adored him with all the passion that centres about only children. How had this all come about? He knew only too well. "For you it's *diplomacy*," said his uncle, Lord Galen, one day, conducting the full orchestra of his self-esteem. His opinion was never asked and he was too weak to resist the little corsair who had become his mother's lover after the death of Felix's father. The boy had been weak and irresolute enough, the man was even more so. So here he found himself in a minor consular post in Avignon – a pro-consul of the career, if you please, but paid a mere pittance for his services. Yes, here he was, half dead with boredom and self-disdain.

The Office had not even had the decency to declare the post an honorary one – which would perhaps have forced

Galen to make him an allowance. He was paid like a solicitor's
clerk. He was only allowed a part-time consular clerk to keep
his petty cash and type the few despatches he ever wrote.
There was nothing to report and if there were any British
subjects in Avignon they had never shown their faces. The
villa was buried deep in dust-gathering oleanders and poin-
settias. If only his mother could see him now – a Crown
Servant! He gave a croak of sardonic laughter and turned on
his side. Yet she must be proud of him. A flood of unformu-
lated wishes and hopes, suddenly floating into view, directed
his memory to a picture which made him always catch his
breath in pain, as if he had run a thorn under his fingernail.
He opened his eyes and saw her sitting withered up in her
wheelchair. Looking at the dusty electric bulb hanging naked
from the ceiling he went over his history for the thousandth
time. His father had died when he was very small; years later
his mother had conducted a long and decorous affair with his
brother, the dashing Galen (extremely discreet, extremely
ambiguous) until the increasing paralysis confined her to this
steel trolley, pushed by a gloved attendant dressed in a billy-
cock hat and a long grey dustcoat. Felix could hear the
munching of its slim tyres on the gravels of gardens in
Felixstowe, Harrogate, Bournemouth. When her illness grew
too severe she had been too proud to continue her affair with
Galen – she could not bear to see herself as a drag on him or
on his career. He accepted this decision with guilty relief,
though he vowed that she would want for nothing. He kept
in touch through her doctors, though he did not write directly
any more – he had always had a superstitious hatred of ink
and paper. He had been taught that things written down can
turn against one in the courts, that was the root of the feeling.
But even had he written she could not have answered for she
could no longer hold a pen; and as for speech, her own was
slurred and indistinct. Her jaw hung down sideways, there

were problems with saliva. Deeply shocked by her own condition, the dark eyes blazed with a sort of agonised astonishment. Her attendant was called Wade. In his billy-cock hat he wore the feather of a cock-pheasant. He was now far closer to her than either her son or her lover. She was impatient for only one thing now – to die and get it over with. . . . Wade read the Bible to her for two hours every night.

Felix groaned and rolled over in bed, turning his face to the ghastly wallpaper with its raucous coaching print. He breathed deeply and tried to hurl himself into sleep as if from a high cliff – but in vain, for other shallower thoughts swarmed about him as the fleas swarmed in his bed, despite the Keating's Powder. This time it was exasperating memories of the official pinpricks he had incurred in trying to obtain a new Union Jack to fly from the mast which had been so insecurely fixed to the first-floor balcony of the villa. During the usual Pentecost celebrations, which were closed by a triumphal gallop-past of the Carmargue *gardiens*, some fool had discharged a gun in the air – *un feu de joie* – and the charge had spattered the sacred flag with smallshot, so that now it looked like a relic left over from Fontenoy. Felix simply could not fly such a tattered object any longer and, having described the circumstances, invited London to replace it. But nothing doing. An immense and most acri-monious correspondence had developed around this imperial symbol; the Office insisted that the culprit should be found and sued for his sins, and lastly forced to replace the object; failing that, said the Office of Works (Embassy Furnishings Dept.), the flag might have to be paid for out of Felix's own pocket – a suggestion which drove him mad with rage. Back and forth went these acid letters on headed paper. London was adamant. The culprit must be found. Felix smiled grimly as he recalled the leather-jawed horseman whose racing steed had struck a bouquet of sparks from the cobbles as it went. The man indeed who had so narrowly missed him, for he had been standing on the balcony at the time to watch the procession. A foot to the right and there would have been a consular vacancy which the Crown Agents would have been happy to advertise in *The Times*. He had even felt the wind of the discharge, and smelt the cordite of a badly dosed home-made charge. And the flag?

And the flag! Should he, he wondered, try to get it "invisibly mended"? There was a new shop in the town which promised such an amenity. But an absurd sense of shame held him back. Would it not seem queer for a shabby consul to sneak about the town with a tattered Union Jack, trying to get it repaired on the cheap? Yes. On the other hand if he flew it as it was just to spite the Office there was a risk that some consular nark from Marseille might see it and report adversely on him. He sighed and turned again, turning his back on these futile exchanges, so to speak. And so then Galen had quietly replaced his father, had taken command of everything, school-fees, death-duties, house-rents, etc. In fact he had actually become his father, and as such infallible. He pronounced shortly and crisply on everything now; his will was done, rather like the Almighty's. The overwhelmed and frightened child could do nothing but obey. Galen had, as a matter of fact, demanded worship, but all Felix could supply was a silent obedience to the little man with the plentiful gold teeth which winked and danced in the firelight as he outlined the splendid life which the Foreign Service held in store for the boy.

So here was Felix listening to the sullen twang of the mistral as it poured across the town, dragging at shutter fastenings and making his flagless flagpole vibrate like a jew's harp. The consular shield below it had also taken a few pellets but the damage was not extensive. It merely looked as if some hungry British subject had taken a desperate bite out of it in self-defence. "Whatever you do, Mr. Chatto," the Foreign Secretary had admonished him before handing him his letters of credence and appointment, "never let yourself become cynical while you are in Crown Service. There will be many vexations, I know; you will need all your self-control but try and rise above them. Sincerely." Well, if he had been in a laughing mood he might have managed a feeble cackle. Indeed his shoulders moved in a simulated spasm but in fact his face still wore the pale, dazed expression of a sinus case which aspirin could not relieve. He could smell the dust being blown in from the garden – dust and mimosa. In the spaces between assaults the wind died away to nothing and left a blank in the air into which seeped fragments of ordinary sound like the bells of St. Agricole. The theatre would be emptying into the square by now and despite the foul wind the cafés would awake for a spectral moment; it was too chill to do more than hug the counters and bars and drink "*le grog*". It was early yet, all too early. Like sufferers from sinus and migraine he was used to seeing the dark nights unroll before him in a ribbon of desolation.

But his real calvary began well after midnight when he rose, made himself a pot of vervain *tisane* and slowly dressed, pausing for long intervals to gaze into the bathroom mirror or stand in bemused silence before the cupboard mirror gazing at his own reflection in it, watching himself dress slowly, knot his old school tie, draw on his shabby college blazer with the blazoned pocket. Who was this familiar shadow? He felt completely disembodied as he looked, as he confronted his own anxious, unfamiliar face. He drew on his black felt hat, stuffed his wallet into his breast pocket; then he stayed in the sitting room gazing at the print hanging over the chimney – a pastoral scene of goats and cypresses. With one half of his mind he heard the throbbing of the wind and registered its diminution with something like satisfaction. Perhaps in another twenty minutes it might sink away into one of its sudden calms. He would pause awhile before setting off on one of his all-too-frequent night walks round the town which he had come to regard as the most melancholy in the whole world. Its eminence, its history, its monuments — the whole thing drove him wild with boredom; mentally he let out shriek after shriek of hysteria, though of course his lips did not move and his consular face remained impassive, as befitted a Crown Servant.

Yes, the wind was subsiding slowly; a clock chimed somewhere and there was the long slow moan of a barge from the river like some haunted cow. He licked his finger and traced the dust upon the mantelpiece. The little hunchback maid who came in for an hour of dusting every morning was fighting in vain against the ill-fitting shutters. As for food, Felix arranged his own light meals, or crossed the square to the little penurious café called Chez Jules where they made sandwiches or an occasional hot dish filled with chili and pimento. He threw open the door of the office and stood for a while gazing down at his own imagined ghost — he saw himself writing a despatch about the flag. What furniture, what entrancing ugliness! He enumerated it all as he sipped his tea and stirred a loose tile with the toe of his suede shoe. There was a mouse-hole in the wall which he had stopped with a pellet of paper manufactured from a particularly exasperating and stupid despatch from head office. It had assuaged his feelings and had apparently discouraged the mouse — though God knows what such a poor creature might expect to find here to eat. Books? He was welcome to the consular library. Felix had a small suitcase of private books under his bed, mostly poetry. But now he was looking at the shallow office bookcase with its reference books which were apparently all that a consul ever needed in order to remain efficient. The F.O. List with its supplements made quite good reading. It soothed him to discover the whereabouts of long-lost London colleagues. When he wanted to gloat he looked up some fearful bore like Pater and read (his lips moved as he did so) the small paragraph which recited all his early posts, sinking in gradual diminuendo towards the fatal posting. Consular Agent, Aden. He could hardly forbear to let out a cheer, so much had he disliked Pater while he was being "run in" in the London office. Then there was Sopwith too – another victory of good sense. He had been posted to Rangoon. On the whole then, Avignon might not seem so bad. But he had no money to get to Nice or Paris, and Galen would never have lent him the large slow Hispano which coasted everywhere with its goggled negro chauffeur – trailing long plumes of white dust across the vernal olive groves. What else was there for a decent self-respecting mouse to feed on? *Consular Duties* in six volumes? A volume of consular stamps and some faded ink-rollers which thumped out a splayed crown if properly inked. *Wagner's Basic International Law* – a huge and incomprehensible compilation. *The British Subject Abroad*, a guide for Residents. Skeat's *English Usage*. *The Consular Register*. *The Shorter Oxford*. All this to keep his despatches in good trim. There were also a few grammars and detective stories. The whole thing was pretty shabby and anyone having a look around would realise (he told himself) that Chatto was very poor, and that Lord Galen was either quite oblivious of the fact or wanted to keep him so. As for pro-consuls in posts as remote as these, they were hardly paid at all, and certainly never got accorded consular *frais*, expense accounts, which they might disburse in the pursuit of pleasure. Moreover Felix had no private income, so that his mind was always pinched by the thought of overspending. Even when people found him agreeable and invited him out to functions he was apt to decline for fear that he would never be able to invite them back. Nothing gives one that hunted look like poverty; and there is no poverty like having to swallow the backwash of extravagantly rich relations, who cannot help patronising you, however much they may try not to. And on such an exiguous budget, in a remote place, everything became a terror – the necessary doctor's visit, an operation, a false tooth, broken spectacles, a winter overcoat. All these possibilities gnawed at his mind, depleting his self-confidence, poisoning the springs of his happiness.

Well then, night after night, as he lay in the coarse sheets, he went over these factors in a trance of sleepless misery; his history seemed to stretch like an unbroken ribbon of distress and anxiety right back to the father's death and his sad schooldays. (His reports always said something like "Could do better if day-dreamed less".) His only refuge had been books; and now he was beginning to take a faked interest in Catholicism because it made one friends and took up time. He felt that unless he could find himself fully occupied the weight of his present boredom and anguish might unseat his reason and lead him towards what was then known as "a brain fever". He whispered, "Oh God, not that," under his breath when the thought came into his mind. Someone to talk to, for the love of God! When he received a note from Blanford telling him of the summer to be spent near Avignon, tears came into his eyes and he gave an involuntary dry sob of pure relief.

In these long night-silences he felt rather like the town itself – all past and no recognisable present. Did Galen know about them coming down – he did not know if Blanford was an acquaintance of the old man. How could one tell? Galen never even bothered to signal his frequent absences and returns – he spent several months a year in the tumbledown chateau which he was too mean, Felix supposed, to restore.

He moved about all over Europe following the threads of the cobweb he had spun with his fortune, playing the game of banking and politics. Everywhere he was accompanied by Max, his negro valet-chauffeur, who in certain lights looked dark violet; and the dumb (literally) male secretary whom Galen had deliberately chosen for himself, saying with a laugh that he knew how to give orders and get them obeyed. A secretary did not need a voice, a nod would suffice.

It should be noted also that where Galen went Wombat went too, seated on a mouldering green velvet cushion with a monogrammed crown printed on it as befitted the animal's pedigree, for Wombat was the imperial cat of this strange, rather sad, motherless household. Max, who loved the thing, carried it everywhere most ceremoniously, as if he were a chamberlain carrying the royal chamberpot of a King. Wombat was half blind and dying of asthma, and if offered the slightest attention or civility like an outstretched hand or a friendly sound, would react unamiably by opening its throat to hiss, and rearing up in anger. When Galen had had a drink or two in the evening he used often to wax sentimental and inform Max that the cat was his only friend; everyone else loved him for his money. With Wombat it was real love. But when he reached out his hand the animal spread its throat and reared like a cobra opening its hood as it hissed – thus avoiding the old man's caress.

No, he had little enough thought for Felix, though every Christmas he received a penny Christmas card of the Woolworth type featuring holly and a robin. It was always signed by Galen but the envelope was made out in the secretary's awkward hand. In summer, then, it was dust and wind and noise, and Keating's Powder and ceremonial processions of scruffy nuns and priests; in winter it was frost and ice and the river swollen to three times its mean summer levels. *Le cafard*, in fact, in its most exaggerated form.

Perambulatory paranoia, they would one day christen his case, of that he was sure.

He had set Blanford's postcard up on his desk as a talisman; he leaned over to read it anew now curbing his impatience by breathing slowly several times. Then he locked up his petty-cash box with its sheets of stamps and the six blank passports in the little wall-safe. He stepped out into the garden of the house, drawing the door to behind him with a soft click. How he hated that door with its ill-fitting lock. It was a glass door with a feverish design executed in squares of cathedral glass; when the sunlight fell upon it it produced extraordinary colour effects on the face of anyone crossing the hall to open it. The features became suddenly the colour of a blood-orange; then, in sharp succession, blue, green and livid yellow. Such theatrical changes often gave the unwary caller a start.

He turned up his coat-collar and, placing his cane under his arm, drew on gloves as he began the slow martyrdom of his night march across the town.

The westering moon drooped towards the battlements and as he turned the dark corner by the abattoir which rang all night to the sound of flushing waters like a public urinal he saw the familiar little lamplighter trotting along ahead of him with his shepherd's crook with which he turned off the street-lights – for only a few corners of the town had been able to afford the new clean electric lighting. He reflected with a selfish pang that he would be sorry when the whole town went electric because the little lamplighters not only marked the hour for him (the lights were turned off at two) but also afforded him a kind of welcome night-company on his walks. He skirted the smoky grey battlements with their crenellations. By now perhaps even the gipsies would have retired to their tents and caravans – they kept up the latest in the town, as far as he could judge; he followed the little

lamplighter who padded along ahead of him making almost
no sound, and only pausing to put out a lamp with his
little crook. It was like someone beheading flowers one
after the other; the violet night rushed in at once with its
graphic shadows. At the rue St.-Charles he mentally said
goodnight to his familiar and turned sharp right towards the
Porte St.-Charles which here pierced the massive walls of the
town. One emerged upon the apron, so to speak, of the
bastion – a dusty *terrain vague* punctuated with tall planes
whose leaves had begun to turn green. Here were great areas
of shadow and few lights – a fitting place for the enactment of
mischief, a corner made for throat-slitting, settling of accounts
and active whoring. The gipsies had not been slow to find
it and to settle on it – in defiance of the law which from time
to time ordered them to leave. In vain. But now their fires
had burned low and they had taken to their caravans where
frail night-lights burned behind curtains. A point or two of
lights could also be seen in the tents and the makeshift
shelters where they lay, piled together for warmth like a
litter of cats. Felix half envied and half feared them, and as
he heard his own dry footfalls change in tone as they passed
between the ramps of the tall gate his hand always strayed
involuntarily to the electric torch in his pocket, though as
yet he had never had occasion to use it in an emergency.

Yes, their fires had burned down to the embers and
even their few donkeys and dogs appeared to slumber. But
from one of the smaller tents a girl, awakened by his echoing
footfalls, arose, seeming to materialise from the very ground,
and sidled towards him whining for alms. Yes, she sidled
yawning towards him like a pretty kitten, stretching out her
slender arms. She could not have been much over sixteen and
she was dressed as vividly as a pierrot in her patchwork
quilt of bright rags. He felt a whirl of desire overcome
him as he saw her beautiful face, so full of the sexual conceit

of her people. He felt almost like fainting. Hereabouts
the stout ravelins made whole barrows of dark blue shadow –
an impenetrable darkness safe from prying eyes. Why did he
not simply beckon her into one of these pools of black and
sink his consular talons into that lithe and swarthy flesh?
She would surely follow him at the mere promise of gold?

Ah! There was the rub – gold! How much would she
want for her caresses? He did not know. Anyway he knew
that he had not the courage to do such a thing; he would have
had to undo the constraints of his whole upbringing. A giant
despondency seized him as he waved away the tempting
creature. He hurried past her, feeling her predatory fingers
brush his sleeve. She was barefoot, and moved soundlessly.
Why didn't she hit him with something and then rape him
sublimely while he lay insensible – then at least he would
not feel guilty about so natural an act? But what about the
dose which would almost inevitably follow such an act? It
would be very expensive to cure a dose here, as well as
unbearably painful. It was a subject on which he could speak
with feeling as he had once accompanied a panicky undergraduate friend to the Lock Hospital in Greek Street. The
poor boy was expiating a twenty-first birthday party spent
at The Old Bag O'Nails in the usual way. Felix out of
sympathy accompanied his friend to his first few drastic
"treatments": he watched these agonising sessions with fear
and repugnance. The background, too, was daunting – the
long marble-walled latrines hushing with water, the rows of
high white enemas and their long slim tubes. . . . Could this
really be the only cure for this foul disease? First the bowel
filled and refilled with permanganate (Condy's Fluid) which
the patient was encouraged to piss away with whatever force
he could command. Then he must submit to the cleaning and
scraping of the sensitive mucus surfaces inside the urethra
where the infection lay. The surgeon inserted a small catheter

shaped like a steel umbrella in the organ and gradually opened it in umbrella fashion, to distend the member. This was supposed to break down and detach the infected parts so that they could be ejected and discharged. It was agony for the patient. Once seen, never forgotten.

And the mere thought of these sessions lent wings to him now, strengthening his resolve to repulse the girl. He quickened his pace and turned away down towards the pretty little railway station with its dark palms. The girl showed some disposition to insist but was soon overtaken by yawns and contented herself by spitting in his wake as she turned aside to regain the tents. The last train had gone out, the first of the new day was still far off. From somewhere among the dark quays came the sharp clanging of milk churns being man-hauled and stacked in the dark sheds against the arrival of the morning milk carts. The refreshment room was also closed at this hour but one naked bulb burned on in it and through the frosted glass he could see the old peasant and his wife washing glasses and teapots and sweeping the flags with tattered straw brooms. He would have liked to drink a grog but they would not open to him until the first train of the day shook the silent station with its clatter and squeals. The *fiacres* still stood outside the main entrance under the clock whose hands had pointed to two-twenty for the last three months. Would it never be mended? The drivers were wrapped in old blankets like effigies, the horses appeared to be asleep standing.

Porte St.-Roche, Porte St.-Charles, Porte de la République – the last led directly to the heart of the town, the throbbing little square around which everything of social consequence was grouped – the Mairie, the handsome old Theatre, the Monument des Morts with its disgraceful but delightful tin cartoon of symbolic lions and the flag-waving Marianne. . . . How well he had come to know it all; he was no longer a hesitant tourist, inspirited by the romance of its history, but one of the forty thousand residents now, his spirit almost embalmed in the boredom of its silences, its frowning churches, its shuttered shops and cafés. The horrifying thing was that this sort of life corresponded most favourably to the best posting available to a young consul, apart from working in a great capital or a town as big as Marseille or Lyon or Rome. After years of expiating his sins like this in places like this he might aspire to the rank of Consul General, though still resting debarred from the mainstream of career diplomacy – for the "real" diplomats were a chosen race, a trade union, a closed circle.

Turning his back to the station he addressed himself to the second massive Porte de la République and entered the inside of the bastions. In the summer he often took the opposite direction and walked over the suspension bridge to the island; but this was rather a sinister place and pitch dark, and he had no stomach to be set upon by footpads. Besides, with the present wind and temperature he could, by taking this anti-clockwise walk, shelter within the walls from the worst inclemencies of the weather. He moved towards the little chapel of the Grey Penitents set incongruously upon its dark canal with the stout wooden waterwheels forever turning with their slopping and swishing sound. From St. Magnagnen one ducked into the terrifying little rue Bon Martinet (the name struck a chord always, though the exact association escaped him for the moment: later Blanford supplied the missing fragment of the puzzle). It was so narrow and dark that one's shoulders brushed the wall on either side and when one passed a dark doorway one prayed that there might be nobody waiting for one in it with a knife or a rope. This emerged – you could see the light at the end of the tunnel – directly upon the canals; this part of the town was the domain of the tanners and dyers, and the paddlewheels, which would have driven a decent-sized steamboat, turned night and day though the actual trade had fallen largely into desuetude.

Here the darkness was like wet velvet; he paused, as always, at the entrance of the chapel and recited the inscription over the entrance to himself in a whisper. Mostly he took out his torch hereabouts to read such things. This was the Grey Penitents – the Black ones were situated in a further corner of the town. He pushed the door and it squeaked open upon blackness. Sometimes he sat for a moment in one of the pews. There was an electric bell in the wall with the name of a priest – a duty-priest, so to speak, always ready to take confession if summoned. One night he had "disgraced himself", as he would have put it if he had been describing it to someone else. In an access of misery he had entered the church with some intention of praying; but when he found himself in the pew facing the cold repugnant statue which was to act as a focus for this novel set of emotions his spirit strangled within him, he became choked. He felt as if the centre was sliding out of his mind. He understood what the phrase "wrestling with the dark angel" meant. But in his case it felt more like the slimy tentacles of Laocoön which closed around him and from which he could not disengage himself. There was nobody in the place, the silence echoed to his deep panting. At last, overwhelmed by these stresses, he crossed the aisle and pressed the bell. Underneath it there was a card with the name of the duty-priest typed on it – *Menard.* Then he stood aghast at what he had done. The sepulchral sound of the bell died slowly away in the further entrails of the building, awakening nobody, arousing no answering sound. He stood there feeling now as foolish and as irresponsible as before he had felt anguished. Ringing for a priest at two o'clock in the morning – it was a scandal! And yet, surely if the religious crisis were a truthful one, a serious one, no priest could complain of the hour – any more than a doctor complain of a night call by a patient *in extremis*? But no, he felt a guilty fool for importuning the church at this time of day. Yet silence was all that his frantic ring had elicited. He stood there with head cocked on one side. In the dark street outside two cats started their macabre love-wails. Where could he be, the priest? He felt stupid, blameworthy, undeserving of consideration since he himself had shown so little. Turning, he ran to the door and opened it onto the dark causeway with its swishing canal and impassive paddle-wheels turning. Then he closed the door of the chapel silently and leaned his head against its oaken panels, as if to cool his feverish forehead with the cold touch of the wood. As he did so he heard the shuffle of footsteps entering the chapel and the clicking of the confessional wicket. A priest had, after all, answered his summons. The thought panicked him anew and turning, he hurried away into the darkness leaving priest and chapel to their darkness and silence. What a bad show this was! It took him an effort to confess it, not to the priest, but to Blanford who later joined him on these night marches, when they were hunting for traces of Livia. It was here too that Blanford untangled the associative strands which made rue Bon Martinet so evocative. The Marquis de Sade!

"It has one thing, this town, for me. The huge span of human aspiration and human weakness are symbolised by two figures from its bestiary, so to speak. I mean Petrarch's Laura who invented the perfect romantic love and the Marquis de Sade who carried it right back into its despairing infancy with the whip. What a couple of guardian angels!"

Felix pushed on doggedly now towards the next bastion, the frowning Porte Thiers where he started to cut diagonally across the sleeping town. Once or twice he passed signs of life, like an old man on a bicycle who passed him riding so slowly that it seemed as if his journey had begun a long time ago – back in the Pleistocene era perhaps. His bicycle bobbed and bounced upon the uneven cobbles and flags of the street, but quite soundlessly. The old man himself looked neither to right nor left – was he perhaps asleep? Then he coughed sharply and Felix nearly jumped out of his skin. The little wooded Place Bon Pasteur slumbered among its dense planes under which the nearby inhabitants had parked their prams and bicycles and carts which would soon be pressed into service when the market opened. From the end of the street he caught a glimpse of a frail light shining in the cavernous tin shed which housed the three trams. At five their squeals would awaken the toughest sleepers in the town – for they traversed the whole length of it. It was all the towns-people had in the way of public transport – the two large and shaky motor buses were a recent innovation and given over to tourism; they slumbered outside the Hotel Crillon and at ten would carry their fares off to inspect Aigues Mortes and the Carmargue. There was a shadowy figure with a storm-lantern moving among the slumbering trams with an oil-can, servicing them for their daily work. Dawn was as yet a premonition in a clear mistral sky prickling with stars – a mere lightening of the sky at the furthest edges of futurity; but it was like a faint chord struck somewhere far away that echoed here, for the bird colonies in the dense foliage of the trees which sheltered the beautiful old market had started to stir and stretch and converse. In the Clinique Bosque he saw a faint bud of flame under a coffee-urn – an alcohol lamp. In the Banque Foix a night watchman stirred and clanked open massive bolts to let in the two shapeless old ladies – the office cleaners. Somewhere in a nearby street an invisible whistler executed a phrase from a popular tango, and then broke off, as if in embarrassment.

This was the hour when Quatrefages at last fell asleep

in the Princes Hotel, with the lights still burning on – he could not bear the dark. What would Felix have done without the *thought* of poor Quatrefages, the knowledge that poor Quatrefages was alone among the forty thousand souls, awake all night as he himself was? The warmth of this thought made his wanderings somehow possible; the lean youth was a sort of symbolic companion for the consul, a poor scholar who was also, like himself, a serf to Lord Galen. Quatrefages looked like some sleepy raven in his rusty black *tablier* which he wore over his clothes when he worked; on this work-apron he wiped his pen with its steel nib during his pauses; his hand was a copyist's Italian cursive, as beautiful as Arabic script or a Chinese ideogram. Though why Galen should retain the services of this poor scholar to decipher and copy medieval documents, was for a time something of a puzzle. . . .

The dark, famished-looking youth had had quite a chequered history before he found himself here, immured in an ill-lit bedroom of the Princes Hotel, working with the savage concentration of a slave on the projects which Lord Galen had proposed for him. His story began with the Church – he had once been a sexton and then a curate of the Church, but a scandal accompanied by the poisonous gossip of a small village had unseated him – he had been defrocked unjustly, or so he felt. His ardent religious faith died in him there and then and was replaced by an overwhelming sensation of loss – as if the whole outer darkness which lay outside the narrow field of the doctrine had rushed in and taken possession of his soul. "Possession" is not inapt as a thought – for he now became convinced that God could not exist and that atheism was the only honourable philosophy for a logical person like himself. He had wasted his whole youth in mumbo-jumbo. In the grip of this despairing belief – for it did not render him happy, this train of thought – he turned his attention to evil with the same single-mindedness as he had once devoted to an orthodox goodness. The path led downwards by obscure stages towards symbolic mathematics, enigmas, emblems and the shadowy reaches of alchemy and astrology. On the way he discovered orthodox mathematics and became, to his own surprise, a very able performer. It was an accident, but a fruitful one, that had resulted in him being co-opted into the department of Lord Galen's business which was called "Trendings"; here a group of four young mathematicians analysed graphs of prediction as to their future movements up and down the scale. It was over these large and pretty graphs that Galen pored at night, wondering whether to sell or to buy. His little band of statisticians provided him with a rough guide to the disposition of his markets, and while they were not infallible there was quite a large element of correctness, in what they found. Here Quatrefages found himself in congenial surroundings; he was well treated, relatively speaking. As he was afraid of the dark and could not sleep until dawn, for the most part he elected to do his work at night. He would sit over the old teak drawing-boards in the uninspiring offices of the firm, his long pointed nose slanted towards his papers. He looked like some sleepy raven; his nails were bitten down to the quick, his fingers always a bit inky, his trousers frayed where the bicycle clips went. His small black mouse eyes were full of a sullen brilliance and impatience. His dry cough and eternal light fever spoke of tuberculosis; indeed his whole physiognomy was that of the old traditional *poitrinaire*, and he had once been placed in a sanatorium where they had collapsed a lung to let it mend. In vain.

But the tell-tale coughing, which sometimes doubled him up and brought tears to his eyes, did not affect the determined steadiness of his work, despite the aching boredom of the matter he had been set to analyse. Always at the end of his night prowl the young consul made a short detour in order to stand for a moment below the lighted window; to breathe in, so to speak, some of the spectral courage and anxiety of his uncle's bondsman. At such a moment his divided feelings about his uncle – hatred and affection and amusement – rose and subsided within him like a sea. Yes, he hated him; no, for how could one? Like everyone with a silly side Galen was endearing. Every afternoon he boxed with the violet negro for a couple of rounds, puffing and blowing and wiping his nose in his glove like a professional. His partner had once been a real professional and he moved round the ring (which had been set up in the garden) as lazily as a moth, fully aware that he must not hit his boss – for Galen would have died on the spot. So they moved in a strange ballet, the dark boxer grazing the ropes with his back. He wore lace-up kid shoes and a much decorated belt whose medals gleamed richly. From time to time he sent out an exhibition punch – a shadow-punch so to speak – which stopped just short of his rival's small chin. Galen's answering blows might have been aimed at the moon, they were so inaccurate. The negro moved aside, but just once in a while, took a flick upon his violet forehead and gave a deep grunt of admiration.

How beautiful Max was to watch! The negro can do nothing which does not aspire towards dancing. Even his exaggerated shuffle round the ring with the hint of gorilla-like menace – the whole thing was light as air, volatile, buoyant and undeliberate; one felt it was almost as arbitrary as the flutterings of a cabbage-white among the flowers. Yet there was science in it even though the arms hung limp as empty sleeves. Suddenly this classical punch would evolve itself like a bee-sting. Max whistled to himself, little mauve tunes, blues. From time to time he breathed a word of advice to his partner, "You gotta breathe with yo bones, sah," he might say, and shaking his head add, "sure damn thing." And

Galen would obediently try to breathe with his bones. After two rounds, speechless and puffing, the old man turned to whoever was watching (most often it was poor Felix) and said: "You see? It's the secret of my iron constitution."

Galen would rise very early in the morning and have himself driven to the main station to see the first train go out towards Paris; he had done this all his life, wherever he might be. Trains were an obsession. The intoxication of the platforms smelling of coal and oil, the bustle and clamour of passengers and porters loading baggage and freight – the whole indescribable chaos and order of the operation never failed to thrill him to the bone. And the farewells! A whole life, a whole human situation is illustrated in the farewells of lovers, friends, married couples, children, dogs. The clang of closing doors, the kisses, the shrill whistles, the red flag, and the steady champ of the engines belching white plumes into the blue sky – it brought him to tears still. It was perhaps by one of those cruel paradoxes in which fate delights that the railway had become connected to the sole tragedy of Galen's life – the inexplicable disappearance of his adolescent daughter. He had spent a fortune trying to trace her or at least to solve the mystery of her disappearance. One supposes that this sort of thing happens every day – to judge by the press, which comments on it for a while and then forgets it. Fifteen schoolgirls accompanied by two nuns from the Sacred Heart Convent took a Sunday excursion train to London from Sidcote. When they arrived at Waterloo one girl was missing – Galen's daughter. It may be imagined what measures were taken to explain this extraordinary fact. Had she fallen from the train? No; had she absconded? The train was a through train. Her fellow pupils said that about half-way to London she absented herself to go to the lavatory. She never reappeared. Galen was beside himself with horror and incredulity. Every field of enquiry was pursued with all the ferocious relentlessness of a father almost beside himself. It was years ago now, but the memory was still fresh, his room was full of her photographs and hand-painted Christmas cards. He wept unaffectedly when speaking of her. One day in London he unburdened himself to his clerk Quatrefages, who was then buried deep in his alchemical studies. In some vague way Galen hoped, by revealing the degree of his own emotional weakness and commitment towards the memory of his child, to move the boy and win a little sympathy from him – he was such a taciturn creature with his bitten nails. To his surprise Quatrefages produced a ring on a pendulum and asked for a scale map of London and Surrey – so that his divining machine would plot the course of that fatal journey and perhaps offer a solution.

Galen watched with fascination as it swung to and fro in the lean hand of the clerk. Finally Quatrefages said, with a note of finality, "She was not on that train, the children were told to say she was. The nuns were lying to excuse their inattention; at the station she was taken by a gipsy." Galen reeled with hope and delight. So she might still be alive, then? After all, through the whole course of Victorian fiction the gipsies were always responsible for the disappearance of children, and often of grown-ups also. "Is she still alive?" he asked in a paroxysm of anxiety, "if so where should I look?" But Quatrefages did not know – or so he said. The truth was he did not want to go too far, as he was making all this up in order to secure a bit of a hold on this funny, aggressive little man. He had found a way. Soon Galen was dropping in for chats, and ineluctably the subject would drift towards his great obsession – the whereabouts of Sabine. He initiated an elaborate study of all the gipsy tribes, a sort of star map of their movements across Europe, and sent his agents hunting equipped with photos. At the yearly world gathering of gipsy legions his agents were waiting for their caravans to arrive from all over Europe at the Saintes Maries de la Mer. He began to find superior qualities in the French clerk – the boy became precious simply because one day he might find the missing clue to the child's whereabouts. As their intimacy grew he offered him a new sort of secret job – one he would not have confided to just anyone. Quatrefages, stupid as it may sound, was now hunting for buried treasure, nothing less, in the tangled mass of documentation which surrounds the Templars and their heresy.

Sometimes Felix stood for a while in the little square beneath the inspiring square of yellow light where once a gallows had stood, and mentally hanged himself; in the pale moonlight his body swung to and fro in the wind, softly creaking and clanking in its chains. A felon of laziness and cowardice if ever there was one. Ineffectual, too. As for Quatrefages, for all his apparent youthful inexperience and all his pretensions to esoteric knowledge, he had kept a fine French sense of proportion where self-interest was concerned. Happily. It was largely through him that Felix had obtained the part-time use of the little Morris automobile, a blessing they shared in amiable enough fashion. The clerk had asked Galen for some form of transport to enable him to travel about Provence, examining ancient sites and ruins and consulting scholars. He used the machine a fair amount, but for the rest of the time it belonged to the Consulate and undertook other duties. Felix drove himself vaguely about the delectable countryside, swollen with his sense of loneliness, and trying to render it endurable by investigating the grand dishes and finer wines of the area; for though Avignon was not Lyon in richness and variety where cuisine was concerned, nevertheless much remained to marvel at in the realm of country cooking. Even in its poorest corners France seemed quite inexhaustible to one raised on ordinary English fare.

Yet the sense of vacuum persisted, and the healthy sleep to which a youth of his age might claim a right, resisted; hence the night patrols in a city where after dark so little life seemed to exist. The few bedraggled and furtive ladies of the night were amiable but hardly appetising; they packed up at two, with the latest *café dansant*. Only the gipsies had colour and movement, and the courage which he himself lacked. Seekers of a late night out were perforce obliged to "go to the gipsies" and risk a police sweep and an ignominious appearance in court. And then the other question ... Felix shook his head. Wandering among the stray cats feasting on fish-heads and vegetable garbage from the over-turned dustbins outside the "Mireille" he pondered on the fate of consuls, and saw with hungry misgiving the manic moon in her slow dejected fall towards the lightening skyline. He yawned. Somewhere he had read that dogs denied sleep for more than four days automatically died. And consuls? He yawned again, this time from the soles of his feet.

Consummatum est. It was nearly over now. In the darkness ahead he heard the sweet whisper of the great underground ovens of the bakery with its cracked sign "*Pain du Jour*" at street level. The shop was open though still in darkness. The sleeping woman sat wrapped in her black shawl like a rook. The clink of the bell woke her and she sat up to serve him. The little cubicle smelt heavenly – with the rack beginning to fill up with loaves and croissants, with *fougasses* and doughnuts and *brioches*. Felix walked slowly home inhaling the two croissants in their slip of tissue paper. The wind had dropped as it always did at dawn. He pushed open the rusty garden gate and let himself into the musty little house, greeting its familiar smell with a renewed spasm of depression. God, even the palm tree in the garden was dusty – while as for a hideous aspidistra on the balcony the maid would have to wipe it leaf by leaf with a damp cloth, as usual.

He went to the kitchen and made some coffee. On the floor in the corner lay a wooden crate he had cracked open; it bore the insignia of the Crown Agents, Gabbitas and Speed. He had ordered it to be sent on to him when leaving London. No sooner said than done, for the Crown Agents had been constituted to offer solace and comfort to diplomatic exiles with their combination tuckbox and gift-parcel deliveries. His was the smallest and most modest order of this kind – two whisky, two gin, two white sparkling Spanish wine and two Bass. That was all for the liquid solace; but there was quite a range of kitchen commodities which might be more welcome in Africa, say, than in Europe; but Abroad was simply Abroad for the Crown Agents: with a capital letter, too, as in Hell. You could also give these damned parcels to your fellow diplomats at Christmas if you wished – it saved time and thought. In the Service they were known as "consolation prizes" – consoling one against the horrors of foreign residence, among the lesser breeds of the Kipling kind, or simply among backward European states like France with its froglegs and polluted water.

Some of the tins like Plum Jam he had already extracted. On the kitchen table stood a tin of Bumpsted's Bloater Paste beside a bottle of Gentleman's Relish and Mainwearing's Pickle Mix. The consul sat down and stared hard at these sterling products. Imperial Anchovies, Angostura Bitters. Pork and Beans, Imperial size. Lea and Perrin's Sauce ... A profound homesickness overcame him. He had seized in passing the postcard from Blanford with all its exciting promises for the coming summer; but their arrival was some way off as yet. He poured himself a large cup of coffee and hunted for milk in his little ice box which was by now iceless and dank. The milk smelt suspect. However ... the sun was coming up; he had defeated another night. Today was his day with the Morris. He started to unpack the crate and put the pots in the cupboard, arranging them like a fussy old maid so that their names were facing forward. Then a sudden impulse overcame him and he did something he should never have done; he smeared bloater paste on his croissant and ate it with a groan. It was delicious.

There would be plenty of time for a couple of hours of sleep before the maid knocked, but lest he should oversleep by any chance he retrieved the little alarm clock by his bed and, rewinding it, set it for eleven. Then he undressed and climbed yawning into his virgin bed, turning off all the lights save the small bedside lamp, for he proposed to "read himself to sleep" as usual; and the book most suitable for this exercise was *The Foreign Service Guide to Residence Abroad.* It had a blue cover with the royal arms, rather like an outsize passport, and the text had not been revised for forty years owing to a mistakenly large first printing. Together with a Bible and a Book of Common Prayer, it was the statutory going-away present accorded to young officers on their first posting abroad. The hints and instructions contained in it had a wonderfully soothing effect on insomniac consuls. Take the chapter called "Hints to Travellers":

Officers should take soft caps for sleeping, in a travelling bag; soft shoes to replace boots, a "housewife", a couple of good mauds, a bottle of bovril, a small spirit lamp, a bottle of spirits with cups and saucers, spoons and biscuits. Also a stout sponge bag with two wet sponges in it, a soft towel, a face flannel, a brush and comb. The pillows should be made to roll up tightly and are best made of thistledown and dandelion-down. A travelling ulster with loose fronts is very useful as one can undo the clothes beneath; it should have deep pockets. Always carry an extra pair of gloves. Always take a small book of soap leaves with a small handbag; thus hands can be comfortably washed with one leaf. With a wet sponge and a soap leaf the dusty and tired traveller can always freshen up his face and hands. It is a good wrinkle to carry an Etna spirit lamp, also a tin of mustard leaves, a medicine glass, sticking plaster, a water bottle, and a flask of good brandy in case of sudden or obstinate illness en route.

On and on went this soothing and comforting rigmarole; across the sleepy vision of the consul passed a long, an endless, line of kindly, colourless yet courageous men in pith helmets followed by their baggage, bulging with brandy flasks and Etna spirit lamps. Now he had joined the long senseless safari – forever deprived of watching the ebb and flow of copper shares on the pretty coloured charts of Quatrefages. And what the devil was "a couple of good mauds"? He would give anything to know. But now sleep had definitely come to claim him: the book dropped from his hand to the carpet and with an involuntary gesture which had become mechanical one hand went out to switch off the little bedside lamp. Felix slept a surprisingly deep and healthy sleep which would be broken by the alarm just ten minutes before the maid arrived to set his little house to rights.

The trams had started squealing and with them came the battering of bells that had once irritated Rabelais so; but he heard nothing.

FOUR

Summer Sunlight

BUT AT LONG LAST THE SUMMER, HIGH SUMMER, WAS upon them, with the promised arrival of the four firstcomers to the old manor house. Felix was in such a fever of excitement that on the expected day he hardly dared to quit the landing stage over the green swift water for fear of missing them when they stepped ashore. He walked distractedly about in the wind, talking to himself and ordering numerous coffees in the little Bistro de la Navigation hard by the river, with its one-eyed sailor host.

There was quite a group of people waiting there, on the *qui vive* for the premonitory whiff of sound from the ship's hooter as it rounded the last bend – as much an accolade to the view of Avignon from the water as a triumphal signal of arrival. In the meantime he had been busy on their behalf; he had visited the house a number of times already, sometimes by car or bicycle, and indeed once on foot; and while he could not get into it until he obtained the keys from Bechet the notary, he had a picnic or two in the dilapidated garden and the herb *potager*, now run hopelessly to seed and weed. Sitting under one of the tall pines, inhaling their sharp odour, he ate his six sandwiches and drank his red wine, dreaming of the excellent company he would enjoy once they arrived. Nor was he wrong – their arrival and their gaiety exceeded all expectation; he was to find himself adopted at once, and the manor of Tu Duc was to become a second home. They were to spend many an evening together sitting round the old kitchen table playing twenty-one; and he even once succeeded in inveigling Quatrefages to accompany him for a dinner, which rendered the boy less morose: the little clerk even expanded enough to show them a series of bewildering card tricks. But the chief factor in his happiness was without doubt the absence of Lord Galen, for the old man had decided to take his liver to Baden-Baden for a cure and had disappeared leaving no word as to when he would return. It was marvellous. The consulate remained closed almost permanently, while Quatrefages downed tools, left his Crusader maps pinned to the walls of his room, and embarked on a series of probably unsavoury adventures in the gipsy section of the town – the quarter known as Les Balances.

Livia appeared, fresh from Munich.

And with her a new element entered the camp, for the icy serenity of the girl, and the hard cutting edge of her character, made an immediate impression on them all – but of course mostly upon the too susceptible Blanford. Yet Felix too in his own fashion was enslaved, for she teased him into a sort of sisterly relationship which tightened his heart-strings with a youthful passion. He could refuse her nothing; even when she asked for the use of the spare room, a sort of glorified alcove, at the consulate (for she was too independent not to find Tu Duc oppressive) he could only limply agree while his spirit performed cartwheels at the thought, and Blanford turned pale. Blanford turned pale.

But despite all the dazzling variety and pleasure of that first summer encounter, more important elements were to form themselves which hinted at future developments and subtly transforming predispositions to come. Sam and Hilary, the inseparables, were the chief inciters to adventure and travel; only when Livia appeared did Hilary seem to take on a new constraint, his ice-blue eyes became evasive and thoughtful as he watched both Felix and Blanford foundering like ships in a gale. Constance and Sam somehow remained in a friendly comradely relationship – something not difficult for a knight-errant born to endure. Sam was not made of flesh

and blood, but of flesh and books. And in the blonde, smiling
Constance he had found a worshipful lady who only lacked a
tower to get locked into. . . . All this, of course, has to be
interpreted backwards – for while events are being lived they
travel too fast for easy evaluation. Blanford noticed many
things which his inexperience could not interpret. In part he
reproduced all these errors in Sutcliffe to record some of the
surprise they gave him when at last the truth (what truth?)
dawned. One day Livia burned Hilary's wrist with her
cigarette and he smacked her – and in a trice they were
tearing at each other's hair like savages. Well, brothers and
sisters. . . .

They had found a hunchback maid who came from the
village every day; she had worked long as a *serveuse* in a
brothel, so they learned afterwards. The experience had
given her insight into the ways of men – she read a bedroom
when she entered it, as one reads a book. She interpreted the
whole scene like a sleuth, the disordered pillows and blankets,
all had something to tell her. She often smiled to herself. One
day Blanford, passing the door, saw her pick up a pillow and
inhale it deeply. Then she shook her head and smiled. Turning
she saw him and said in her hoarse way, "Mademoiselle
Livia!" Yes, but it was the bed of Hilary that she was making.
Things do not strike you at the time; ages later Livia bit his
hand with her white teeth and he suddenly remembered the
incident. And with it the kind of strained attention with
which Hilary heard him say at the end of that summer:
"Hilary, what would you say if I asked Livia to marry me
one day?" The hard blue eyes narrowed, and then flared into
rather factitious congratulatory warmth; he squeezed his
friend's shoulder, however, until it hurt, but he actually said
nothing. Later when they were having lunch he said, out of
the blue, "I think you should make sure, Aubrey." And
Blanford knew at once that he was thinking of Livia. It takes

years to evaluate such tiny glimpses into the multiple mean-
ings of any single human action. As Sutcliffe one day said to
him in one of his notebooks: "Right girl, old boy, but wrong
sex. Hard luck!" At another moment in another notebook the
poor old novelist had jotted down the remark: "My mother's
sterile affect was cocked like a trigger to fire me into the arms
of Livia, or of one of her tribe." Then another thing, another
glimpse – for Livia had now spent several days, or groups of
days, lodging in the box-room of the consulate – with its
clumsy cupboard in which Felix had found a place for a small
wardrobe. When Blanford, at the end of the summer, said
to Felix, "I am going to propose to Livia when we leave here,"
he received a strange wondering look from the youth –
which he rather condescendingly interpreted as jealousy.
Several thousand light years afterwards when Blanford was
recording the strange manoeuvres of his double Sutcliffe,
he met Felix by accident on a rainy platform in Paris, as he
was just setting off for the south; and now Felix told him
what that lost and forlorn glance portended. He did not
repeat the scathing estimate of her character by Quatrefages,
who at that time spent one afternoon a week devilling at the
Consulate, keeping the petty-cash box in order. This report
on her was quite gratuitous and spontaneous on the part of
the little clerk and somewhat shook Felix by its terseness.
Yet ... he himself had strayed into his guest's room while
the maid was cleaning it and had seen, hanging up in the
shabby cupboard, some articles of male wear which aroused
his curiosity. And there was no doubt that late in the evening
she often disappeared in the direction of the gipsy encamp-
ment. Why not? She was young and adventurous and may
well have felt the need of a male disguise. Indeed Felix said
as much, on a note of mild indignation, to the little clerk; but
the latter shook his head and said laconically: "I know. I
myself frequent the *gitanes*." And this too was true. Mind you

(as Blanford told himself) it did not matter – he would not, for anything in the world, have renounced an experience which had literally scorched him awake, precipitated him from raw youth into adulthood. In a sense this was the worst part of it; somewhere, in some dim corner of himself, he must have perversely enjoyed the kind of suffering she was to inflict on him. When he said as much to Felix, the latter warmly praised his loyalty and generosity, which naturally disgusted our hero. "O God, Felix," he said in anguish, "it's not that. I'm trapped. I can do no other. I am fuming with impotent rage."

But he was not the only one to be grateful to the girl; Felix was hardly less so, for Livia, by joining him more than once on his night walk, had performed a miracle – she had made him fall in love with this small and dismal city. *Venite adoremus* said the chipped gold sign above the chapel of the Grey Penitents, almost as if the church had divined his mood, his abandonment to his love for this mysterious and eccentric girl. She sat so docilely hand in hand with him in the silent pews, listening to the thresh and swash of the paddles revolving. She said, whispering, "Go on and pray, if you wish. I have never been able to." But his shyness constrained him and he felt himself blush in the darkness. Nor would he have changed his position for anything, for the feel of her rough little hand in his was bliss. How marvellous, how romantic it all seemed, and how beautiful she was, this Livia who talked about painting and seemed to know everything about the history of the place which had for him been up to now an echoing prison. As for the gipsy side of her character – why, she had been the most brilliant student of the Slade School in the years when the influence of Augustus John was at its height; all students worth anything ached to become Carmen. One night when she disappeared he ran into her by chance in the eastern sector of the town, and she was walking arm in arm with a gipsy girl; behind the couple, as if offering protection or surveillance, came a couple of lean gipsies leading a mule. They were shabby as pariahs, and had a brilliant scavenging gleam in the eye – as if they had just done a successful robbery. Livia dressed in tattered pants and was bare of foot – another passion of hers was to walk about barefoot. That summer she cut her foot on a piece of tin and the wound turned septic; this immobilised her for a while and she accepted the ministrations of Felix with brusque good grace. In the evenings the gipsy girl hung about the consulate quarter, but she always made off when Felix appeared.

Only with Quatrefages nothing worked; Livia and he simply hated each other, and hardly bothered to hide the fact. Later they came to an interesting compromise, for the little clerk blackmailed her into co-operating with him in one of the numerous enterprises of Lord Galen – one which also concerned the gipsies.

What had happened was this: the gipsies had taken up a second headquarters in the corner of the town known as Les Balances, where a number of disreputable and tumble-down houses offered them precarious shelter. Prompted by a hint from Quatrefages, they had removed the heavy stone flags of the floors and started to dig down beneath these shacks, to arrive at a layer of civilisation much anterior to the Papal period of the town. Amphoras, grave headstones, armour, domestic remains, tessellated pavements, they had made one of the richer archaeological finds of the period; and all this material was surreptitiously placed in sacks and sent up to Galen's chateau by mule. Livia, details of whose doings among the gipsies had come to the ears of Quatrefages, was content to lend her good offices to these ventures rather than have him tell anyone about her own tenebrous adventures; and indeed was responsible for securing one or two of the larger pieces which might have been salted away by the band who were vaguely aware that someone was making a larger profit than they were from these finds.

But for Felix the real felicity of that first summer was not merely the marvellous evenings spent at Tu Duc, it was to walk half the night with this dark girl with her haughty face and bare feet; her thin body was erect as a wand, and she seemed to feel absolutely no fear in the darkest corners of the town – some of which made the flesh of poor Felix creep; like the terrifying rue Londe for example with its one gas lamp set askew in a wall so mossy and so dribbling with damp that it exuded a death-chill. Here the shadowy doorways were set in such a way as to afford perfect cover for a footpad. Obviously she felt nothing of all this, for she did not cease her quiet conversation as they travelled down it – perforce in Indian file to avoid the contact of their shoulders with the rotting walls. One thing she had determined to find – a famous Avignon shawl such as her mother had had as a young girl. Alas, these fine kashmirs were no longer made in the old town.

But it was Livia who made him sit and listen to the wakening birds in little squares like that of Le Bon Pasteur, or the Square des Corps Saints with its ragged plashing fountain; or Saint Didier, set slightly at an angle to the rest of the universe, but not the less evocative. And with these night rambles the whole harmony of the Mediterranean south swept over him, filling his consciousness with gorgeous impressions of star-sprinkled nights in the old town – the six of them seated under a tree in front of some old bistro like The Bird, drinking the milky anisette called *pastis* and waiting for the moon to rise over the munched-looking battlements of the city. Once Livia managed to procure them horses from the gipsies and they rode across to the Pont du Gard, to picnic and camp the night on the steep hillsides, overlooking the jade-green Gardon as it swirled its way to the sea. Sometimes, too, Blanford invited himself into town for a consular walk with them both, much to the chagrin of Felix, who looked quite crestfallen when his friend appeared on the scene. But Blanford was as much subject to the magnetism of Livia as Felix was – he simply could not resist forcing himself upon them, though he inwardly cursed his lack of tact. Yet it was Livia who seemed glad, and who indeed seemed to favour him quite unequivocally over Felix. The crestfallen consul was forced to witness, with exquisite pangs of jealousy, the two of them walking tenderly arm in arm, while he followed wistfully after them in his college blazer, uttering fearful imprecations under his breath. Nobody took any of this with high seriousness – it was simply youth, it was simply the spirit of an intoxicating summer felicity among the olives and cherries of Aramon, of Foulkes, of Montfavet or Sorgues. Often, looking back on this halcyon period, Blanford had the sudden vision of them all, standing upon the iron bridge at the Fountain of Vaucluse, gazing down into the trout-curdled water and listening to the roar of the spring as it burst from the mountain's throat and swept down past them, thick with loitering fish.

But if ever in the years to come Blanford might feel the need to account for the enigma of this fierce attachment to Livia there was one scene which quite certainly he knew would rise in his memory to explain everything. Once when Felix was away for a few days Livia gave him a rendezvous at the little Museum in the centre of the town – at four-thirty in the morning; punctually a sleepy Blanford turned up to find the barefooted girl waiting for him at the dark portals of the place with a swarthy gipsy. Dawn was just breaking. The gipsy had a massive pistol-key in his hand which fitted the lock; the tall doors swung back with a hushing noise and ushered them into the red cobbled courtyard; and as they did so they heard the inhuman shrieks which came from the interior garden with its tall dewy plane trees. It was the crying of peacocks on the lawn. They passed through tall glass doors to reach this interior courtyard which exhaled a strange sort of peace in that early light of day. The taciturn gipsy took his leave, having confided his key to the girl. Together they loitered through the galleries with their massive water paintings of the Italian school – lakes and viaducts and avenues depicting imaginary landscapes during the four seasons of the year. Portraits of great ladies and forgotten dignitaries stared urgently at them in the gloom. Then they came to the Graeco-Roman section and after it to a small glass-roofed room with manuscripts and documents galore.

Livia, who seemed to know the place by heart, opened the cases one by one and showed the bemused Blanford medieval documents which mentioned the marriage of Petrarch's sweetheart, and hard by, some pages of handwriting torn from the letters of the Marquis de Sade. It was strange in that silent dawn to hold the white paper in his fingers and read some lines etched in a now rusted ink. He had forgotten that both the libertine and the Muse were called Sade, and were from the same family. . . . Now Livia was at his side, then in his arms; she closed the precious cases and led him back to the cool lawn where they sat side by side on a bench trying to feed the peacocks with scraps of stale sandwich which he had had the forethought to bring with him. "Soon I shall be going back to Germany," the girl said, "and you won't see me until the next long vac – unless you come with me; but I know you can't as yet. Such wonderful things are going to happen there, Aubrey; it's bursting with hope, the whole country. A new philosophy is being built which will give the new Germany the creative leadership of Europe once more." It sounded rather puzzling, but Blanford was politically quite ignorant. He had heard vague rumours of unrest and revisionism in Germany – a reaction against the Versailles treaty. But the whole subject was a bore, and he presumed that some new government would bury all these extravagances once and for all. Besides, a new war was unthinkable and specially for such trivial reasons. . . . This is why Livia intrigued him with her romantic talk. So, more to humour her – for he adored the flushed cheeks and the joined hands which showed her enthusiasm – than from real interest he said: "What was the old world, then?" Livia shook a lock of hair impatiently out of her eyes and said: "It died in 1832, with the death of Goethe; the old world of humanism and liberalism and faith. He exemplified it; and its epitaph was pronounced by Napoleon after he met Goethe; it was an unwilling tribute to the world which the French Revolution was then destroying. '*Voilà un homme,*' said Boney, himself a child of the Directory, and the harbinger of the Leninised Jewish coolie-culture of today. With the death of Goethe the new world was born, and under the aegis of Judeo-Christian materialism it transformed itself into the great labour camp that it is. In every field – art, politics, economics – the Jew came to the forefront and dominated the scene. Only Germany wants to replace this ethos with a new one, an Aryan one, which will offer renewed scope for the old values as exemplified by Goethe's world; for he was the last universal man of the Renaissance. Why should we not go back to that?" Blanford did not see quite how; but her sweet enthusiasm was so warming, and the tang of her kiss so unmanning that he found himself nodding agreement. Livia's new world sounded like the Hesperides – as a matter of fact any new world which had a Livia in it elicited his instant support. He said: "I love you, Livia dear. Tell me more about it, it sounds just what we need to escape from all this fervent dullness." And Livia went on outlining this marvellous intellectual adventure with heart-breaking idealism and naivety. When he mentioned Constance she cried: "I can't bear her devotion to all the Jewish brokers of psychoanalysis, to the Rabbinate of Vienna. It's dead, that whole thing. Its barren mechanism betrays its origins in logical positivism." Blanford was far out of his depth here – he knew very little about these factors and personalities. Livia went on in torrential fashion: "Long before these barren Jewish evaluations of the human psyche, the Ancient Greeks evolved their own, more fruitful, more poetical and just as reasonable. For instance, before that bunch of thugs who ruled Olympus there were others like Uranus who ruled the earth and was castrated by Chronos. Those severed genitals were thrown still frothing and writhing into the sea, and the foam they generated gave birth to Aphrodite. Which world do you prefer? Which seems the more fruitful?" Blanford could only repeat, whispering in that small stag's ear the stupid words, "I love you and I agree."

She touched his face – the haptic sense – and the poor fellow was mesmerised; he was in love, and so full of glory and distress that he could have accepted anything without query provided Livia was part of it.

Here on this moist fresh grass they lay, with their arms under each other's heads, staring up into the clear warm sky with its rising sunlight and light musical clouds – herald of another perfect day. It would soon be time to slip quietly away, locking the doors behind them, and make their sleepy way back to Tu Duc through the olive groves turning to silver in the breeze. The kisses of her hard little mouth with its thin lips, sometimes cut in expressions of smiling contempt or reserve, held a world of promises for him. She had promised to spend her last few nights in his room. "I shall be back in Paris again in three months if you want me," she added, and Blanford began actively, resolutely, planning ways and means to accept this marvellous invitation. Gazing into the *camera lucida* of the eye's screen he saw a vastly enlarged version of Livia, one which filled the whole sky, hovering over them both like some ancient Greek goddess. It seemed a fearful thing to have to share this marvellous creature with the others – but there was nothing to be done for the terms of reference dictated that they should do almost everything together. As their departure began to shape itself into a fact – at first the summer seemed endless and their return to the north a figment – it became imperative to go on as many excursions as possible, to see as much of the country as possible before the fatal day dawned. Constance was staying on in Provence to try and fix up Tu Duc a little against future habitation; Sam and Hilary and Blanford were to affront their final examinations before selecting a profession. The centre of gravity was slowly shifting. At dawn, unable to sleep, and heading for the lily pond for a dip, Blanford came upon the two sisters naked upon the flagged path, walking with sleepy silence towards the same objective in the dusky bloom of daybreak. Slim and tall, with their upright carriage and hieratic style they looked like a couple of young Graces who had slipped out of the pantheon and into the workaday world of men, seeking an adventure. Blanford turned aside and waited until he heard the ripple of water; then he too joined them, sliding soundlessly into the pool like a trout. So the three sat quietly breathing among the lotus flowers, waiting for the sun to rise among the trees.

It was like a dream – the wet stone heads of the sisters, like statues come to life; the dense packages of silence moving about the garden suddenly drilled by a short burst of bird-song. "Perils and absences sharpen desire," says the ancient Greek poet. In all the richness of this perfect summer Blanford felt the pang of the partings to come – vertigo of a desire which must for the time being rest unrequited. Her wet hair made her look shaven; her pretty ears stood out pointed from her head, like gnomes at prayer. From the sunny balcony where breakfast waited they could see the swifts stooping and darting; how beautifully the birds combined with gravity to give life to this wilderness of garden which Constance had sworn never to have tidied and formalised. It was full of treasures like old fruit trees still bearing, strawberry patches, and a bare dry section of holm-oak – a stand of elderly trees – which had a truffle bed beneath.

Days had begun to melt and fuse together in the heat of Provence, their impressions of heat and water and light absolutely forbade them to keep a mental chronology of their journeys, jogging about the gorges of the Gardon in the old pony-cart, or taking the little toy train down to the sea to spend a night on the beach and attend a cockade-snatching bullfight at dusty Lunel. Ah! the little pocket train, which plodded down to the flat Carmargue, to take them to the Grau du Roi. It had such a merry holiday air; the carriages were so bright – red for the first class, yellow for the second, and green for the third. All with the legend PLM modestly painted on them. The long waits in tiny silent stations where the guard sometimes braked to a walking pace so that he could loiter in a field beside the track and gather a few leeks. When you were dying of thirst how good the fresh water from the pump at Aimargues tasted; it was really intended for the engine, but once the machine had drunk its fill it was the turn of the passengers. Once Hilary even used it as a shower while they were waiting for the connection which was to carry them down to the Saintes. In the dry heats of summer the odours of the sand and the sea came up to them from the beaches – and from the inland maquis that of thyme and rosemary bruised by the flocks of sheep. Sometimes they sat in a siding and let a train pass through from Nîmes which was full of the little black Carmargue bulls used in the cockade fights. Small stations on the roads to paradise, signal boxes at the end of the world; they would return after these excursions dazed with the sun and sea. And then in the evening Blanford would hear the sweet voice of Livia intoning the AUM of yoga as she sat in the green thicket behind the tower, re-charging her body, re-oxygenating her brain. Remembering a phrase from another life, "The heart of flesh in the breast is not the *vagra* heart; like an inverted lotus the valves of the flesh heart open by day and close by night during sleep."

The sleep of the south had invaded also their love-making, giving it a tonality, a resonance of its own; with Livia it was simple and rather brutal. He would never forget how she cried out "Ha" as she felt the premonition of the orgasm approaching; it was the cry of the Japanese swords-man before the shock of his stroke. And then, so extreme was the proof that she lay in his arms as if her back were broken.

Eating their picnic lunch among the brown rocks above the Pont du Gard, watching the eagles wheel and stoop, they all – as if by sudden consent – felt their minds drawn towards the thought of the impending future with the inevitable imperatives which choice would force upon them. Blanford was perhaps the luckiest for he would inherit a modest income which he would have no difficulty in supplementing by academic work – or so he thought. The brown-skinned Sam was less self-assured as he mused. "I shan't have a private income, and with the little intelligence I have in-herited I don't suppose I could get anything sensational in the way of a job. To tell the truth the Army seems the likeliest *pis aller* – though I am not very militant." He had been an active member of the Oxford Officers Training Corps and could with luck get a commission in a line regi-ment. Constance rested her arm lightly in the crook of his brown arm and smiled up at him, confident and at ease. There was no stress in their loving, while between Livia and

Blanford there was a kind of premonitory hopelessness; they were in that limbo where destiny, like an undischarged bankrupt, waited for them. They had gone too far to retreat now even if they had wished.

Hilary said: "I am going to surprise and perhaps pain you. I have been seriously tempted by the Catholic faith. I have the notion of really taking it up – if that is the word. I thought after next term to go into a retreat and receive instruction in it. I can easily do a little tutoring for a living. Then we'll see if the thing is lasting or wears out." He smiled round at the others, feeling suddenly abashed and unsure of himself; once these sentiments had been uttered aloud they seemed far less substantial and enriching than they had been before. He climbed down to his favourite diving plinth, above the river, poised, and suddenly fell like a swift to furrow the jade water far below. Sam sighed and rose to follow, followed by Blanford. Suddenly, by this brief conversation, the future had materialised before their eyes.

Blanford had brought a pretty little ring which he hoped to give to Livia, but the act seemed somehow embarrassing and confusing; he had not sufficient courage to indulge in definitive declarations – the only kind which would approximate to what he felt. And Livia needed none; she stared at him, smiling her hard little smile, holding her hand in his. They would meet again in Paris! Ah! in the cafés of that great epoch one arrived, distraught with love, and called for ink and paper, envelopes and stamps, while a concerned waiter, having supplied them, rushed for a *cassis*. Thus were great love-letters born – they would be sent by *pneumatique* and a helmeted motor cyclist would deliver them, like Mercury himself, within the hour.

Blanford decided to send her the ring by post when she had returned to Paris. On the last evening but one they went for a short walk together among the olive groves and Livia surprised him by saying: "I always think of you as a writer, Aubrey; people who keep copious diaries like you always have – they are really writers." She had noted his habit of scribbling in a school exercise book nearly every night before he got into bed. It was a self-indulgence he had, like most lonely people, permitted himself from early adolescence. And it was here, unwittingly, that Sutcliffe got born. Once at school one of his diaries had been pilfered from his locker and a teasing youth read out some passages aloud to a circle of laughing and taunting schoolmates. It was fearfully humiliating; and to guard against a repetition of such a torture Blanford had attributed his thoughts and ideas to an imaginary author called S. He also firmly lettered in the title "Commonplace Book", and put a few genuine quotations into it, to suggest that he was simply copying out things which struck him from the books he read. But slowly and insidiously S began to take shape as a person, a flippant and desperate person, a splintered man, destined for authorship with all its woes and splendours. To him he attached the name of the greatest cricketer of the day – also rather defensively; Sutcliffe was, in the cricket world, a household name. Yet over the years he was fleshed out by quotations which suggested the soliloquies of a lonely and hunted intellectual, a marginal man; Blanford took refuge in him, so to speak, from a world which seemed to him quite insensitive to intellectual matters, in fact calamitously philistine. Later when the great man actually emerged on paper and started his adventurous life of sins and puns Blanford was to adapt a hymn for his use, the first line of which was "Nearer My Goad to Thee." But this was much later. Now he simply looked into the eyes of Livia and replied steadily: "I don't think I could be imaginative enough, I'm too donnish I think."

But she was right.

And looking at her, watching her smiling at him, a

simple thought came into his mind, namely how marvellous not to be blind! Livia said: "Who is this S you are always quoting?" So she had been reading his exercise books behind his back! He answered "Schopenhauer" without a flicker of expression. But in the back of his mind was already looming a large fleshy man with pink knees pressed together, penis *en trompe-l'oeil* as he might say, whirling dumb-bells before an open window. The original Sutcliffe who was to keep his emotions in a high state of chaos; one of those novelists all out of shape from too frequent childbearing. Perhaps he was a poet? Yes, he wrote verses. Some had been published in *Isis*. He would send some to Livia in order to bolster her faith in him as a creative person. She had taught him several yoga *asanas* and now every morning he obediently performed them while he thought of her sitting somewhere out among the olives beyond the tower in the lotus pose which seemed to cost her no effort at all, intoning the Aum; or lying in the corpse posture, snuffing out her whole will and body, and by her meditation "swallowing the sky". He was rather afraid that all this was very much a fad, though he admitted to feeling better after it.

It was by these strange byways and unfrequented paths that years later he was able to track down that corpulent soak, that ignoble ape, Sutcliffe, whose vulpine quivering nose reddened at the approach of whisky, and whose shaggy body rejoiced to feel the warm thrust of alcohol in the nerves. Where did this extraordinary *alter ego* come from? He was never to discover.

Livia was looking at him curiously – a snake with a trigger in its tongue, a cat with afterthoughts. . . .

And now Felix Chatto came up the drive on a derelict bicycle and brought them an invitation from Lord Galen; it was for a farewell dinner before he took his own departure for Berlin. It would be agony to squeeze their swollen feet into socks and shoes, to unearth shirts and ties. . . . But they could not refuse the old man. Anyway it would be a good training for their return to the city after this bemusing Provençal holiday.

FIVE

Lord Galen Dines

W HEN I WAS A BOY", SAID LORD GALEN WITH A massive simplicity, "I read a book called *The Romance of Steam* and I have never forgotten it. It had a red and gold cover with an engine on it and it began, "The steam-engine is a mighty power for Good." Nobody could tell if he were joking or not. He fell into a muse and pulled his upper lip. Max the chauffeur, now transformed into something between a major-domo and an Italian admiral by a costume specially created for him, diligently carved the roast chickens in their chafing dishes before serving them. His black dress-trousers had a broad gold piping, and in the lapels of his dress coat he carried the insignia of a *sommelier* – a master of Cellars. It was he who had trundled up to fetch five young people in the Hispano, and they had been very grateful for the lift, for the walk was a long and dusty one from Tu Duc.

The house Galen owned and occupied sporadically throughout the year was as characteristic as the old man himself – it had been built quite recently by a Greek armaments king with whom he had business dealings; one old tower was all that was left of the original chateau which had stood on the site. All the rest had been rased to clear the ground for the modern villa – architecture of calamitous joviality – which, however, stood in handsome shady gardens. "Nothing old-fashioned does for me," said the old man forcibly; adding, "I have never drunk life through a straw, you know." Jutting out his chin.

The original name of the house had been "The Acropolis", but Lord Galen, with characteristic Jewish modesty, had renamed it "Balmoral"; the large painted board which announced the fact always gave Felix Chatto a twinge of horror as he turned into the drive – his taste had been educated to a very high pitch of refinement. The inside of the house also caused him pain by its exuberance; it was the kind of house that a successful but ignorant actress might order in Cairo. Masses of marquetry and leather and cretonne; the salon was raised on pillars so convoluted and painted that they resembled barbers' poles of the old style. It was wonderfully modern and slightly profligate in atmosphere. And on this particular evening they found a new visitor present who seemed to belong to it, to be most appropriate to the satin and damascene and scarlet leather. They had none of them met the Prince before, nor even heard of him; but it soon transpired that though he was an Egyptian prince of the blood he was also a business associate of old Galen. His presence lent a singular and appropriate touch to all this oriental décor for he wore dove-grey clothes, and dove-grey London spats over tiny boots polished like mirrors. His grey waistcoat sported pearl buttons, and he wore a stock which set off to admiration a lean and aquiline face which was almost as grey as the rest of him. In his lapel he wore a gold squirrel, on his finger a scarab ring.

Lord Galen performed the presentation with just the slightest trace of unction, adding afterwards, "Prince Hassad is an old business associate of mine." The Prince seemed extraordinarily meek, he ducked shyly as he shook hands; his hands were small, bird-like, twiggy, and he seemed glad to reclaim them after every action. Beside him on a chair lay a richly chased fly-whisk and a gorgeous fez with gold tassels of great lustre; the green band indicated not only his royal antecedents but also the fact that he had made the traditional pilgrimage to Mecca. At first blush it seemed that what was striking about him rested on the fact that his dress was exotic, his person foreign. But within a few moments the impression changed; they felt they were in the presence of some sort of oriental saint who sat so modestly but vividly before them, his face bowed, looking shyly up under his brows as he gazed from face to young face. His English was almost perfect, his French without a trace of a foreign accent or intonation. If ever the fact was commented upon the Prince was apt to say, smiling: "I learned both languages young. There is nothing else to do in the Royal harem but study."

"Champagne," said Galen with a lordly wave and there was a suggestive popping among the rock plants in the winter garden where the dumb secretary presided over a cocktail cabinet; and what a treat it was in all that summer thirst! The Prince sipped a glass and placed it beside him on the table; he was much reassured by the fact that they all talked French as well as English.

Constance, of course, won his immediate attention and admiration by her smiling good sense and swift French; it was to her that he chiefly addressed himself in order to explain himself and expound his habits to all of them – aware perhaps that he must seem a story-tale figure in the French country-side. "I am travelling north into Germany in my carriage, and Lord Galen is coming with me to transact some business on behalf of Egypt." Galen looked rather doubtful about this; he had offered to drive north in his elegant car, but the Prince had quietly insisted on the huge state landau with its four horses – a desperately slow method of getting about. He had also expressed a somewhat alarming wish, namely to visit a cathedral or two on the way north – a sentiment that Lord Galen found slightly morbid. But the little Prince was proposing to enjoy himself as a deeply civilised oriental should do when abroad, and there was nothing for it but to fall in with his wishes. But at night, in bed, Lord Galen gave a groan when he thought of their slow progress across

Europe in this royal contraption. At the moment it reposed in his garage where the two uniformed black Saidhis were currying the horses and watering them.

Needless to say, the Prince made an instant hit with the inhabitants of Tu Duc, though hardly less markedly with Chatto and the taciturn Quatrefages who had put on a tie for the occasion and whose flushed face suggested that he had perhaps had a drink or two to stimulate his courage for such a frightening occasion. Perhaps the Prince sensed this, for he at once paid the boy some special attentions, questioning him softly in his patrician French, and soon the clerk was quite at ease and sufficiently self-confident to venture on talking in an English which was not bad despite his marked accent. So the exchange of politenesses proceeded until Max with a grunt announced that they could come to table if they wished. The Prince put down his gold-tipped cigarette and asked permission to wash his hands; his body-servant, a tall Nubian clad in the scarlet sash of the royal *kavass*, helped him, holding the towels for him to wipe his hands on, and then sprinkling the royal fingers with scent at the end of the operation. The Prince dabbled some scent on his face also. Then he came modestly to table, where they all stood and waited for him; Lord Galen placed him between the two sisters which seemed to please him very much as he instantly engaged Constance once more in small talk.

From the kitchen came the clatter and chatter of the three young farm women who had been conscripted for this fête by the secretary; he himself took his meals apart in the study. "Every year", said Lord Galen happily, "I have this little beano as a farewell treat before leaving France. But it's the first time I have welcomed the Prince to my table." He beamed round him while Prince Hassad with his shy smile made a little self-deprecating *moue* of the lips, as if the allusion embarrassed him. "I am glad to be here," he said, and added:

"particularly because of the work you are doing on your romantic project, in which I find it very hard to believe. We Egyptians are very suspicious people."

"Quite right. Quite right," said Galen with approval, "but our little project is not all fancy, you know. We have certain definite lines of enquiry laid down. This treasure is not a will o' the wisp, eh Quatrefages?"

The Prince shook his head doubtfully. "As an investment?" he murmured, almost under his breath. He motioned to his servant, who had taken up his traditional food-taster's position behind his chair, to leave. It was as if he did not wish for an eavesdropper in the room in case the conversation became confidential. He looked prudently round the table and said: "Perhaps after dinner I could be given some facts about your search. Then I will be able to judge." Then, turning aside with a more definite air, he asked Livia to tell him what monuments he should see in the vicinity, and in her usual forceful way she offered to be his guide if he should so wish, at which he looked hesitant but grateful. "There is so much to see," said Lord Galen with a regretful sigh, "but I never seem to have the chance." The grotesque cat of the household which lay on its velvet cushion in the corner of the room gave a croak. It had smelt the chicken. Lord Galen regally cut a piece from his own portion and had it despatched to her by Max who got a serpentine hiss for his efforts. For such a frail-looking man the Prince was surprisingly adroit with knife and fork, and was soon deeply involved with second helpings and vegetables which he forked on to his side-plate, preferring to eat in the French fashion – to enjoy meat and vegetables separately. Nor did he neglect his glass of Tavel, which he held up to the light with a professional expression of appreciation, to admire its topaz glow. "Though a Moslem," he confided in his host, "I am anything but a fanatic. But I never overdo things in case my wife catches me." He gave a small sweet chuckle and lowered his eyes again.

"Of course," said Lord Galen soothingly, "to drink a little – it's all harmless jollity." Quatrefages had been taciturn and talkative by turns, had been flushed and pale also; Felix knew him well enough to decipher these indications. They betrayed that he had been drinking absinthe again; it made him fiery and apathetic by turns. Now he produced his little pendulum from his vest pocket and allowed it to swing over his glass of wine for a moment. Everyone watched him with interest, as if he were about to do a conjuring trick. But no. After a moment of intense study he put away his divining instrument and drained his glass, giving an involuntary belch as he did so. They all smiled indulgently but he gazed about him with a bloodshot eye and made a sign for Max to refill his glass, which the butler did, but not without an anxious glance in the direction of his boss.

Lord Galen was talking, however, and had not noticed this small diversion. He was talking about the pleasures of Germany, of the pleasant journey they were soon to enjoy together. "Pleasant and I hope profitable," he added. "The brothers Krupp will come in their special train into Austria and we shall become good friends, yes, very good friends." An emotional man, he felt the tears of friendship rising to his eyes. It was to be a most meaningful meeting, he assured the Prince. The Nubians would get what they wanted cheap because of his other interests. Felix whispered an aside to Blanford: "He doesn't seem to know what is going on over there." If Quatrefages divined by the pendulum, Felix divined by the stock pages of the *Financial Times*. The sinister drift of events in Germany had been an object of his concerned study for some time; why, even the Foreign Office Intels had been showing diplomatic unease about the situation – and here was Galen blithely chatting about financial speculations and business interests for all the world as if the country was stable and productive, and in a fit state to welcome foreign investment.

Normally Felix would have said nothing but now his curiosity got the better of him and he said: "I personally don't at all like what appears to be going on there. I am surprised that the situation has not alarmed you." Lord Galen bridled and said: "Situation?" And this gave Felix the chance to give a brief and rather succinct outline of the state of affairs in Germany and the possible issues. To all this Lord Galen listened with a condescending smile, but attentively; he rolled bits of bread in his side-plate and popped them into his mouth. But he politely heard his nephew out, and seemed no whit abashed by the nods and murmured agreement of the old Prince who seemed at least as well informed as Felix if not quite as anxious as the consul. In fact he was delighted at this diversion which he had been too polite to initiate, but which might clear up a lot of points which were still obscure to him. He glanced from one face to the other, trying to divine whether Lord Galen, under his somewhat ineffable air of serenity, was not playing a game with him – a game of investor's poker, so to speak.

But Livia, too, seemed to be on the side of Felix, for she too nodded agreement to the propositions which he put forward. When at last the question of Jewry came up Lord Galen had had enough of his nephew's presumptuous exposition and he held up his hand in a kind but firm way. "Everything you say sounds true, but I can assure you, Felix, that I know the contrary – I know because I have been there, and I have seen with my own eyes. You will imagine when first the press started these rumours about anti-Semitism that I took note, and indeed I felt a vague alarm. As a Manchester man I could not ignore it." For some reason he disliked and avoided the word "Jew" – perhaps because of old schoolboy associations? He preferred to use the circumlocution "Manchester man"; it sounded almost as if one were a member of an Oxford college. He repeated on a lower note, and more impressively: "As a Manchester man I could not ignore it. I was both personally and financially concerned, as you might say. So what did I do? Why, I went into the whole thing, I went over myself and investigated the state of the country and nature of the opposition to the government. Now, if I had had the slightest doubt, would I have invited you to come from Egypt? All the way from Egypt, eh? An old friend, eh?" There was a long pause in the conversation during which he and the Prince beamed at one another. But Felix shook his head and Livia stared at Galen with profound curiosity – was he just ill-informed, or just pretending in order to deceive the Prince?

Lord Galen was deceiving nobody but himself. "I went so far as to see the leader of the National Socialists himself. I spent a whole weekend with him in face-to-face discussion about his plans and sentiments." He looked round triumphantly and paused.

Then he lowered his voice and went on: "It was not possible to distrust the assurances of such a man; his sincerity was absolutely convincing. Mark you, he was no hotheaded youth but a mature man who had been through the whole war as an ordinary sergeant. He had seen the whole thing from the inside. He spoke most movingly and simply of the sufferings of his country, and of the political indignities the Allies had forced upon it. His only desire was to redress these wrongs and live at peace with the world. He gave me the most explicit outline of his policies and convictions – it was really heart-warming, I was touched almost to tears. We had been really very hard on the Germans. He was right to feel a certain mild resentment about the fact. But his whole attitude was grave and measured and his views long deliberated. And this is where I was first able to question him closely about the

alleged anti-Semitism of his party. There was no doubt that
the man was sincere – his whole face and manner betrayed it.
He knew, he said, that nobody could pull the wool over my
eyes, and that I was free to judge as best I may, but for his
part he could guarantee that the whole press campaign was
false, and had been stage-managed by political opponents.
His party were even thinking of creating a second Jewish
state, more stable than mandated Palestine, somewhere in the
East. He spoke with passion and conviction – and if ever I
trusted a man I trusted him. He showed me a long memorandum prepared by the party department of demography
about a Jewish state of ten million souls and asked me what I
thought of it. You can imagine my excitement. It was the
dream of the race to have a place of their own. It was most
reassuring to feel that a modern political leader could think
along these lines. He said with a smile: 'You see, Lord Galen,
in some ways we are more Zionist than the Zionists.' I found
him very splendid indeed."

Galen gazed round at the company whose expressions
varied from polite incomprehension to incredulity. Felix
listened to his uncle with startled astonishment, Livia with a
sort of tremulous doubt – was he roasting the Prince? The
rest of them neither knew very much nor cared whether these
views were true or false; only the Prince seemed delighted by
this brief exposition, and not unfamiliar with its details. His
clever grey face was like a silk handkerchief, folding itself
into smiles. He said with an air of elation: "And the contracts,
P.G. eh?" Lord Galen nodded.

"I was coming to that," he said; "it was right at the end
of our talks that we discussed the financial situation of his
party. It was, to say the least, precarious, for he was facing
powerful vested interests who wished to see other leaders
take the helm of state. If he did not get into power what
would become of his dreams of founding a small Jewish

state? This is what made me think. I sounded him out on the whole question of foreign investment and he told me that he would offer substantial concessions in the future against present aid. In the light of all that had gone before I felt that the situation held out great promise for myself and my associates. Nevertheless, I never act hastily, and I once more went over the whole ground. It was clear to me that this was the chance of a lifetime – to offer a massive contribution to party funds which would be paid for later by wholesale business concessions. I consulted everyone – naturally some were highly doubtful of my good sense, or of his good faith. But my arguments prevailed, and pretty soon we hope he will get in, largely thanks to us; meanwhile, the document which we spent half the night discussing was signed solemnly by us both in the presence of witnesses. I brought it down tonight to show everyone."

He inserted his fingers in a cardboard tube and eased out a scroll which he unrolled and held up before them. It was typewritten and the seal looked expensive with its wax eagle. But it was too far for anyone to read the text, and after a brief exposure of it to the company, he prudently replaced it, smiling the while at the memory of his astuteness. The Prince made as if to clap his hands in appreciation of his host's business acumen.

Livia said she was feeling unwell, and rose with her napkin to her lips; it was nothing, she said, she wanted a breath of fresh air, that was all. They all rose from their chairs to register concern, but were ordered to remain seated, while Constance said: "It's nothing, but I'll go with her," and the two girls made their way out of the house on to the warm green lawns where Livia sank on her knees and then lay fully down and began to turn slowly from side to side. At first it seemed like some sort of paroxysm but in fact it was only an attack of laughter so strong that she was forced to cram her fist between her teeth as she laughed, rolling back and forth. Her sister squatted beside her and watched her with smiling curiosity, waiting patiently until the laughter died away into exhaustion. Livia produced a small pocket handkerchief and mopped up her eyes. "The old fool is giving them money," she said, still a trifle tremulously. "How they must be laughing." She rose now, sighing, and allowed Constance to dust her down. "I thought I would explode at table," said Livia, "and be forced to explain my laughter. Sorry for the diversion. But it's the joke of the year."

Constance knew little and cared nothing about all these problems, so she held her peace; but she linked arms with her sister and together the two women re-entered the dining-room once more where the Prince was just saying: "I also have a car to carry my luggage – but it is a lorry really because I travel with so much luggage." He sighed. In fact, as they later found, the auxiliary vehicle was a very large removers' van – the kind known as a pantechnicon. It carried, apart from the Prince's personal belongings, a crew of three servants. At the moment it was drawn up outside his hotel in Avignon, watched over by a kindly policeman; the Egyptian Embassy had signalled the authorities that the Prince was travelling in France.

The French customs had already been dazzled by the extraordinary contents of the van; all the Prince's boxes were made of rare wood and covered outside with coloured silk and inlaid with metal filigree. There was a royal coffin worthy of Tutankhamun. Expensive bridge tables. Enough plate and cutlery to give a banquet for thirty people. When later he showed them these wonders, which included four of his favourite hawks in case he might be in the mood for hawking, he was good enough to explain that what might seem rather superfluous to them was really very necessary for an Egyptian prince, because one never knew. One never really knew. But all this transpired a little while later when their acquaintance with the Prince had ripened. For the moment they sat at table still, but now over brandy and cigars, while Galen cracked walnuts vividly and chatted knowledgeably on the subject of investments. The Prince drank off quite healthy swigs of cognac for a man who looked so slender. "Of the other matter – your buried treasure – we will speak later!" His tone was bantering, amused, which somewhat nettled Quatrefages, who glared at him.

The clerk was rather suffused now with drink and his mood was, from the point of view of an outside observer, fretful and precarious. Felix eyed him with curiosity and affection and wondered whether he was going to break out into an impassioned speech about the treasure. As a matter of fact the French boy, always a bit touchy, resented the Prince's smiling scepticism about the seriousness of the work they were doing; why, he wondered, did not Lord Galen insist upon it and say something in defence of it? But he sat mildly rolling bread balls and thinking while the weight of the Prince's scepticism grew and grew.

At last Galen said: "The tradition is a long one and it's been hunted for by many people; a lot of money has gone down the drain hunting for it, so far in vain. More than one consortium of interests has tried its hand. But it is only recently that some documents have come to light which might pin-point the *place*. There is no doubt that there was a treasure and that it disappeared during the trials of the Templars for heresy. After all, the Templars were the bankers of kings with enormous fortunes in their care. In the documents of the trials which are being deciphered and printed in Toulouse it is clear that the burning question for the investigators who tortured them was financial rather than ecclesiastical. Where had the treasure gone? The questions of heresy were all very well – the Inquisition looked into that very thoroughly; but what the Chancellor of Philippe le Bel wanted to know was where the hell they had put the boodle. This is why the trials were so long drawn out; they could have popped off the whole lot of the Templars in a few months. Why did they hang about? They were hoping for a lead which would guide them to the treasure. That was the only thing that obsessed the King – for the state was bankrupt."

He paused and turned to his clerk for confirmation and support. But Quatrefages glared at his plate in a brown study. The Prince was unsmiling now; he had suddenly remembered the stories of buried treasure which figured so largely in Egyptian folklore and the idea appealed to him. His doubts began to be qualified by the reflection that if there were nothing to the story but hot air surely it would not have attracted the attention of a renowned business baron with a reputation for flair and strong dealing? But he realised that he had offended Quatrefages by his bantering tone and he made amends now, reaching out to touch him on the wrist in an apologetic way which quite won the boy's heart and put him once more into a very good humour. "*C'est vrai*," he said to the smiling old man, "it is true; we have some very precious indications. It is probably a crypt now covered in grass. Part of a chateau or a chapel or a monastery. The sign was an orchard of olives planted like this...." He drew an envelope from his pocket and with his fountain pen sketched a quincunx of trees.

"I think", said Galen, "the thing would be for you to visit Quatrefages' little office at the hotel and see how he is tackling the matter. It's great detective work. The scent has led us as far as Avignon or its immediate surroundings. We are going through the records of the chateaux and chapels in the immediate vicinity of the town; there are plenty of them, as you may imagine, because of its importance as a religious centre during the period when the Popes made it their headquarters. But there's hope; o yes, we have hope. That little affair with King John gave me confidence in my own private intuition. You remember? That also looked foolish, but we won through, didn't we?"

It was perfectly true. Chatting one day to a young Oxford historian at a reception, Galen had been intrigued by a remark dropped at random; the subject of treasure had come up – heaven knows in what context – and the young don enumerated several examples of buried treasure from his history studies. Among them, and one which he found perhaps the most curious, was the loss of King John's treasure in the Wash. One would have thought that that at least was traceable; the depth of the channel was negligible and clearly marked. The local movement of tides and sand bars at the ford was extremely limited. Yet despite the efforts of several generations of treasure-seekers nothing had ever come to light. The treasure itself was the most important ever to be lost in England – almost priceless indeed. This stray remark was enough to fire the admiration of Lord Galen who had always fancied himself as a sort of poet of the commercial instinct. He made a note in his little red morocco notebook and called a meeting.

He knew, of course, that in law all treasure trove belongs to the Crown which has the right, but not the obligation, to reward the finder with a bounty. Lord Galen felt that if he could secure a government promise to reward him to the tune of fifteen per cent for anything he might find, the project might prove to be worth his while. The Prime Minister was a personal friend and was coming to dinner with him the following week. He took the opportunity to explore the situation. He was given a fair wind. Dealing at such a high level with such matters one does not ask for guarantees or formal contracts. He would, he said, be content with an exchange of letters serving as a declaration of intent. Of course it was a risk. The project was a costly one and might end in failure. The Government had nothing to lose. The upshot of the matter was that he was able to attract finance for the project and indulge his sense of romance by having the Wash surveyed from the air and inviting engineers to devise the sort of machinery necessary first to locate, then to raise, the buried treasure. It had taken over two years, but had at last been successful. Lord Galen became as famous in Fleet Street as he was in the City. The profits were extremely handsome.

"I agree," said the Prince on a note of contriteness. "It was fully justified by the outcome, and a lesson to sceptics." Galen accepted the accolade gracefully, nodding his personal agreement with the remark. "That is why I thought of you, my dear Prince, when we embarked upon this little venture – which is perhaps a trifle more risky even than old King John. Many more people have tried to locate what we are hunting for – and there is always a chance that someone might have found it and kept the matter secret in order not to surrender it to the French Government. But I have made exactly identical arrangements with the Government here, and have reserved a fine meaningful percentage for my shareholders. The rest is a matter of science, of luck, and the flair of Quatrefages who will bring you up to date on what we have so far found."

Quatrefages looked steadily at the Prince and nodded gravely. "We will speak," he said on a note of confirmation. And the Prince stroked his hand once more with a warmly oriental gesture, saying: "Of course; we understand each other, no?"

At which the conversation once more became general and the contingent of guests from Tu Duc began to feel a faint disposition to yawn despite the earliness of the hour. The candles had burnt down and begun to drip. Max docked them and changed some for new. "I think", said Felix, "we should consult the clock and perhaps start moving off in good order." But a sudden loneliness assailed Lord Galen at the thought of spending the night alone with his asthmatic cat. His voice became quite quavery and pleading as he said: "O do not go so early. Let us have a last stirrup-cup on the terrace. After all who knows when we shall meet again?" Blanford felt the words entangle the muscles of his throat as he looked at Livia across the table. She smiled at him with a slow affectionate expression, but he was so deeply sunk in his own conjectures that he did not respond. How brown she had become – almost the colour of a gipsy! All of a sudden he too was assailed by a fearful sense of anguish and disenchantment – later he would recognise this as premonitory; but an irrational and boundless fear of what might come to pass for them all, and in particular for himself and Livia who inhabited so temporarily this little enclave of passionate feeling in the immensity of a hostile world. The darkness inside was now (for they were on the terrace) matched by the darkness without.

They sat over new whiskies and coffees to accustom themselves to the faint glimmer of stars. Occasional fireflies snatched in the deep grass of the lawns which that year had not been mowed. The faint wind had turned a point or two northwards and brought with it a welcome and refreshing chill which towards dawn would cause (Felix noted this) a heavy dew upon the leaves and window-panes. "It's beautiful," said Lord Galen with an unwonted warmth of feeling as he gestured towards the star-scattered darkness where the dense mists turned and shifted, now hiding, now revealing the vibrating depths of the Provençal night sky. They heard Max yawning his violet yawns within as he disencumbered the table; each time he passed the stricken Wombat it snapped blindly at his ankles.

Lord Galen contemplated the long empty reaches of insomnia which awaited him as a condemned man might think of an age of servitude ahead. He had started taking sleeping pills which guaranteed him some rest but was depressed to notice that he needed increased doses to maintain the equilibrium. It was the time of night when the thought of his daughter echoed and ached within him with a dull neuralgic insistence, poisoning his peace of mind. Sometimes after midnight he rang for his secretary and bade him produce the chessmen. They would sit silently hunched over a game until the first pale streaks of dawn woke the birds in the park. Sometimes he took a stroll in the icy dew, his footfalls silenced by the deep grass. It was rare that he could return to his bed on such occasions. He hung around until five-thirty when he heard the alarm go off in Max's room. Pretty soon the yawning black man would come and give him breakfast in the kitchen – waffles and maple syrup. Galen ate hungrily. By then he had already despatched his yawning secretary to his room. Soon it would be time to dip down the dusty hill into the town and watch the first passenger train set off for Paris. . . .

Rehearsing all this in his mind he felt the weariness and spleen assail him anew. "I suppose you all want to go to bed," he said at last, rather bitterly. "I can see you yawning and stretching, Felix – not very polite." Felix sprang to attention, metaphorically speaking, and blushed his apologies. He too was quailing at the thought of the night which confronted him; this temporary sleepiness would serve to get him to bed all right, but after an hour or two he would find himself switched on like a light and unable to prevent himself rising to make coffee, and at last, to walk the silent town. They smiled now at each other but the weariness engendered by their thoughts suffused the air, and at last the Prince, fearing that people could not leave before a prince of the blood took

his leave, called in soft Arabic for his landau. The tall major-
domo was standing just inside the drawing-room, and relayed
the message in a low voice. There was a long period of confused noise and at last the travel-apparatus of the Prince
rumbled round the house and came to rest before the flight
of marble stairs where the restless horses struck sparks from
the cobbles with their hooves and whinnied softly. *Noblesse
oblige.*

The Prince accepted his fez and fly-whisk from the
hands of his servant and then turned smiling to take his leave.
"Well, if you young people will forgive me. . . ." he said,
pressing their hands for a second in his. "I will expect you all
to a drink tomorrow in my hotel at seven." He did not wait
for a formal acceptance, but turned to embrace his host in the
French fashion, giving him a dab on the cheek with his lips.
He smelt aromatic, he smelt of camphor like a mummy – so
thought Lord Galen as he returned the accolade. Now the
Prince climbed into his coach and turning back said: "Can I
give anyone a lift? Surely Mr. Chatto? Quatrefages, no?"
They accepted his offer in order to spare Max an extra detour.
As they stepped into the landau and sat down beside the
Prince he remarked rather unexpectedly: "I feel like a bit of
fun tonight, to be sure."

They rumbled off into the darkness and the Prince
began a long and animated conversation with his staff in
guttural Arabic. He seemed to be asking them for information
about something. Then, aware perhaps that it was somewhat
impolite to talk in a language the others did not understand,
he ventured on an explanation directed largely at Quatrefages. "I am asking them to take us to a good house – surely
there must be a nice *pouf* in Avignon?" Felix choked with
astonishment but Quatrefages acted as if he had foreseen such
a departure and chuckled as he slapped the Prince on the knee
in a manner as familiar as it seemed to the dismayed consul

downright vulgar. "Of course, of course," said the clerk with a gesture towards the night sky, as if invoking all its starlit bounty upon the head of the grinning Prince.

Felix found that something distasteful had entered the expression of the Prince; those grave, sweet expressions, those silent modesties, had given place to a new set of facial looks – a trifle perky and monkey-like. He looked elated and full of zest; it seemed as if his intentions and desires had become a trifle debased, a trifle vulgar. "You aren't taking him to a brothel?" he said *sotto voce* to Quatrefages, who himself had changed but in a milder degree. He looked slightly tipsy and insolent. "Indeed I am," he said in an airy way, "the old darling is a Gypp and needs a cleanser. He will absolutely love Riquiqui. I will hand him over to old Riquiqui and see what she can provide." Felix looked miserable and alarmed. The Prince was talking Arabic again, heedless of them. "If he catches something," said Felix, "my uncle will never forgive you. Anyway I shan't go; it's too risky. If my uncle thought . . ." Quatrefages said simply but trenchantly "F**k your uncle."

The advice, Felix felt, was apposite and chimed with his own feelings. But it was all too easily said. Moreover he was not at all sure how the sentiment could be implemented. It was partly his cursed uncle and partly the dignity of the Foreign Office which nagged him. He sighed under the importunity of these ideas and set his mind firmly against this frivolous excursion, stifling all his regrets. Actually he would have given anything for an evening of good fellowship and a touch of profligacy. Ah well! The coach went stumbling and swaying through the dark olive glades to where at the outer edges of the darkness the lights of the city gleamed; from the quarter of the gipsies there came a thin plume of wood-smoke. It was still early. Owls whistled in the secret trees. The faint rumour of the city gradually evolved itself

from their own noise of creaking coachwork, jingling harness
and clattering horseflesh. The Prince was in a great good
humour as he sat with an arm thrown round the shoulders of
Quatrefages. He was occasionally slipping into his elegant
French now as a concession to his companion. "I have a few
small oddities of conduct", he said thoughtfully, "which are
not unusual for a man of my age. Do you think they will
understand?" Quatrefages gave a reassuring grin as he
answered. "At Riquiqui they are used to everything, they
cater for everything. And as they are frequented by the chief
of police they are very much à *l'abri*." Reassured, the Prince
beamed and squeezed his knee.

Felix had never been to Riquiqui's sordid establishment
except with Blanford – and that for no questionable purpose.
Once they had hunted for Livia during a night walk and the
gipsies had directed them to try Riquiqui. The sordid
surroundings and the darkness did not commend themselves
to the two young men; and the personage of Riquiqui herself
inspired the worst misgivings. She had opened a cautious
inch in response to their tapping upon the rotten oak door.
The little side street in which the house stood was pitch dark,
and smelt of blocked drains and dead rats. The houses
immediately to right and left of Riquiqui's had fallen down
or been knocked down; their foundations gaped. Weeds
sprouted everywhere. Blanford professed to find the place
sinister but romantic – but of course he was lying. Felix
was plainly nervous.

Riquiqui had enormous breasts bulging out of the top
of a sort of sack dress, divided at the waist by a primeval
drawstring. She had a wall-eye which gave her the air of
looking over your shoulder while she spoke to you – which
they found disconcerting. Moreover, lupus had ravaged her
impure face – a burst of purple efflorescence covered one side
of it. She tried to present her clear side rather too obviously,

but from time to time she was forced to turn and present the diseased profile with its great splash of suffused blood vessels turning to crimson-lake and purple. A faint candle illumined the scene – the gaunt stairs behind her. She could give them no indication of Livia's whereabouts though she seemed to know, from their explanations, the person they were speaking about, for she nodded a great deal and said, "Not today" repeatedly, which suggested, at any rate, Livia was in the habit of calling in at this disreputable establishment. Curiously enough the information, far from depressing Blanford, elated him; he admired the insouciant and courageous way Livia went her own way, busied herself with her own affairs, without expecting their protective company. But Felix found this attitude inconsequent, even compromising.

But tonight, he told himself, there was to be no such excursion for the consul. Pleading a slight headache he had himself dropped off at the station; there was still time to sit and relax at the buffet over a coffee – after the bustle and conversation of a party he loved to spend a few moments alone, thinking his own modest thoughts. A train had pulled out for the north; the engine gave a whiff or two, as if it were calling back over its shoulder. The little *fiacres* stood anchored in the monotony of their function as train-waiters. Later when he set out on his walk he might feed the horses a sugar-lump or two if he felt lonely; this would lead to a conversation with the sleepy drivers.

But for the moment he had had his fill of conversation. The Prince had rumbled off into the darkness with his coach. From the neighbouring livery-stables came the noise of horses coughing and stamping. A bell trilled and wires hummed. Avignon was beginning to settle down for the night – that long painful stretch of time which must somehow be affronted. Felix yawned – yes, it was all very well, but would it last? He paid for his coffee and sauntered across under the frowning darkness of the Porte St.-Charles. It would not take him long to return. Then he would undress and go to bed doggedly; yes, doggedly. But as he neared the villa his nerves gave a jump for there was the figure of a man sitting on his front door-step smoking and waiting for him. It was a mere silhouette; he could not at first make out his identity.

For a moment he hesitated timorously, and then, cursing himself for a coward, advanced with a deliberate *sang-froid* to reach the garden gate. "There you are!" cried Blanford cheerfully. "I wondered if the Prince had taken you off on a binge." Felix recounted his journey home in the coach and Blanford chuckled. He said, "I suddenly decided not to go to bed; we got Max to drop us off and walked the quarter of a mile home – it's not far, after all." Felix opened the front door and entered the musty little villa. "I wondered if you would be walking tonight," said Blanford; and suddenly Felix seemed to sense the loneliness and misgiving behind the words. "Is there anything wrong?" he asked unexpectedly and Blanford shook his head. "No, it's just the end of this perfect holiday and one doesn't want to waste the time on sleep. I went home dutifully with the others but couldn't get to sleep, so I headed for town."

Yes, there was something lame about this long explanation. Felix put a kettle to boil and prepared to make some coffee. Then the explanation of Blanford's tone struck him forcibly and made everything clear. Livia had disappeared, and he had suddenly missed her and decided jealously to come and see if she were with Felix! It was true. Blanford could not help it – though he cursed himself roundly for butting in. He was propelled, as indeed Felix was, by a quite uncontrollable jealousy, which came and went in spasms, and which both struggled to surmount by reminding themselves that they should really be above such feelings. It was no good.

Thinking of all this, Felix poured out the dreadful Camp coffee which was made of liquid chicory and smiled acidly upon his friend as he said (unable to disguise the tone of quiet malice in his voice): "I suppose it's Livia again?"

"Yes," said Blanford surrendering reluctantly to the truth, "it's Livia."

Felix was suddenly furiously contemptuous of this spoilsport friend of his. His pent-up feelings broke loose. "And just suppose that she wanted to be alone with me, to walk with me?" Blanford nodded humbly and said: "I know. I thought of that, Felix. I am most awfully sorry. I just couldn't resist coming here. I felt I had to find her. I am so sorry, I know you care for her too. But I have asked her to marry me later on. . . ." His voice trailed away into silence while his friend sat opposite trying to convey his disapproval and annoyance by small reproving gestures. As a matter of fact, at a deeper level than all this superficial annoyance, he felt a certain misgiving about Livia as a suitable person to marry. To love and if possible lie with – yes. "Marriage", he said sharply, "is quite another affair." Blanford detested the curate's tone in which Felix uttered this sentiment. "Yes," he said, becoming rather acid in his turn, "it happens to be my affair at the moment. That's why I took the liberty of coming. But if my presence upsets you I can take myself off. You only have to say." Felix was on the horns of a dilemma here; for if he were alone and sleepless later on he would welcome company; but if Livia was driven off by the presence of Aubrey . . . it would be far better if he went home now. Which solution was the better? He went into the bedroom to consult his little clock. The hour was pretty advanced now, and the likelihood of Livia coming rather remote. He returned to the disconsolate Blanford and said: "Were you thinking of a walk, then?"

Blanford shook his head and said: "Only as far as

Riquiqui's to see if I can pick up her trail. It's a lovely night."

It was a lovely night! The words echoed in the skull of Felix as he apportioned the last of the coffee and decided that he would not go to bed, he would after all walk. Moreover he now sensed that behind Blanford's tone of voice lurked an anxiety, a fear almost of the gloomy and ramshackle quarter of the town which he proposed to visit in search of the girl. He couldn't resist a slight touch of malice in his own voice as he said: "I suppose you'd want to go to Riquiqui's alone?" Blanford looked up at him and said, somewhat humbly, "On the contrary. I'd welcome company. You know that that whole section of the town scares me a bit – it's so disreputable with its bordels and gipsies."

This went some way towards mollifying Felix who betook himself to the bedroom where he changed out of his formal suit into something lighter, and topped it by his college blazer and a silk scarf. Through the half-open door he caught a glimpse of the glorified alcove which served as the so-called spare room where Livia sometimes lodged. The little cupboard stood there with its door ajar; he had already shown Blanford the male kit hanging up in there. He himself had never seen her in full disguise, though once or twice she had worn trousers to wander about the town. Blanford had made no comment – no comment whatsoever. What did he think? Felix could not say. For his part he found the whole question of marriage unreal – despite the magnetism of her beauty to which he was as much bound as Blanford. But there was something else which had qualified his passion. It was something he remembered with a certain shame – it was not in his nature to spy on people; yet, one evening, in a sudden fit of curiosity and without any conscious premeditation, he had walked into her room, opened the wardrobe and felt in the pockets of her brown cheap suit for all the world as if he knew that he would find something there – which indeed he did. It was a slip of paper torn from an exercise book – a love letter no less, but written in arch, lisping style, as if by an adolescent girl.

"*Ma p'tite Livvie je t'aime*," and so on in this vein, but riddled with misspellings and turns of phrase which suggested an uneducated and very youthful author. Felix examined the hand with the magnifying glass which was always on his desk, and decided that it was not the writing of a gipsy but of a schoolgirl. But his investigations went no further and after a moment of hesitation he replaced the note where he had found it and went whistling light-heartedly back to his office, glad in spite of himself that his rival was being betrayed. From time to time he frowned, however, and tried to banish the uncharitable and unfriendly feeling – for he was a good-hearted boy who believed in friendship like the rest of us. Yet it kept coming back. Sometimes, walking beside Blanford he repeated the words in his mind, "*Ma p'tite Livvie je t'aime*", almost letting them come to the surface and find utterance. It was very vicious, this sort of behaviour, and he did not approve of it; but he could not help it.

They finished their coffee and Felix put the cups and saucers into the sink in his usual somewhat fussy way. Blanford waited for him, smoking thoughtfully with an air of profound preoccupation touched with sadness. A curious polarity of feelings had beset him – somewhere in the deepest part of himself he was actually glad that Livia was going, that they were to be separated for a time. It would take a weight off his mind, as the saying goes; he had indeed become a little impatient with himself, with the extent of his complete immersion in this unexpected infatuation for a girl who, more often than not, seemed hardly to know he was there, so remotely distant did she seem from all thought of him. The force of this attachment had somewhat exhausted him, and he knew for certain that it had prevented him from enjoying

Provence as deeply as he might have done. Loving – was there some sort of limitation inherent in it? This was the first time he had ever asked himself the question plainly. But the answer eluded him.

"*Avanti*," said Felix, who out of boredom had started to study Italian; and together the two young men crossed the withered garden and advanced among the criss-cross of tenebrous streets and alleys which led them towards Les Balances, that desolate and ruined quarter sloping down towards the rustling Rhône. "I don't suppose she really gives a damn about me," said Blanford unexpectedly, throwing his cigarette onto the pavement and stamping it out with petulance. He was dying for Felix to contradict him, to come out with some reassuring remark, but Felix was not going to pander to his mood. "I suppose not," he said composedly, looking into the deep velvety sky, smiling to himself. Blanford could have strangled him for his composure there and then. He made up his mind to find Livia if they had to walk all night; and when he found her to pick a quarrel with her, to try and make that dry little lizard of a girl cry. Then they would make it up and . . . here he lost himself in pleasant reveries. But what if she had returned home and was snug in his bed while they were wandering about like a couple of fools? It was amazing how his spirits soared optimistically at one thought and then sagged earthwards at its successor. Somewhere at the bottom end of this keyboard – among the bass notes – there lurked migraine and the ancient neurasthenia. They waited for him. He always carried a couple of loose aspirins in his pocket. He took one now, swallowing it easily. *Absit omen*. "It is not easy, I have never been in love before. And whores scare me a bit."

Felix took on a man-of-the-world tone as he said: "O pouf! I regard them simply as a disagreeable necessity in a puritan age."

"I once got clap after a bump supper," said Blanford gloomily, "and it wasn't at all gay. It took ages to get itself cured."

Felix felt an unexpected wave of admiration for his friend; so he had suffered in some subterranean lavatory decorated by horrific posters depicting all the possible ravages of sexual intercourse indulged in without a rubber sheath? The man was a hero after all! "It must have been dreadful," he said with a suddenly alerted wave of sympathy and Blanford nodded, not without pride. "It was, Felix."

They had started downhill, sloping along a set of streets which straggled from the height of the Hotel de Ville to the actual medieval walls which alone prevented them from seeing the scurrying sweeps of the Rhône. A glimpse of Villeneuve on its great promontory – that was all; and a coffin-like darkness in whose soft shifting exhalations of mist prickled a star or two. Felix had brought a torch, but used it sparingly in the deserted streets. The noise of their footsteps sounded lonely and disembodied in the night. The municipal lighting hereabouts was haphazard and sporadic. The last two streets they crossed to reach Riquiqui were in dense darkness; the pavements had melted away, and occasional cobble-stones lay about ready to trip them up. The quarter was an undrained one and smelt accordingly. Riquiqui's establishment stood at an angle in a *cul de sac* and its doors opened into the street. Bundles of old rubbish lay about – broken chairs, bits of marble, sheets of tin, lead pipes and refuse. It stood, the house, like the last remaining molar in a diseased jaw; on either side there was a weed-infested waste land with the remains of low walls. A window gave out into this gloom with a yellow and baleful light. But the hallway of the house seemed to be in darkness, to judge by the blind fanlight over the door.

There was no sign of the coach either – which Blanford

had christened "The Prince's Pumpkin" – but this could have been dismissed and sent away to the livery stables where its horses were lodged. Or perhaps they had gone to some other establishment of the same category – though there were not many in the town which enjoyed the reputation and indeed the official protection of Riquiqui, for she also lodged people and operated (if such a thing can be believed) as a foster mother to waifs and strays. But she nevertheless remained in a somewhat ambiguous position as one who kept a house of ill-fame and was a friend to the gipsies; they called her "angel maker" for the children confided to her care were unwanted ones and would soon – so the popular gossip went – be on their way to heaven to join the angels. The very fact of her existence was explained by her payment of bribes, in cash and in kind, which was at least plausible; for she was fairly openly frequented by minor officials and the lower echelons of the police force. The two young men trod the streets of this raffish quarter with a certain native circumspection, though Felix once or twice whistled under his breath as if to register confidence.

At last they stopped before the door of Riquiqui and Blanford advanced to tap upon it with timorous knuckles. It was not much in the way of a summons and it evoked neither light nor voices in response. They waited for a while in a downcast manner. Then Felix picked up a brick from the gutter and made a more reasonable attempt at a knock – he didn't like making a noise in the street at this time of night. Supposing that nearby windows were thrown up and exasperated voices urged them to go to hell? They would scamper away like rabbits. But no windows were raised, no voices admonished them; worst of all there was no sound from behind the unyielding front door of the brothel. An exasperated Blanford tried a couple of kicks, but this was not much use either as he was wearing tennis-shoes. They waited and then knocked again, without the slightest result. The silence drained back into the darkness. The only movement was the stirring of large birds in the ragged storks' nests on the battlements. Somewhere – not really so far, but sounding as if it were situated at the other end of the known world – the Jacquemart struck an hour, though they were not quite certain which hour. "Not a sound," breathed poor Blanford with a sigh of despair. "There must be someone there."

Reluctantly they started to move away when Felix had a brainwave; his torch played among the rubbish heaps which filled the abandoned ruin at one side of the brothel. There were some oil drums in the corner and they gave him an idea. He rolled one over the mossy surface and placed it against the wall under the lighted window, mounting it very slowly, with a thousand precautions; for he did not wish to fall among the foundations and break his back. At last he levelled off, and, holding onto the wall, craned his neck towards the light. "It's a lavatory," he said in a low voice. "They've left the light on and the door open." Then he drew a deep breath and said: "Jesus! There they are! Just look at our old Prince!"

Blanford, consumed with curiosity, hurried to take possession of his own olive oil drum and was soon standing up against the wall beside Felix, gazing into the lavatory and, through it, into the relatively well-lighted hallway leading to an inner courtyard full of divans and potted plants of somewhat decayed aspect. And sure enough there was the Prince, spread out on a sofa, and perfectly at ease; while Quatrefages, clad only in a shirt and red socks, sat by his side sipping whisky and talking with the greatest animation. It took a moment or two to register the more piquant details of this scene which had all the air of taking place in some small theatre – it looked a bit unreal.

The Prince had divested himself of everything that covered the top half of his grey little body; he sat, so to speak,

clad only in his heavy paps, and had a sort of chinless gran-
deur. His nether half was clad in lightweight Jaeger combinations which stretched to the ankle and through the fly-slit of
which depended the royal member with its innocent pink tip.
Quatrefages also presented a somewhat equivocal appearance,
being clad only in a shirt and socks. He was clearly engaged
in a long explanation or exhortation addressed to Riquiqui
who stood almost out of range and half in shadow – so that
it seemed that the clerk was talking with animation to two
outsize breasts bulging out of a dirty shift. Beside them stood
a puzzled female dwarf with a hideously rouged face as if
ready for the circus; she was clad in white organdie with a
marriage veil. Moreover, she was jingling with trinkets and
had obviously been dressed against a very special occasion.
As a matter of fact she had been specially dressed for the
Prince, but now his companion was expressing the Prince's
discontent with her, and indeed his general discomfiture,
presumably because of her age. Yes, it was not hard to follow
the train of the argument. The dwarf was too old and too big
to appeal to the Prince. But they were being polite about it
and the horrible little creature bobbed her agreement and
dipped lovingly into a big box of Turkish Delight which the
Prince had pushed towards her. She had huge, discoloured
teeth like rotting dice.

As for Riquiqui she appeared to be at her wits' end to
meet the unusual demand. Languidly the little man extended
a hand and indicated that what he desired was much smaller,
very much smaller. He lent weight to his argument with
flowery little gestures which indicated clearly that there was
no question of ill-feeling or bad humour involved. He was
asking, not commanding. His tone was civilised and equable.
He proffered the box of loucoumi and Riquiqui in her turn
dug out a cube of Turkish Delight and wolfed it, licking the
powder off her talons, before dusting her shift to remove the

last traces of it. Then she held up her finger as one who sees daylight at last and bustled off, leaving them to their whisky. The misshapen little phantom of pleasure followed her, ripping off her bridal veil with an abrupt gesture like an actor quitting a wig as he left the stage.

Left alone, the two occupants of the centre of the stage – the suggestion of intimate theatre was irresistible because of the severely framed scene and the brilliantly stagey lighting – reloaded their glasses and conversed in low tones. The clerk was flushed and jovial-looking in his somewhat unclean shirt. The Prince in his long combinations looked quite regal still in an attenuated sort of way. He scratched his small decoration and exuded amiability. They had not long to wait, for at last Riquiqui burst in, flushed with success, hand in hand with two little girls dressed in a manner appropriate to a First Communion. Their faces were heavily rouged, which gave them the appearance of wearing painted masks through which they peered with unafraid but puzzled wonder. She paused, the huge woman, for dramatic effect as she entered, presenting her charges boldly but hesitantly. *Eureka*! She had remembered the existence of a couple of "angels", no doubt.

The result was a foregone conclusion. The Prince's radiant features expressed his delight and relief; he looked like a small boy who was turning cartwheels from sheer elation. Quatrefages folded his arms after setting down his glass and beamed upon the lady while the Prince extended his hands to take hers and move them half-way to his lips in a simulated kiss of congratulation. The two little children stood mum-chance, but with a kindly air. They were sucking sweets. The Prince stood up and embraced them warmly; then he waved his arms and muttered something in Arabic and his major-domo (who must have been waiting in the shadows, the wings, so to speak) entered the lighted stage leading two large and beautifully groomed Afghan hounds on a gold leash.

The Prince clapped his hands in ecstasy and gave a little crow of laughter; he beamed round on the assembled company. Clearly everything was in order now. The next stage. . . .

Riquiqui threw open a side door which gave on to a bedroom of the house which had been decorated in the most extravagant fashion; a vast damascened bed lay under a lozenge-shaped pier-glass. It was covered in a gold cloth, and the shelf above it was full of children's dolls clad in folklore costumes. The walls themselves were draped with scarlet shawls and the whole context suggested a scene from *The Phantom of the Opera*. The little manikins looked as if they were the shrunken bodies of real children which had been patiently and fastidiously pickled before being dressed as harlequins, Arlésiennes, Catalans and Basques. Into this décor she ushered the Prince, now amiably holding the hands of the two children. The dogs, now off the leash, followed at his heels like well-drilled servants who knew their duty. The stage-set was so piquant and the actors so unaware that they were being observed that the two eavesdroppers almost forgot to feel the anxious disgust which had started to seize them.

But it was at this moment that Quatrefages entered the lavatory right under their noses and closed the door on this equivocal spectacle. He sat himself down on the throne and proceeded to more primitive business. They soon could hear his grunts and sighs right under their chins. It was quite a dilemma – they did not wish to be discovered in this spying posture. And they were suddenly aware of the precariousness of their station, for they could not simply jump down and run away. In the darkness one could have broken an ankle. So they stayed on, mentally swearing at the wretched clerk, and hoping that he would soon finish and restore them the lighted stage and the grotesque Egyptian. On the other hand, they could hardly pass the rest of the night standing up there on the oil drums watching the sexual evolutions of this Mecca-blessed libertine. A wild indecision reigned which matched their general situation; neither spoke because neither could think.

No doubt their frustration and gradually mounting discomfort would have sooner or later forced them to take a decision, but fate determined otherwise, for Quatrefages completed his business to his own satisfaction and pulled the chain; and as if by the same token the door was thrown open and the brightly lit stage once more revealed to them. There was a slight change of disposition – the door of the inner room was almost closed and even by craning the neck it would not have been possible to see with any clarity exactly what the Prince and his livestock were up to. Riquiqui was sitting down in a manner so relaxed as to suggest the puncture of an inner tube; and she was profiting by the absence of the Prince to renew her attack on the box of gummy sweets.

The little hunchback crossed the stage – now nude – and seated herself at what appeared to be a small upright piano covered in coloured shawls. She began to pick out monotonous little tunes on it with one finger. Quatrefages firmly retrieved his drink and spread himself over a divan with a relaxed and gluttonous air. The conversation flagged. There were a few indistinct sounds from the direction of the Prince's room but nothing very concrete that might be interpreted. The whole atmosphere had become now slack and humdrum, lacking in great interest, and Blanford began to find his toes going to sleep. It was clearly time to get down and go home. He was about to express this thought to his friend when there was a sudden irruption onto the little stage which all at once reinjected vitality into the drama, brought everything alive again.

The major-domo burst clucking and chattering into the room once more (apparently through the front door, for they heard the bolts shriek) and demanded the presence of his master at once. When he was advised to be patient his voice jumped a whole octave and his hysteria mounted to the ceiling. Greatly daring (so they thought) he threw open the door of the bedroom and revealed a scene of almost domestic tranquillity – the Prince on the bed surrounded by children and dogs and himself wearing a communion veil at which the children were both laughing heartily. He shot up indignantly, forgetting to remove the veil, and let fly a stream of Arabic oaths at the head of his servant, who, however, continued to babble and gesticulate. Apparently the gravity of what he had to relate alone justified this intrusion. After a moment of wild rage the truth dawned on the Prince and he sat up to listen to what the excited man was actually saying. Whatever he at last began to comprehend had an altogether electrifying effect upon him for he leaped out of bed with commendable agility and dashed into the next room, heading for the direction of the front door and crying in a high bird-like tone and in the English of Cairo, "They have pinched the bloody coach."

Such was the excitement of the two men, such was the velocity of their movements, that everyone took fire, everyone was sucked into the procession in spite of themselves, whirled into the drama by the sheer momentum of the Prince's dramatic dash. The two young men balanced on the oil drums outside also gave way to a wave of panic as they realised that the whole of this sudden surge led towards the open street, where they might be discovered in this igno-minious posture. They jumped down and by the beam of the torch picked their way through the shattered detritus of the old foundation walls.

But the Prince and his servant, with the trajectory of comets, had rushed into the street, and as if quite mesmerised, so had the rest of them – Riquiqui, Quatrefages, the little naked dwarf, the dogs and the communicating children. They all stood gazing about them in a daze of wonder and confusion and anger, for the coach, which had apparently been standing before the front door, had disappeared. The Prince stamped his naked foot on the pavement with a gesture of febrile vexation, while his servant, as if to make quite sure, ran to the corner of the street and quested about generally like a gun-dog trying for a scent. Then he came back shaking his head and muttering. The Prince gazed around him, his regard travelling from face to face as if for sympathy. "Who could have done it—" he said, and Riquiqui, who had shown less surprise and consternation than the others, replied, "It's the gipsies. Leave it to me. Tomorrow I will find them."

The company was so absorbed in this little drama that they greeted the appearance of Felix and Blanford in an almost absent-minded way, hardly greeting them; but when they brought evidence to suggest that the coach had been stolen some good time ago (for it had not been there when they arrived) they managed to kindle a little interest. They were, after all, potential clients – so thought the little dwarf, who tried to link her arm in that of Felix, to his pained horror. "I will call the police," said the Prince in a sudden burst of childish petulance. "I will telephone to Farouk." It carried little conviction, for there he was with his little member protruding from his long woollen combinations.

Quatrefages, after a moment of reflection, led him muttering back into the house of pleasure and this time Blanford and Felix followed them in order to have a drink and to reassure themselves about the absence of Livia. Quatrefages, overcome by a sudden pudicity, became aware of his naked condition and hunted for his trousers before pouring out more whisky; the Prince retired haughtily to the inner room with his dogs and children and banged the door, leaving instructions that he was not to be disturbed for at least an hour. Blanford sipped his drink and heard the tinny piano tinkle. He felt suddenly terribly sleepy. Quatrefages said with a malicious grin: "Livia has gone to the gipsies."

So she had been there that evening, and had given them the slip as usual! Felix could not repress a slightly malicious side-glance at his fellow sufferer; but Blanford looked more angry than sad. He was telling himself that this would have to stop – this infatuation would have to be brought to an end. "It leads nowhere," he said aloud, talking to himself. At last the real truth of the matter had dawned on him – but like every glimpse of truth it was only fleeting and provisional. With the other half of his mind, so to speak, he was still lamed by his inner vision of her, of her sullen magnetism, of those expiring kisses which had ignited their minds. He did not care for the sardonic remarks of the clerk nor the cynical looks of Felix – the matter was too important, went too far into the gulfs of hopeless sentiment, of bewitchment, for the others to appreciate it.

He hugged his mood to himself, ignoring the rest of them, treasuring every little stab of pleasure or pain which it brought. What did it matter what Livia was or what she did? A strange metaphor came into his mind which expressed the exact nature of this attachment – a metaphor which centuries later Sutcliffe would use when he tried to define his gross attachment to the pale wraith Pia, who was a diluted version of the girl Constance, Livia's sister. But in his present mind it was Livia who provoked this thought which one would have had to be an alchemist to understand. What he loved in her was her "water" – as of a precious stone. It is after all what is really loved in a woman – not the sheath of matter which covers her – but her "signature". In the middle of all the chatter and movement of the brothel he found himself brooding upon this fact in all its singularity and wishing for a scrap of paper on which to jot it down. He would have liked to incorporate it into his diary but he knew that by the morrow he would have forgotten it.

Suddenly an enormous lassitude had taken hold of him. "I want to go home," he said yawning, and to his surprise Felix pronounced himself of the same disposition. Blanford felt so lonely he could have gone out into the dark street and waved vigorously to imaginary people. Quatrefages said he would come too – "*J'ai tiré mon petit coup*," he said modestly. And the Prince? Why, he was to be left; the major-domo would see him safely home to the Imperial where he had taken up his headquarters. Already a substitute pumpkin-coach in the shape of a town *fiacre* had been summoned and stood at the door. But the night was no longer young, and the three young men felt sallow and spent. So they set off across the town on foot, finding some refreshment in the dark coolness which was full of the scent of lemons and mandarines and honeysuckle. Felix would be the first home, then the clerk; Blanford wanted to sit somewhere and watch the dawn come up, to let his thought of Livia ripen like some huge gourd. The pain was in the pleasure – a novelty for him, he realised.

The night had waited for them – a great paunch of silence upon which the ordinary sounds of the city hardly impinged. Somewhere an ambulance raced with its tingling alarm; there was something vengeful in the peals of its bell, he thought, as it hurried back triumphantly to the hospital with its trophy of maimed flesh. They heard its signals diminishing as it dived through the outer ramparts towards the suburbs. Felix yawned. Blanford, sunk himself, felt the whole weight of his unexpressed narcissism heavy inside him, like dough or wax, waiting to be kneaded into some sort of significant shape – by what? – but he did not as yet dare to think of himself as an artist. It was like a blind boil which could not discharge itself except in insomnia or in those sudden dispositions towards tears when some great music stirred him, or the glance of light on some ripe landscape pierced him. For others these vague intimations of beatitude, these realisations of beauty were enough in themselves simply to enjoy. But he came of that obstinate and unbalanced tribe which longed to do something about them – to realise and recreate them in a form less poignantly transitory than that vouchsafed by reality. What was to be *done*? That was always his thought, and he fretted inside himself at the notion that there was nothing, that he could do nothing, there was nothing to be done.

A brief wind ran the whole length of the street and turned a corner, disappearing in a gusty whirl of dead leaves, pouring itself into the throat of the invisible river whose slitherings and strivings they could hear as they approached it. When the sun came a thousand leafing planes would mirror themselves in its greenish waters. Here at last was the Consulate. The pavements were still warm and, because they had been washed with water and Javel, gave off the smell of incense. Felix too felt the gnawings of a nostalgic sadness. "I am sorry you will soon be gone," he said, but comforted himself with the thought that after such a summer he had happy enough memories stored against the winter with the rains and snows it would bring to the city. "I must ask for some leave," he went on, enlivening his thought with the prospect of meeting the others somewhere, perhaps in London. But Blanford's thoughts were of a graver cast – for there was to be no more Oxford after this term. Life was spreading its wings. What was to become of him? He would have enough money to live on – but what would that serve if he had no passionate aptitudes which he might fulfil? Tinker, Tailor, Soldier, Sailor ... what was he to do with his life? He had shown Livia the two little lyrics in the University magazine and he thought that she had looked at him with a new respect; but this was probably imagined. As for the poems they were quite nice pastiche, without an ounce of real feelings in them. Could she not see that? He sighed aloud as he walked. Quatrefages also seemed to be touched, through his fatigue, by the prevailing nostalgia. He gazed at the dark sky and shook himself like a wet mastiff. "Life is only once," he said unexpectedly. Felix now turned yawning into the gateway of the Consulate. "Remember the car is mine tomorrow," he told the clerk who shrugged his shoulders with indifference. Felix paused inside the front door for a moment to listen to their receding footfalls on the dark pavements. Soon the lamplighter would emerge to gather his blossoms of light, shy as a squirrel. Soon he would be alone again in this oppressive city which could only be enjoyed if seen through the eyes of Livia. In spite of his yawns he made the effort to clean his teeth before subsiding into his bed – for he was rather proud of their evenness. He told his sleepy reflection sternly: "I shall not cry myself to sleep because there are no golf courses on the moon." It was a declaration of faith, in a manner of speaking.

The two others walked silently side by side, each absorbed in his thoughts: but as they began to near the little square where Quatrefages' garish window shone out of the dark mass of the darker hotel, their steps began to lag. Despite the fatigue the clerk was reluctant to part with his companion. Truth to tell he was of a timorous nature and was always afraid to return late and alone to his room for fear of finding someone or something waiting for him. He imagined perhaps a very old tramp, sitting in the armchair waiting patiently for his return; or a blind man with a white stick and a great white dog. They would have come to propose some sort of compact with the Devil. He frowned and shook his head at his own stupidity; yet he wondered at the same time what excuse he could give which might persuade Blanford to mount the stairs with him and enter his room – just to reassure him so that he could now turn off the light and get some sleep.

It seemed absurd to propose yet another drink but that is what he heard himself doing, and to his great delight Blanford, who seemed in some obscure way to have divined his feelings, accepted the invitation. The clerk could not believe his luck. His dejected walk became all at once buoyant and nervous, his lassitude slipped from him. As a matter of fact Blanford was always intrigued by a glimpse of this extraordinary office whose walls were covered with death charts of the Templars, each with his date of execution. In the corner lay an unmade bed and a side-table covered with the impedimenta of the insomniac in the shape of bottles of pills and tinctures of opium, packs of cigarettes, and a cluster of books on alchemy and related topics, all bearing the marker of the Calvet Museum.

A pile of children's exercise books were propped up on the mantelshelf. A white chamberpot stood under the bed decorated by a cluster of roses in bloom. The whole centre of the room was taken up with the sort of trestle tables with angle lamps such as an architect might set up to draw a project in detail – or else perhaps the kind of tables upon which a paperhanger might set out his wallpapers before brushing the glue on to them. There was a small alcove in which stood a crucifix together with a bottle of whisky and several small mineral water bottles. The room smelt damply musty. It was situated on the blind side of the street and never got any light. It was heavy with dust and the little lavatory-douche was in a dreadful mess – towels covered in hair cream and, strangely, lipstick. The drains stank. Everywhere cigarettes had burnt out and left a dark burn – even on the wash basin. One wondered how there had never been a fire there. Quatrefages poured out a warmish drink and dragged out an uncomfortable chair for his guest to sit upon.

But Blanford preferred to stand and examine the charts on the wall with their suggestive datings, and the now lively Quatrefages followed his gaze with an air of pride. "We are down to the last of them," he said, "and we know for certain that they had managed to hide the treasure where neither Philippe nor his Chancellor Nogaret, who conducted the persecution, could lay their hands on it. This is why things dragged on so. The Templars would confess to anything but they would not divulge the hiding place. From other documents, some pretty enigmatic, we know that five of the knights were in the secret. But we don't as yet know which. But we have some clues to go on which seem pretty definite." He paused to drain his glass and cough loudly. Blanford, whose curiosity had got the better of him, asked a few questions and then suddenly and perhaps rather rudely said: "Livia told me that she thought you had discovered the place, the vault, the chapel or whatever, and that there was nothing in it. That the treasure had been pinched ages ago. . . ."

The change in Quatrefages was as sudden as it was marked; his sallow complexion had become strained and laboured. He sat down on the bed and croaked out an oath: "Livia knows nothing," he said, "nothing. The gipsies tell one all sorts of things, but it is false. I have not found the place as yet. But of course Provence is full of ruined chapels and empty vaults destroyed during the various religious upheavals. But nothing that so far corresponds with the evidence of an orchard – the 'Verger de Saint Louis' – where the plane trees were set in a quincunx like an ancient Greek temple grove. No, as yet we have not found the place."

Blanford felt all of a sudden apologetic for having made this intrusion – the more so because he suddenly felt that Quatrefages was probably lying to him. Or was it Livia? At any rate none of this was his business, and he had no intention of making the little clerk feel that he was not to be counted upon, or that his word was not believed. "I am sorry," he said, "it was not my business and I should not have repeated gossip."

Nevertheless, whatever the truth of the matter was, the agitation of Quatrefages seemed somehow excessive, and Blanford could not help speculating upon this fragment of gossip which had slipped from Livia's lips quite casually, seemingly without malice or premeditation. "When we do discover it," said the clerk, his eyes glittering malevolently in his nervous paleness of feature, "that will be the day to rejoice." Blanford turned away to the great wall charts of the dead Templars and as he did so the dawn broke softly in the open street below. Its faint tinges of yellow and rose coloured the walls of that sordid room, almost like some signal from a past full of mystery and significance.

The dead names glowed like jewels, like embers still breathing in the pale ashes of the past. The names slowly recited themselves in his mind, each with its hush of death and silence cradling it. Dead cavaliers of the piebald standard! Raynier de Larchant, Reynaud de Tremblay, Pierre de Tortville, Jacques de Molay, Hugues de Pairaud, Jean du Tour, Geoffroy de Gonneville, Jean Taillefer, Jean L'Anglais, Baudoin de Saint-Just. Inhabitants now of history, destroyed by blind circumstance, by the zeal and cupidity of the lawless ages. "One wonders what they were guilty of," he said aloud, more to himself than to anyone. His eyes traversed the great names again, lingering over them, savouring the mystery and sadness of their premature deaths by starvation, torture, or the burning pyres of the Inquisition. It was a riddle which would never be read, an enigma which still intrigued and baffled new generations of historians.

Quatrefages sat on the edge of the bed leaning forward and concentrating – as if he were trying to follow Blanford's train of thought, to read his mind. His face was flushed now, the fever had come back; and he was full of drink and beginning to feel it. "What were they guilty of?" he repeated aloud in a sharp cracked voice, so curiously at variance with his natural tone that Blanford turned curiously upon him and said: "Well, what?" But it was now clear that Quatrefages was very drunk indeed; he stood up and swayed and began to snivel. "The greatest heresy the world has ever known," he said in an exalted way; he clenched his fists and raised them on high, for all the world as if he himself were standing on a high pyre, feeling the flames rising around his feet, and testifying to the truth of a belief which ran counter to the whole structure of an age's thoughts.

Blanford watched him burning and crying there for a moment, and then reached out a tentative hand, as if to soothe or console him against so much excessive feeling. He felt also a little guilty – as if his idle remark had somehow provoked this orgiastic recital. Quatrefages was now a-tremble with emotion. He was like a wire through which passed a current of a voltage almost too powerful to bear. "You don't know the truth," he said incoherently and his lips began to wobble as he spoke, his tears to choke him.

Blanford was able to glimpse now the zealot who lived underneath the external guise of the young man – the carapace of industry and probity and politeness which made up the outer man. But now it was as if a switch had been thrown, first by the drink and then by Livia's remark – the image of a dam came into his mind, or one of those *écluses* on the Rhône through which their barge had slid. The current had pushed down all the debris of Quatrefages' solitary and secret life – sitting there agonising over long-dead knights, and trying by guile and science to pick their pockets. "We are like grave-robbers in the pay of Galen," he cried with a bitter vehemence, still standing in his theatrical attitude of human sacrifice. "They have reduced the whole thing to a vulgar matter of *fric*, of booty. They have missed the whole point of this tremendous apostasy. Blanford, *écoutez*!" He took his companion by the shoulders and shook him so violently that his drink was nearly upset and he was just able to set it down and free his elbow in time.

Quatrefages sank back on to his bed and plunged his chin moodily into his fists. "That is what is killing me," he said in a lower key, suppressing the drama in his voice a little; "the ignominiousness of what we are doing, and my own part in it." Blanford's reactions to this sort of outburst were typically Christian public-schoolboy; he felt shy, alarmed and overwhelmed. He cursed himself for having unwittingly provoked this storm. He did not want to witness Quatrefages' self-recriminations and breast-beatings. If he so much disapproved of what he was doing why did he not resign? It was easy to simplify matters thus – he knew that. But he suppressed a sigh as he sat down, prepared to let the clerk talk himself out. "I began in good economic faith, and then I began to get more and more curious about the Templars – not about their fortune but about the nature of their heresy. To defy the reign of matter as they did, to outface the ruling devil – that was what intrigued me. Yes, they quietly built up an almost unassailable temporal power – they were the bankers of the age. And these great constructions were their banks, their prisons."

He waved an arm vaguely in the direction of the Papal Palaces on their elevation above the river, now doubtless turning rose also, petal by petal, spire by spire. "The knights were systematically destroyed by the hooded anonymous butchers of the Inquisition in order to secure the succession of what they now knew was evil – the pre-eminence of matter and will in the world. They were the instruments of Old Nick himself who was not going to have his throne shaken

by this superb refusal of the knights; he was not going to
submit without a struggle. The death wish against the life
wish – God, you know, is only an alibi in all this, only a
cover-story. The real battle between the negative and positive
forces was joined here – and all Europe in the coming ages
was at stake." He paused and licked his dry lips. Then,
draining his glass in a wobbly way, he said, almost in a
whisper, "They lost, and we lost with them."

The two of them stared at one another for a moment and
then Quatrefages gave a hopeless little chuckle and put his
head on one side and, half closing his eyes – like a bird
putting its head under its wing – said: "I know why you
look at me like that. You are saying to yourself that it is
preposterous to feel so strongly about a mere historical event.
You are right. But we are living out the fateful destiny of
European man which was decided then – right here in
Avignon. We are taking part in this materialist funeral of
living man. Yes, they were suppressed and deafening clouds
of propaganda were pumped out over them to obscure the
real issues and blacken their names. They were accused of
every kind of sorcery, whereas the only conjuring they
indulged in was the flat refusal to continue living the great lie
of civilisation as it was then ordered. Of course it had to be
kept secret, for it was heresy, in the strict terms of the
epoch."

He fell silent at last. Blanford stared at the great wall
maps: among them was a series of architectural studies of the
various Temples and their disposition. He was, he concluded,
in the presence of a harmless young maniac who had allowed
his head to be turned by the bogus speculations of the
popular mysticism which was at the moment all too fashionable. The Rosy Cross, the dimensions of the Great Pyramid,
Madame Blavatsky. . . . He knew the line of country fairly
well and indeed had read quite a few books about these

matters – but without being swept off his feet by what he regarded as enjoyable fantasies. "What does it *matter* if there is a treasure or not?" cried Quatrefages passionately, waking up temporarily to resume his theme. Bang! "To add a little more *fric* to Galen's fortune? But I think there is no treasure; I think Philippe Le Bel got it all. I have not mentioned this to anyone because I am not absolutely sure – but our search for the quincunx of trees concerns another sort of treasure. That is what I really believe. But who can I talk to about it? Nobody! Nobody!"

Again he banged his fist upon the bed until the springs twanged. The whole confused details of his own apostasy, his own refusal of the body of Christ, the cannibal totem, rose up to choke him with a sense of his unworthiness, his insufficiency. He let out a groan. Blanford said rather primly, "I do understand a little bit. You mean the Philosopher's Stone, don't you?" But the clerk was plunged in his reveries and only nodded abstractedly, as if he were listening to some distant music too absorbing to allow him to shift his attention to what Blanford was saying. "But that is not the sort of treasure one finds in the ground, like a crock of gold containing a liquid rainbow . . . is it?" The question was useless and deserved for answer the silence it got. Quatrefages now whispered something to himself, quietly and confidently, nodding his head sagely and with resignation. Then he sank sideways on to the pillows, cradling his heavy head in his hands as if it were a Roman bust, and fell asleep. Blanford watched him for a while with curiosity and sympathy; his mind seemed to burn with such pathetic intensity in his lean body. Now, sleeping there, with his long nose aimed at the pillow, he looked touchingly defenceless. His wrists were so very thin. As the light had already been turned off there was nothing left but to tiptoe from the room and down the creaking staircase.

He paused to whisper a word to the sleepy night-porter who was putting his improvised bed to rights. Then down to the icy river and the bridge which steered away from the wakening city to the wide green hills beyond. He set out in a new burst of energy to walk back to Tu Duc. Everything on that joyful morning seemed to gleam like a new coin – a newly minted currency of vivid impressions. He felt words stirring inside his mind, like some long-hibernating species which a tardy spring had wakened only now, struck by the romance of the green swirling river and the cypress-punctuated hills he was approaching. To really appreciate a place or time – to extract the poignant essence of it – one should see it in the light of a departure, a leavetaking. It was the sense of farewell in things which impregnated them with this phantom of nostalgia so important for the young artist.

He felt the lure of language stirring in him, like a muscle stretching itself, cramped from long disuse. He did not know how to contain nor what to do with all this happiness. He approached the sleeping house across the unkempt lawns, cutting the dew with every step and feeling the moisture soak into his tennis shoes. A black cat sat on the mat by the kitchen garden – just like in his first nursery-book. But more wonderful still; from the rumple of bedclothes which hid the secret form of the naked Livia he could only pick out one slender hand with its long fingers relaxed and extended – one finger yellow with tobacco stains. He stripped and crawled in beside the sleep-sodden half-drugged nymph and, glad that she slept on, set himself to studying every feature of that slender expressive face with its striking alignment of bones and planes.

He tried to pierce with his eyes the very real bewitchment which transformed it; he realised that what he saw was not Livia but his own transfigured version of her – the reflection of his love. Beside the bed was the little box with the cheap wedding ring he had bought in Lunel from an old Jewish lady in a booth which sold lottery tickets and betting slips. He slipped it softly onto her unresisting finger and, like the unwise mooncalf he was, kissed it. He made love to her at her whispered request, though she neither opened her eyes nor in any way altered the disposition of her body; he moved her about as she lay there, quite limp, rather like one of those articulated "lay figures" that artists and dressmakers use.

Their united spirits seemed to wash down the long river together, entangled in one another, and then far away out to sea – the deep sea of a new sleep. But in order to leave her undisturbed he took a blanket to the balcony and curled up on the stones in the vanishing dew, his sleepy head pillowed upon a damp towel. In the half-sleep of fatigue the whole gorgeous gallery of Provençal images unwound inside his mind as if on a giant spool. There were so many memories he did not know what to do with them. He heard Livia stir and, turning on his elbow, gazed through the open balcony door. Yes, she was sleepily awake and sitting up in bed; but he was not prepared for what he saw now. She was gazing at her ring-finger with a curious expression of horror he had never seen on her face before. It was the expression of someone who suddenly finds a scorpion on the lapel of a jacket they are wearing. Her lips all but cried out: "Who would have done this?" and with a gesture which combined anger with repulsion she snatched off the ring and flung it with all her might into the corner of the room.

He heard its sour tinkle as it bounced about on the floor. It was quite a shock – something went dead and cold inside him as he took in this involuntary gesture of rejection. He too sat up now, to watch her sink back with a sigh into her bed and draw the covers over her head as she foundered into a deeper sleep. The ring! Blanford reflected on these mysteries and on the independence of Livia as he crossed the wakening garden and plunged into the icy waters of the lily pond; what did it mean? It was Livia who had entertained his callow addresses and his suggestions about marriage. She had shown no distaste for such a thought before. But here she was standing beside the pond, poised for a dive. "What has changed?" he asked her quietly, rather painfully, though he did not know what he might have to fear in her answer. "I was not ready for it," she said. "Not yet. Perhaps I shall never be. We'll see."

But then to make up for this disturbing hesitation she launched herself into the water and came swirling into his arms to kiss and embrace him anew, her body glittering like a fish in a net. So their peace was restored and their solidarity of feeling – yet in the heart of the matter Blanford felt the prick of sadness, of some unachieved intimacy which lay between them like a shadow. "I missed you everywhere, gipsies, Riquiqui's, Felix, Quatrefages. . ." He smiled at her but he all of a sudden seemed to wake up with a jolt and tell himself: "She lies as simply as she breathes – about everything." Later he hunted for the ring but it had gone. She had reclaimed it, then? He did not ask her.

SIX

Talking Back

THE LONG SERPENTINE THOUGHT, AFTER SO MANY parentheses, came at last to rest in his silent mind. A very long silence fell, which seemed to both of them as if it might prolong itself unto eternity. "Hullo!" cried Sutcliffe twice, on a note of almost childish anxiety. (Ghosts always get alarmed when they are not in full manifestation – when they are off duty, so to speak – for it seems to them that they are in danger of ceasing to exist.) Yes. Suppose, I mean, that Blanford forgot to think of *him*! What then? It would be the end! And Blanford himself was, at that moment, bowed under the same thought, for he knew that once the ghosts, which together go to make up the collective memory, cease to care . . . why, one goes out like a light. Ask any artist! For a moment he was quite tongue-tied, he could not answer; in his imagination he had let the old-fashioned receiver fall upon the arm of his chair as he gazed into the fire with frigid intensity, for he had seen the face of Constance there, and it was curling up with the flames, it was disappearing. Sutcliffe could hear his uneven, heavy breathing. "For God's sake," he cried, "why don't you say something, Aubrey?"

But a sudden sense of helpless inadequacy had over-whelmed the writer as he wondered how to compress and condense into a few pages all the events and impressions of that short period which had come so abruptly to an end with the outbreak of the war. This brief glimpse of Constance had suddenly revived it all. It had been so extraordinarily rich, so bursting with promise; then abruptly the whole period had sunk out of sight, into the dark night of Nazi Europe. But what was he saying? For almost a whole year the war had actually been declared, though nobody had moved. The French lurked among their block-houses, wondering at the extraordinary paralysis which had gripped the whole of Europe. Meanwhile the life of Paris and London appeared to continue unchanged – the postal services were normal, for example, the telephone worked, the skies were as yet empty of planes. Yes, a few greasy-looking barrage balloons had appeared above the Thames. Somewhere, in some dim and amorphous region of the group-mind, feverish preparations were being made to forge a weapon which might contain the launching thrust of the German forces. But somehow nobody could believe in it. In all the soft paralysis there was a luxurious hopelessness, a valedictory sensation of the doom which must overtake the great capitals, one by one. Bye-bye to Paris and Rome, to Athens and Madrid. . . . One had a wild desire to revisit them quickly for a moment, to feel their living pulse before it was stilled forever. But even this was late in the day, after the formal declarations had been made. Yet for months, even years, before one could see some sort of war coming, see the horizon darkening. They had lived with this thing and knew that there was nothing to be done.

Tiny incidents, mere crumbs, remained still in Blanford's memories of that epoch, as if they had been simply markers to point the direction of the prevailing wind, the death-wind. How he had lent Sam the money to buy himself a uniform, while down in Provence Constance waited for him, for Sam, with a calm and smiling solicitude which so expertly masked the depth of her feelings. It was no time to decide to marry, but that is what they had done, and walking into his room at Tu Duc she came upon him awkwardly examining his fancy dress in the mirror with an air of rapturous astonishment. She did not actually weep but he put her head on his shoulders and began to laugh at his foolish expression. Meanwhile he said to himself, aloud, in the mirror:

"If she doesn't love me in this get-up she never bloody will."
The trousers had to be altered, the waistcoat set more snugly.
And here Felix came to the rescue and found a tailor in
Avignon. Sam had only a few days' leave before returning
to Oxford and the war. It was not entirely in bantering terms
that he said: "I was really worried about being unemployable,
and now look at this excellent job, so well paid. And bags of
promotion, too, if one is energetic." This was on the platform waiting for the train to Paris. Blanford saw Constance
turn away to hide her emotion and he engaged his friend in
banter to hide his own. The whole world was breaking up
under them like some old raft. It was deplorable to be so
callow, so undemonstrative.

Yet there were certain modifying certainties, among
them the general belief that the Germans would never
penetrate the Maginot Line whatever their bombers might
do to the cities. If there was war, even a long war, France
would remain geographically intact, so that some sort of
civilian life would go on until it ended. The famous Line
was to France what the Channel had always been for the
British. In the back of everyone's consciousness there must
have been obstinate archaic memories left over from 1914,
stalemates on the Somme, and so on. Nobody thought
about mobility, even later when it was clear that things had
gone well beyond compromise. What then? Felix had received
orders to stand by and aid the evacuation of British subjects
should the storm break – and then to hand over his Consulate
to the Swiss. And here came a remarkable and most welcome
discovery. The three of them – Hilary and his two sisters –
were of dual nationality and would claim Swiss citizenship.
Their clever old fox of a father had had them all born in
Geneva. Neither Sam nor Blanford, however, could claim
such an immunity from action, while for his part the latter
wondered whether he should not declare for conscientious

objection. Felix offered him all the necessary documentation but he was gripped by conflicting uncertainties. The fate of the Jews had become clear, and while one could be against war in general one could not really turn one's back on this one, when such terrible issues were at stake. Yet for the time he did nothing.

And then somewhere in the middle of all this period comes a spell in Paris with Livia, a spell which ended in that fatuous marriage anchored by a wedding ring which was never to be worn. A disorderly, roughcast sort of student existence in the fourteenth arrondissement. A Livia who was always busy and preoccupied though he never found out what she was doing. But she was out at all hours in all weathers, and she talked in her sleep and drank absinthe with disquieting application. The little rented flat was a shabby enough place, but there was a table at which he could write so that one basic need was satisfied, though at this time he wrote mostly long letters. Yet stirring deep in the jungle he could hear the rustle of those animal doubts which came creeping upon him. He began to wonder what he had indeed done. At times when she was drunk her laughter was so extravagant as to be insulting. At times he caught glimpses of unusual expressions on that pale face – hate, malevolence, disdain. It made him feel fearful and sad, as if some vital piece of information was missing – the presence of a shadow which stood forever between them. There was. She had become so much thinner that her looks had changed. The head of the cicada had become narrower, the face an adder's.

Then his mother's health began to falter and flicker and he was called back to her bedside where he gazed long and earnestly into that once familiar face, now pained to see that the long illness had altered all its stresses, composed it in new planes and lines, as if to copy on the outer skin the fearful loneliness and despair of the inner mind. She had things to tell him about her small fortune, and she had discovered that she could not trust Cade, the valet. He opened her letters and in general kept a spying eye out over her affairs. She had longed to give him notice but in all his other duties he was so perfect and so dependable that she had not dared. In this, as in all other things, she was lucidity itself, and even when she sank back into a last deep coma he did not think that she would die – indeed the doctor warned him that she might linger on a long time yet, so strong was her heart. Nevertheless he spent that day at her bedside, holding that frail hand in which the pulse continued to beat like that of a captive sparrow. In these long silences his mind went about its business slowly and densely. He wondered much about Livia and about his own future. His mother was leaving him a small marginal income, as well as the London house which could be let. There was also a small cottage on a farm outside Cairo where his father had spent many summers pursuing his entomological passion with silent assiduity. This was a mere shack, though, and there was hardly any land around it. Nevertheless, it was like a window open upon another country.

Another problem: if she should by any chance wake, ought he to tell her that he was married to Livia, or was it better to keep the whole matter a secret? Already there was a sneaking premonition that he had embarked upon something which might become a capital misadventure. Sitting in that grey light of a suburban nightfall, trying mentally to align her ticking wrist with the ticking of the grandfather-clock in the hall, he wondered a little bleakly what would come of it all. In a sense it was good to have the war to think about – for it dwarfed purely human schemes, and one could shelve them temporarily. And yet he did not think there would be a war, despite all the signs; history was like some lump of viscid porridge sliding slowly down a sink, but with such an infinite slowness! Their gestures, their hopes and schemes, seemed to be somehow insubstantial, chimerical. Meanwhile the frenzy of Paris was still teaching, and he realised how pregnant were the lessons he had learned in this all too brief residence there – the capital of the European nervous system. So many valuable acquisitions: how total freedom did not spell licence, nor gastronomy gluttony, nor passion brutality.

The old streets down at the fag-end of the rue St.-Jacques which smelt of piss and stale cooking were the mere folklore of life lived in a relatively waterless capital where the women did not shave under their arms, and preferred stale scent to soapy bath water. In summer the smell of armpits in the cafés was enough to drive one mad. Yet everywhere the river winds cradled the velvet city and one could walk all night under a canopy of stars worthy of grand opera – the brilliant glitter of outer space impacting upon the shimmering brilliance of a world of hot light.

Appropriately enough she had given him a rendezvous (for the marriage) at the old Sphinx, opposite the Gare Montparnasse, where the respectable exterior – a family café, where families up from the country came to eat an ice and wait for their train – masked a charming bordel with a high gallery and several spotless cubicles. A simple bead curtain separated the two establishments, but such was the pleasant naturalness of things in the Paris of that day, that often the girls, dressed only in coloured sarongs and with the traditional napkin over the arm like waiters ("no spots upon the counterpane, please") came out to meet friends and even play a game of chequers with elderly clients whom time had ferried lightly into *impuissance*. "How marvellous," she said when she came, "if you could take all this with you to smoky

Euston." He had told her about his mother, that she was dying; he would leave immediately after the ceremony, which was performed by a very deaf consul and duly entered in the Consular Registers. The Minister then offered them the traditional glass of champagne under the tactless portrait of an idealised Wellington. He was a kind old man but he could not keep his horrified gaze off the dirty feet of Livia in her sandals. Later, much later, when Blanford asked Livia why she had done it at all she replied with a contemptuous laugh: "It seemed so unimportant; so I made you a present of something you wanted."

All this and much more passed through his mind as he sat holding the wrist of his dying mother – a flight of impressions like a brilliant surge of tropical fish across the dim aquarium of his student life. On the other side of the curtain of adolescence was a Paris full of bountiful surprises – a Paris where all the whores had started to take German lessons. The teachers of the German Institute were overwhelmed with requests for classes! A Paris where nobody shaved under the arms. At the Sphinx where he went rather sedately to play *belotte* and drink (with a timid air) an absinthe, which he hated, he had met a charming friend of his new wife, a negress of great beauty with a smile from here to there, and hands which roved into any pocket that presented itself. Livia found her "killing", and derived such amusement from her Martinique French that he was forced to enjoy her as well. Curiously enough she did shave under the arms, though she said the girls in general did not because a swatch of hair excited the customer and was good for business. He was extremely frightened of these unexpected revelations of turpitude, but it was after all romantic and he was in the rapt middle of Proust, and France was after all ... what exactly? He had never been in such an extraordinary ambiance before, a sort of ferment of freedom and treachery, of love and obscenity, of febrility and distress. A life which was so rich in possibilities reduced one to silence.

Nor for that matter had he ever been really in love before, whatever that might mean. The brilliant little taxis which flashed about the town like shooting stars were their favourite transport. Whenever they rushed off the macadam on to a cobbled thoroughfare the kisses of lovers in the back began to hobble and shake as if with an extra passionate emphasis conferred by the *pavé*. And quite apart from the greater beauties of this most beautiful of cities they were made freemasons of the company of its lovers, holding hands dutifully on the Pont des Arts, sitting heart joined to heart at the Closerie des Lilas or the rumbling Dôme. Floods of new books and ideas swamped them. He read relentlessly to keep abreast in quiet cafés and parks. It was the epoch of puzzling Gertrude Stein, Picasso, and the earlier convulsions of the American giants like Fitzgerald and Miller. He was sufficiently mature, however, to reflect that Europe was fast reaching the end of the genito-urinary phase in its literature – and he recognised the approaching impotence it signalled. Soon sex as a subject would be ventilated completely. "Even the act is dying", he allowed Sutcliffe to note, "and will soon become as charmless as badminton. For a little while the cinema may conserve it as a token act – as involuntary as a sneeze or a hiccough: a token rape, while the indifferent victim gnaws an apple." He added: "The future is more visible from France than anywhere because the French push everything to extremes. An audio-judeo-visual age is being born – the Mouton Rothschild epoch where the pre-eminence of Jewish thought is everywhere apparent, which explains the jealousy of the Germans."

Standing at night on a quiet bridge with the whole of reflected heaven flowing beneath them, silent, rapt. "One day you will despise me," she said, talking as if to herself.

One star was ticking over the lemon water. He said to himself: "Pity and she don't match and never will." And here he was – most inappropriate of men, a writer, watching from the abolished tower of his male self-esteem refunding his youth into these silences with this dangerous girl. "In two months' time I am going away, perhaps for good," he said, but he didn't take it seriously, just as he didn't really take the war seriously. Sutcliffe chided him from Geneva where he had landed a temporary job tutoring. "It's all very well to sit up there in your private Pisgah," he said, "but kindly note that Pisgah is the Hebrew word for an outdoor shithouse. It was here that old Moses quietly, while shifting the load of guilt, in the posture of Rodin's *Thinker*, *thunk*. My last words on leaving the school were as follows: 'The school will get no more half holidays unless secret practices cease and a new detachment is born, say a detachment of dragoons, firing off maroons.'" He went on after a pause, "But when I left, after my scandal, such is a frailty of the female organism that there was an outbreak of mumps, chiefly among the nuns."

But in spite of the confusion of this period Blanford was thinking, he was looking around him and taking stock as well as taking notes in his little student's *calepin*. Like: "The old seem to be praying for a war to carry off the young; the young are soliciting a plague to carry off the old. Fortune's maggot, I nestle in the plenitude of my watchful indifference."

She was his, and yet she was not really completely present. Reality, fine as a skin on milk, was called into question the whole time by this disturbance of focus aided by alcohol or tobacco or other unspecified drugs. Shaving himself in the bathroom mirror he realised that he had been pretending to be sane all his life. Now, even while kissing her he did not know which state of mind to assume. To overhear a thought thinking itself, to eavesdrop on a whisper of a truth formulating itself – this was his new state of mind. He began a book – the whole thing seemed to write itself. It was the purest automatic writing. It was a vignette of life in the country somewhere – a country which he himself had never seen. It was overwritten and shapeless so he destroyed it. Yet something important had happened to him – on the mystical plane, though that seems a rather pompous way of speaking about the intervention of "reality prime" into his scheme of things. (He tried saying "I love you" in several ways, in several keys, at several speeds, just to try and imagine what it was she heard when he did.) But what he realised was that from that moment onwards nothing he did was frivolous. It could be bad or good or even just inadequate or indifferent but it would be fraught with his own personal meaning, it would have his finger-prints on it. When he dared to say as much to Sutcliffe, his bondsman groaned aloud: "I see it all," he declared, "another novel written by the automatic pilot," and when Blanford looked at himself in the mirror he could see that in fact his expression was a trifle portentous – swollen, as if he had a gumboil. His self-esteem had boiled over.

Anyway, would there be time? They were pushed by the anxieties of the age to try and drink in everything before the war swallowed it up – that meant Edith Piaf looking like a cracked plate and singing like a cracked dove. "*Mon coeur y bat!*" That meant the new cinema – which had by now forfeited its chances of becoming more than a minor art by the invention of sound-track. It meant piles of saucers growing up under one's drinks at the Dôme while voices spoke of Spengler and the thirteenth law of thermo-dynamics. . . . God! it was good to be alive, but it was an agony also, and he felt it all the more when the slow measured rhythm of England replaced the throbbing Paris rush. He managed a brief visit to Oxford to see friends and collect belongings, and found it strange and secretive and tongue-tied – "theological dons in their Common Rooms dancing round the *filoque*," as Sutcliffe was to put it. For his part the great man had started to do yoga by the lake. "Come," he said in magisterial fashion, "sharpen your intuitions in the cobra pose."

Blanford did nothing of the kind. His thought-glands were too soaked in alcohol, his mouth tasted itself through a coat of fur. He was happy in a distressing sort of way, dwelling in the great shadow of happy fornication with this buccaneer, this bird of paradise. "I am young and handsome," he told Sutcliffe, "and self-possessed as a cervical smear. I want to enjoy myself before age sets in and I suddenly go blue as cheese with a heart condition. . . ."

Publishers, he pretended to himself, were bursting their braces with desire to receive a new masterpiece, and here he was destroying everything he wrote as fast as he wrote it. In a friend's studio here was a grand piano on which from time to time he would practise. He played Schubert for her until she wept, and then innocently fell asleep, chin on paws like a Persian cat, a catspaw. Self-pity engenders oxygen and she was very sad to be sad. He started to write the memoirs of The Superfluous Man, but found he lacked the art. A pelican, he was trying to drink a little blood from his own breast.

> The tirra lirra of the public purse,
> The piggy bank whose use we learned from Nurse;
> The affect cannot hoard its wild regrets
> Except as dark repressions in cold sweats.

"I see you have a poetic turn?" said the patronising Sutcliffe. "I too dabble, and before leaving England I tried my hand at everything, even Sapphics which have never been done well since Campion. Listen!

"Deliciously sapped by the swish of thy swansdown chemise
I perch on a porch in Belgravia pansexually pooped."

It was full of false quantities and not at all a real Sapphic,
but what was the point of arguing with Sutcliffe? It was clear
that he was pained and lonely, and probably had toothache
as well. He struck a chord, a sad diminished seventh, to wake
the sleeper but she slept on.

> If pianos could polish themselves
> They would be turned to cats;
> In mirrors of self-esteem efface their lust
> Licking their likenesses to dust.

Suddenly Constance appeared in Paris and strangely
enough with her the war became suddenly real – as if she
herself had declared it. She was very much thinner and yet
calmer, and she had had what she declared was a momentous
series of meetings with Freud in Vienna. She had attended a
conference of psychs at which he had presided and they
had taken a fancy to each other. Other meetings followed
and the result was that now she was a wholly submitted pupil
of the old man whom she now vehemently declared to be the
foremost thinker in Europe.

"Here! Wait a moment!" said Blanford, shocked by so
uncompromising a hero-worship, and of course she laughed.
It was obvious to her that he, in common with nearly all
so-called intellectuals of that epoch, understood next to
nothing of the modest provisional theses of the old professor.
How to make it clear? She took him by the shoulders with an
affectionately admonishing air and said: "From now on it
has become impossible for anyone to write *Hamlet* again,
do you see?" He did not see, did not wish to see much beyond
the dancing points of her bright eyes and the grand flush
of colour with which she announced that she was meeting
Sam secretly that evening, and they were going to get

married before the war broke out. "It will be a long sad stalemate of years perhaps," she said. "They will never get through the Line and we will never have the force to go after them. Meanwhile, lots of bombing and short rations and stalemate." It was of course the general view, hence the strange kind of stagnation in which they lived. But she had other fish to fry as well for she suddenly changed her expression from gladness to bitter gloom. "Where is Livia?" she asked with a kind of waspish sharpness. How should he know? Nobody could keep track of Livia's movements; sometimes in desperation he left her little notes on the notice-board of the Café Dôme for she turned up there from time to time.

Constance paused for a long moment with her chin on her breast, thinking; then, as if coming to a decision, she said: "All right, well, I shall tell you then. In Vienna I saw a German newsreel of some great Nazi rally in Bavaria – there she was, plumb in the centre of things, dressed in a German uniform."

The news was electrifying and numbing at the same time. What could it mean? "Are you sure?" he said weakly. Constance nodded and said: "Never surer. She was full in the camera for about ten seconds, singing and giving the salute. She looked out of her mind. I am terrified for her."

Blanford did not know what to say, so acute was his shame. "She has never confided in me," was all he could think of in the way of self-defence. But even at this late stage the full extent of the tragedy which was slowly being enacted in Germany failed to register – its impact skilfully dulled by false propaganda and censorship to which they were as yet unaccustomed. They walked a little together in the Luxembourg, mostly in silence, trying to shape some sort of true perspective for their future lives – but only vague prospects and qualified hopes stretched away from them into ... what? But at least Constance was sure of her basic direction. She had joined the Red Cross on the medical side, and with her Swiss passport proposed to be of some use in the crisis to come. Sam had a fortnight before rejoining his unit in Britain. Tonight, after getting married, they would take the old train from the Gare de Lyon, and spend a brief honeymoon in Tu Duc. She asked: "Why don't you two come for a few days? Hilary can't, he is still in his Scottish seminary." But he sensed that it would not have done. They parted with warmth, and on his side with a pang of vague and imprecise regret, as if he feared that their friendship might be qualified by his marriage. It was silly of course. The old certain stability of things had melted into something new – a sort of state of limbo. And in the midst of all this, glowing like a precious stone, was the memory of Provence and all it had held for them on this first rich encounter with it. The richness was overwhelming, and in his own dreams he returned again and again to the old house lying so secretively among the tall trees, in a silence orchestrated only by the wind and the ripple of river which passed through the garden.

As they parted she said in a sudden little flurry of agonised feeling: "Do you think I am doing the wrong thing? I wouldn't like to hurt Sam." He shook his head but he felt the shock of her words. The question meant that, in fact, she *was* doing the wrong thing, and that somewhere in her inner consciousness she knew it. But what made him feel ashamed was his own sudden feeling of elation as he recognised the fact. He felt it was horrible and quite unpardonable. He would seek absolution in thinking up some extravagant present for her in London.

Cremation is a clean and unemphatic way of disposing, not only of your dead, but also of your thoughts about death and any fears and misgivings they might engender. The rain melted down over everything, a soft blue rain which pearled

down the windows of the old respectable Daimler they had
hired for himself and Cade, the only two mourners. The
coffin looked small and very light. It lobbed slightly as the
hearse gathered way. He had been extravagant about the
flowers because he knew she had loved flowers, yet an
obstinate parallel thought crossed his mind as he wrote out
the cheque, namely: "I never received a moment's affection
from either side of the blanket." He felt aware of some sort
of emotional attrition, of a withering away inside himself –
a kind of poverty of affect which art and literature might
only pretend to redress. Perhaps later, in middle life . . . yes,
but would there be a middle life, with all this war business
going on? To his surprise he bought a new car on an impulse
and paid for driving-lessons. He retained Cade's services
for a year, but offered him an extended leave to revisit his
family in the north. When all this was over he would drive
down to Provence and wait there for history to declare itself.

The crematorium was a gaunt-looking place, of an
architecture so frivolous that it resembled an abandoned
Casino in Southern Italy. The plume of smoke which rose
from behind the main building flapped upwards into the
rain and then flattened out across the fields of concrete which
surrounded the place. The whole area was tastefully laid out
with gardens full of daffodils and other Wordsworthian aids
to memory. But there was quite a waiting list of bodies for
cremation and they were a few moments early. They were
set down to wait, and optionally pray if they wished, in a
small ante-chapel which did duty as a waiting-room. The
suburban church architecture of the chapel was of glacial
coldness and infernal ugliness. The altar with its cheap
cathedral-glass saints wallowing in the crepuscular gloom
shed a dreadful Sunday School light upon them. On the wall
in the corner there was what the cricketer in Blanford
recognised as a score board such as every school buys for its

cricket field. Instead of a score however there was the pro-
gramme of the day neatly indicated in detachable lettering.
Theirs was to be preceded by three other cremations – those
of Mrs. Humble, Mrs. Godbone and Mrs. Lamb; then came
Evelyn Blanford. They must wait their turn? Cade ostenta-
tiously prayed and the chief mute sycophantically followed
suit. He was a Dickensian caricature of fruitless respectability
in his old and scruffy top hat and withered tail-coat. His
cuffs were dirty and had been arranged rather impres-
sionistically with the help of nail scissors. He was wheezy
with asthma and false devoutness. Blanford closed his eyes
and breathed deeply through his gills, praying that this might
soon be over. It was astonishing how deeply upset he found
himself to be – he would not have suspected this wave of
intense sorrow and loneliness.

The officiating clergyman was a robust and pink young
man with a touch of bustle about him, as if he were anxious
to get through the work of the day as soon as possible. But
he was very detached and otherworldly as well, and one
might have supposed him to be cremating some headhunters
from darkest Borneo rather than respectable suburban
matrons from fondest Folkestone. Blanford felt rather put
out by his offhand manner and the hint of cockney in his
speech which made Holy Writ read like an advertisement for
Glaxo. But at last the session wound to its end and Blanford
was suddenly aware that throughout the length of the
service his mother had been slowly sinking into the ground
before their eyes: the coffin slowly sinking down the trap
into the operational part of the concern. The young man
achieved perfect timing, for the last word of his peroration
coincided with the muffled clap of the doors closing, after
having launched the coffin onto the rails of a subterranean
railway. They heard it whirring off down the chute. The
machinery was a trifle squeaky. Then followed a long

silence during which the mute turned to them and said, "Of course you'll be wanting an urn, sir?" "Of course," said Cade sternly. "*Two* urns!"

The man tiptoed off after saying: "I will meet you outside at the car." The parson shook a pale pork-like hand and took his leave. They were free. Blanford was wild with relief and regret. And yet speechless as an anchorite.

They had not long to wait outside the chapel before the beadle-like mute stalked round the corner of the building, holding in his arms two grotesque *bonbonnières* a little larger than the traditional Easter egg, which he distributed with an air of conscientious commiseration. Cade almost snatched at his, and to Blanford's surprise, actually beamed with pleasure, as if he were receiving a gift which brought the greatest joy. Then he caught the curious eye of his master upon him and scowled his way back into his normal taciturnity. Blanford felt a fool sitting in the back of the Daimler with an urn in his lap, and as soon as he could he placed it gingerly on the nearest mantelpiece. Ashes to ashes, dust to dust. . . .

But he was aware that a deep fault had opened in the ground under his feet – the past was now separated from the future by it. The taste of this new freedom was unnerving, as was the knowledge that if he chose to live modestly on what he had inherited he need not seek employment. A life of quiet travel and introspection seemed to sketch itself upon the horizons – yes, but with Livia? Yes, but with a war? History with the slow fuses of calamity smouldering away . . . He had selected a modest hotel from which he started to take long afternoon walks in the rain, passing more often than not the gates of the school where Sutcliffe taught and read music so many moons later. Once he even went into the close and sneaked a glance into the chapel which would so often echo with the great man's voice. On the white cliffs mewed

up by seagulls with the voices of sick kittens he felt the
(valedictory?) rain pouring off the peak of his hat, the
shoulders of his coat. Is there only one sort of death for us
all, or does each death partake of the ... valency, so to
speak, of the life it replaces? It would be marvellous to know.
Suddenly there came into his memory the dark intense face of
Quatrefages saying: "I believe Eliphas Levi when he says
that the devil is God's ruins. If you embark on the path to
sainthood and fail to achieve your goal you are condemned
to become a demon."

Suddenly Tu Duc rose up in his mind's eye and
vibrated with an almost unbearable longing; it had all been
too brief. What he must try and do, he suddenly thought,
is to drive down there and await the war in the seclusion of
that little village of Tubain. If he was called up, well and
good. (He was still envisaging a 1914-type war.) Yes, he
would leave this week and see what Livia thought of the
notion – would she come too? If they had to start a married
life together surely that would be the most propitious way
and the right place to do so? From the window of his bedroom, which gave out onto the recreation ground of the
local school, he could stand and watch the boys during
"break" and marvel at the unchanging habits of schoolboys
through the years. Their habit of buying a tin of condensed
milk and punching a hole in it – the sweetened version.
This they would suck like monkeys all day long. The older
Victorian versions of sweets were still on the market – like
the Sherbet Dab, which made you dream you were in bed
with the Queen of Sheba. It was rather expensive. Other
boys bought an orange and screwed a sugar lump into its
skin. This wound could be also sucked with pleasure. Most
magical of all was the Gob Stopper, almost the size of a golf
ball, which shed successive coats of colour as one sucked. . . .
His own schooldays seemed half a century away. He often

stood there in a muse until dusk fell, and then darkness, while once in a while the moon, "in her exaltation" as the astrologers say, rose to remind him that such worldly musings meant nothing to the hostile universe without. Even war meant nothing? Yes. He would write poems in invisible ink, then, and post them to himself. Was he then *doomed* to be a writer? All circumstance seemed to be at his elbow to prompt him.

> Mirrors will drink your image with intensity
> and bleed your spirit of its density,
> for they are thirsty for the inner man
> and pasture on his substance when they can.
> The double image upside-down
> They drink their fill – you never drown.
> They echo fate which is not kind
> O sweet blood-poisoning of the mind!

It was not too bad a description of the acute narcissism necessary to become a poet. He was anxious to be away south but the Probate people kept him an extra week. It was a strange new sensation to have money in the bank, to be able to write out quite decent-sized cheques. His allowance had been a very modest one, and he had tailored his needs to meet it. Now he bought some clothes which he much needed. But the result of all this was a bad attack of panic-meanness, and for a few days he lunched in a pub on short commons, almost choking himself with Scotch eggs and other such heavy fare. Back in London things were rather different. There was some sense of urgency. He met fellow under-graduates already in uniform and talking of foreign postings. Air raid sirens were in full rehearsal. The newspapers were full of hypothetical battle fronts bristling with arrows. A national daily asked "Where are the War poets?", and the Ministry of Propaganda set about creating some, though this was difficult, as to be really efficacious they would first have to die, and at the moment there was so little chance. Or so it seemed.

But Austria! The bombs, the parades, the curfews self-imposed from panic, the bands of uniformed thugs roaming the streets all night, surely all this was moving in the right direction? In London the left-wing poets announced that Plato was a Fascist and his mature thought was exemplified by Hitler. It was Syracuse all over again. Blanford had no literary contacts, only a few donnish ones. He aspired mildly to be a historian and apart from a few sporadic attacks of verse had little interest in the world of so called literary values. The scene was not wildly exciting. It was still fashionable to fustigate Lawrence, while at home the "serious critic" devoted energy to wondering if Walpole had genius. But Austria was another matter!

All this was preoccupying Sutcliffe no end, for he was stuck in Vienna, waiting for the treatment of Pia to yield some "concrete results" – what a cliché! He was waiting for her to "come to herself" – what a cliché. And this new science was a sort of hedgehog of cross-reference in which one could only have an approximate faith. He spent most of his time in a pastry-shop round the corner, on the square by the Somethingstrasse, 'twixt the so-called Rathouse and the office for the registration of foreign labour. His German did not exist, so he lived in a sort of fearful fog. He waited for his darling, engulfing the while, at breakneck speed, those ponderous sweetmeats, puffs and flans for which the capital was famous, and feeling himself covered with spots at each new intake of sugar. They lived in a small hotel-room where they returned each night in trembling silence to eat a sandwich while he brewed a coffee in the lavatory. Then slept. She turned her back to the horrible folksy wallpaper and sighed and trembled and talked in her sleep all night. There was no more communication between them; there was nothing they could say to one another that would not wound, would not spoil the chances of this fragile "treatment". It was a real war situation, and moreover it was a costly one. Blanford was touched by his plight and sent him quite a large cheque which was no sooner cashed than swallowed up by the treatment. But Rob had discovered that all the barbers in the capital were females – there were no male figaros. In black dresses with white frilled collars and cuffs they attended to the male scalp at all hours of the day and night. It was his only solace, to be soothed by the fingers of one of these amiable maidens and have his scalp tingled by some alcoholic concoction which made him feel as if he had gathered a halo.

In that small world of neurological patients and terrified Jewish intellectuals who could see the world coming to an end, they made a number of good friends, but the best among them was a dramatic and beautiful Slav whose extravagant and fleshy *ampleur* was somehow wonderfully sexy and composed. She was a writer and a new disciple of Freud, and she spoke of poets then unknown like Rilke and even of Nietzsche whom she claimed to have known – which made them laugh in secret. But they liked her, and she developed a deep fondness for poor Pia.

He stood in the late spring wind – cutting despite the time of the year – and watched his newly acquired motor-car hoisted up into the air at Dover and then plonked down with a shudder on the deck of the ship in which he proposed to travel. He was fearful lest the bump damage its interior – which he visualised vaguely as something very fragile: an engine made of china and supported by hairpins. But it worked well enough when it was discharged again and he set off in a gathering twilight for Paris, driving with immense devoutness on the wrong side of the road. He had been assured that he would soon get used to it and indeed by the time he reached the capital he felt quite at home in the new vehicle. He had avoided thinking too explicitly of Livia partly because he was still in a state of concern and distress about the news Constance had brought, and feared to force a breach between them by demanding an explanation: and partly because with one side of his mind he was troubled by the vague intimation of a side to her life which might in the long run prove fatal to this painful attachment to her.

To his surprise, he was reassured to find the flat empty – or apparently empty, for after a long moment of questing about for evidence of her possible presence in the form of cigarette-butts or journals, he became aware that there was indeed someone in the bathroom at the end of the corridor. He heard the flush clank, and then the sound of running water in the basin. There was light also shining through the fanlight over the door. In this new mood of hovering irritation mixed with sadness, he tapped lightly with his finger and turned the handle, to find that the door was unlocked. As he did so the girl standing naked in front of the long mirror turned also and confronted him with a bold and impervious stare. No, both adjectives were quite incorrect – it was simply the calm animal quality which made him qualify her gaze thus. It was as if he had interrupted some self-assured pussy-cat at her ablutions. In fact she had just finished shaving under the arms with a small safety razor which he recognised as his own. She had swabbed the pits with a sponge and patted them with a rolled towel. Now she was simply there, and her great bronze face with its marvellous Easter Island eyebrows gazed equably at him full of a keen friendship. A vivacious light shone in those sumptuous eyeballs, the light of tropical islands, where all thinking is muffled by sunlight. "She went this morning," said the Martiniquaise hoarsely, setting her fine head back to clear her helmet of dark hair off her shoulders. "But only a moment ago."

This was the girl whose French was so "killing"; and in her satiny nakedness she was of great beauty but also of great strength. The figure was athletic – that of a discus thrower or an Amazon of the javelin. But she was friendly, and had no thought but to please.

It was indeed her professional cue to be so and an endearing paganism shone warmly out of her eyes and mind. Those little tip-tilted breasts she leaned towards him now in a soft gesture of shy friendship. "Take me," they said, "I am all antelope. I am all musk-melon. I am spice-islander." He raised his hand perhaps to slap her but she did not flinch, she almost appeared to welcome the blow – perhaps as a sort of expiation; his hand fell to his side again. He stood there quite still and listened to the ticking of his own mind – no, it was his wrist-watch. The woman said, "All finish with her – *fini. Elle a dit à moi!*" She tapped herself on the breast-bone, stretching her long throat-line the while, with the dignified mien of some Polynesian queen. Yes, it was finished. He suddenly realised that, and, wondering at the irrationality of the human mind, he asked himself which of two reasons was the stronger. Was it because of the sexual betrayal as much as because he had discovered her opening his letters? Curiously enough the second reason seemed every bit as wounding as the first. He had old-fashioned notions about marriage and privacy, the fruit of his English education. "You say nothing?" said the woman, and he agreed, shaking his head and staring steadily at her until he felt the small prickle of incipient tears starting up. He felt ashamed of them.

She moved towards him in sympathy and then his hand, groping for a handkerchief, encountered the black rubber dildo which was still attached to her pubis, buckled on to her body by a section of dark webbing with a fastening at the back, over her rump. He took it awkwardly in his hand. There were little metal buckles round the crown of the penis, presumably to add pleasure. But what an extravagant invention, and how coarse compared to the tender and sensitive organ for which it was so pathetic a substitute. She poked it against him and laughed. Then with hands behind her back she undid it, with the gesture of one who unbuckles a sword, and let it flop to the floor where it lay, a grotesque trophy of their coupling minds. He turned on his heel and went back into the small salon, where a tremendous confusion reigned. In his haste he had overlooked this tangle of lipstick-marked towels and torn paper wrappings – marks of a hasty packing-up and departure. Through the open door he could see the unmade bed, with the pile of old newspapers lying beside it. Standing there, breathing softly and con-sidering, he felt the weight of his grief mixed with both anger and relief. But where was the letter of farewell which she must undoubtedly have written and left somewhere? The dark girl must have scented his confusion and divined the reasons; she went to the cupboard and opened the door. It was there with a few of his clean shirts. It was terse and to the point. She was going into Germany and not coming back if she could help it. They must divorce.

About the sense of failure there was no doubt, but it was perplexingly supplemented by a feeling of freshness – the fresh wind of freedom which quickened all the staleness of the last few weeks, all the doubts which he now realised that he had been stifling. It was with a pang of remorse for this feeling that he watched the dark girl change into a clean frock and express herself as ready to accompany him towards the inevitable consolation of a drink which would topple sadness and free him once more to see the world for what it was . . . an absurd way of putting it. The new world that was

beginning to emerge from the slime of history – would it be
so very different from the old?

> Boys and girls come out to play,
> Children of the *godmichet*
> Now let each seraphic mouse
> Between the thighs keep open house
> Let their uncanny kisses rain
> Upon the upturned face of pain
> In grief at having lived in vain.

In the Sphinx all was light and the pleasant frenzy of
welcome by all the acquaintances he had made when he was
last there. The Martiniquaise disappeared about her tasks of
pure ablution round earth's shores – his Keats was rusting
visibly – and left him to the silence and introspection of his
notebooks which even by then had started to gather their
aphoristic fungus, their snatches of verse and prose. He
plunged his hearing into the swathes of coarse talk and
laughter, his sense of smell with delection into the smoke of
cigars and Celtique cigarettes. Friends came up to salute
him, students from the Midi with warm accents so different
from the curt Parisian parrot-accent. *Didonk mon gar comment
sava* – his ears transliterated sound and conveyed it to his
limping understanding. No, his French was not bad, just
rather slow. It would have been appropriate to reply: *Cava
très mâle* – with the circumflex. But really he was too
despondent about his circumstances to appreciate his own
feeble witticism. He set himself to drink ardently in the
traditional manner of the jilted Anglo-Saxon. Later he would
break up the bar, get himself knocked out and put in custody
for the night. This would obviate sleeplessness and idle
thoughts about suicide which would be simply anachronistic –
since the whole of Europe was bent upon that course. It
would be pretentious, an individual act of the kind. Even
if the hemlock, love's castration-mixture, worked. Who did

he think he was, Socrates? Passing to and fro, leading her clients up the stairs or dismissing them at the foot, the dark girl took the time to stroke his shoulder or hair. Was she trying to fire him? He bent more closely to his book.

The fatal absinthe did not so much fire the blood as alter the heartbeat, anaesthetise one; one became steadily gloomier and more wretched until, just before the cataleptic trance of oblivion, one was seized with a positive epilepsy of joy, a frenzied ecstasy in the mode of St. Vitus. One pulled beards, danced with chairs, imitated famous ventriloquists. The police came. He had never as yet gone beyond a second glass of the mysterious and milky liquid. Yet already the first stage – that of an unsteady torpor – had seized him. His desires had become unwieldy, infused by a sort of sulky passion. He gazed around at the long bar with its patient and attentive clients sipping their drinks and allowing themselves to be fondled into heat by the all-but-naked girls. Trade was brisk. In the outer café beyond the bead curtain a harsh music burned like straw – *la vie* forever *en rose*. The next time she passed and placed her hand on his head he was sufficiently emboldened by hemlock to run his fingers up into her fork and touch the moist fountain of youth under her sarong. "*Viens, chéri*," she breathed, and buttoning up his *serviette* to secure his precious notebooks he lurched to his feet and obeyed. Quick as a swallow now she ducked back to where the Madam of the house sat, enthroned in wigged splendour like a very very old ice cream of a deposed empress, watching keenly over the form of her female stable. The girl took a *jeton* and was given a fresh towel which she draped over her arm like a waiter. They then mounted the stairs, negotiating them very successfully, and at last entered the little cubicle which was white and clinical and decorated only by a hideous eiderdown on the bed and a crucifix over the bidet.

The divine spasm assuaged nothing, nor did it modify the hunger it was intended to cure. He saw it now – with a phantom of disgust – as an act of barren retaliation. But skin was as glossy as ivy, breath as sweet as newly minted cocoons, so who was he to challenge fate, especially after his second hemlock? It was later that he discovered that she had managed stealthily to empty his wallet; happily his rentier's low cunning had foreseen something of the kind and he had placed two-thirds of his *fric* in the hind pocket of his trousers which he kept firmly in view at the end of the bed. It remained only to catch a homely clap now and he would be all artist. The serpent lay beside him breathing softly, waiting for him to recover his strength, fondling him the while to see if there wasn't another kick in the old *manivelle*. As a sort of testimonial to his masculinity she sowed a few love bites, little *suçons*, upon his throat and shoulders. Heigho! So this was the creative life as lived in this seamy capital? He had begun to feel somewhat of an initiate by now, though his mind still flirted with anger and sadness.

But here was a new problem – his walk had gained a strange swaying amplitude which was unwonted; coming down the stairs he had sudden flashes of vision which made him feel that he was falling backwards into a prism of yellow light. Dismayed, and a trifle alarmed – he was perfectly sober, only his legs flirted with gravitational fields beyond his knowledge – he hung himself on the bar again, in order to gain time. Though he asked for nothing he found another bloody hemlock standing before him and in his shy confusion drank it. Faces were pivoting in the mirrors, other girls seemed eager to share their favours with him. He clutched the wad of notes at his bum and allowed an attack of meanness to overwhelm him. By breathing deeply and evenly he steadied the optic nerves and then steered his way majestically into the night, tenderly unhooking the ivy-soft arms and fingers which sought to stay him, and keeping tight hold of his diary-notebooks.

At the Dôme there was a crowd gathered in the inner dining-room around a radio from which poured stream upon stream of terrifying rhetoric in a voice which by now the whole world had come to know only too well. The barmaid – a rather handsome little second-hand widow in a good state of repair – had provided this curiosity for them, though she knew that almost none of her customers understood German. It was simply the spectacle that riveted them, the phenomenon of that grating snarling voice; the sense they might well guess. And then the roaring applause. He thought of Livia. But what was he doing here? What had prompted him to enter another bar? The answer was a thirst, a raging thirst. He realised the folly of drinking so much Pernod, and called now for a pint of champagne. It hardly mended the situation, except that the coolness was invigorating. But now he was really drunk and his subsequent wanderings gathered impreciseness as time wore on. He lost his briefcase and his umbrella. Thank goodness he had had the sense to leave his passport back in the flat with other and more valuable papers. . . . He nearly fell over the Pont Neuf, enjoyed the conversation and esteem of several hairy clochards, and was finally knocked down by a taxi in the Place Vendôme, whose driver, appalled by what he had done, had the humanity and despatch of his profession, and loading him into the back raced hotfoot to the American Hospital in Neuilly where his confusions were worse confounded by drugs intended to secure him some sleep while they investigated his bones.

He informed the doctor seriously: "The whole of humanity seems simultaneously present in every breath I draw. The weight of my responsibility is crushing. A merciful ignorance defends me from becoming too despondent." He was told to shut up and sleep, and was reassured that while no bones were broken he had been much "concussed", which accounted for some of the bells ringing in his head.

Deus absconditus, the shaggy God of all drunkards' slumbers, now invaded him, and in his mind's mind he found himself wandering the ever green lanes of a southern landscape, hand in hand with the sort of Livia he had dared to imagine – one he was never to see in reality; or else seated at the stained old table in the garden covering page after page of his notebooks in a hand which he vaguely recognised as that of Sutcliffe. Time stretched away on either side of the point-event of each drawn breath, back into the subfusc suburban past, forwards into a veiled future, but somehow as yet void of significance. The writer, *l'homme en marge*, writing the Memoirs of a Marginal Man. On the title-page he had written, in this large flamboyant and rather hysterical hand: "All serial reality is by this writing called into question." The radio went on and on in his head, roaring and foaming. An ape fingering a safety catch – Europe was holding its breath. He bent his aching head lower and wrote on, "I have no biography; a true artist, I go through life like a character in one of my own books." To this S added, "My first experience of an audience was when, as a fattish youth, I played Adipose Rex in the school play. Since then I have often dreamed of living in a deserted school (life?) full of empty rooms, open doors and clean blackboards; yes, life waiting for the scholars of breathing. Comrade, continue that poem in invisible ink, ask yourself why the Dalai Lama has no Oedipus Complex." "Silly, because he has no parents. . . ."

The sirens wailed once or twice briefly like supercats *en chasse*. These were practice calls only but they wrung the heart. Marriage to her would be like drinking wine from a paper cup. What he had really needed was the smell of warm sirloin, smell of cooking in fair hair which had bent over the stove, the scent of celery in the armpits. Already he seemed to have lived a dozen lifetimes with her, all in the same cottage. For years afterwards they would remain, the claw-marks on the door where every night the dog scratched to be let in, the scratches she had made with her key around the lock. Suddenly the voice of Sutcliffe admonished him: "Aubrey, you have a mind like a fatty chop. Be silent or be completely fascinating. Never bore." The poor fellow could not have felt in any better humour than his bondsman yet he persisted in being flippant – though at times his voice was quite squeaky from fatigue. He quoted:

> Our old telluric artichoke,
> We sucked her leaves but nothing woke;
> The cactus of the primal scene
> Had mogrified her sweet demean.

Blanford, always slow to retort yet determined to get some of his own back, sat up and said: "Rob, you haven't the talent to rub a bit of polish off the primal apple; you are simply an old football full of pus."

Somewhere in the course of his military training at Oxford he had come across the expression "omega grey", and had been told that it was the scientific designation of the deepest grey before complete blackness; now as his troubled sleep swirled about him, changing form and colour and resonance, it seemed to him that the whole of the outer world beyond the window of the white ward was painted in this colour – the almost black of death. Omega grey – the phrase echoed on in his mind, though whether he was asleep or awake he could not guess. This drug-bemused reality was filtered through a mesh of discrete sensations, containing fragments of the recent past juxtaposed or telescoped upon fearful contexts. He saw the body of his mother transformed by a neo-Cubist painter into a series of porpoise-faced nudes. Her teeth were all but opaque, her gums fashioned in gelatine.

Swollen to enormous size she floated over the Thames to
defend it against enemy aircraft; moreover she was all grey,
camouflage grey, *omega* grey, the last colour before the dark
night of the soul settled over them like a new ice age. There
would hardly be time enough to achieve that state of beatitude
and equilibrium which for him was already associated
(wrongly) with the creative act. What was he doing here in
this molten bed, fuddling while Rome burned? He should
have been telling his beads and praying aloud.

He pressed his palms on his eyelids and sent showers of
sparks flying across his eyeballs. Yes, it was there, the state
he vaguely hankered to achieve! It already lay somewhere
inside him in a completely unrealised form – or rather he
knew it was there without being able to locate it. It was like
hunting through the house for one's spectacles when they
were on the top of one's head, perched on one's crown. A
vomit of words, linked by pure association, floated below
his visions like the subtitles to an incomprehensible film
written by a lunatic. (The drunkard's word list is sometimes
the sage's also.) A vision of Livia with her finger to her lips.

The weather is breaking up, my puss,
The cards are down in autumn stars

In his dream he told her: "The maddening thing is
that what is to find cannot be looked for. You are trying
desperately to acquire what you already possess but do not
recognise. Meditation brings on a state of perilous heed – it
is not mere daydreaming. All this would be risible if it were
not so serious a matter." To which she replied sweetly,
shaking that fine cervine head: "At any moment tell yourself
that things are much better than they have any right to be."
What sophistry! In the streets he saw the faces passing,
omega-grey glances upon pavements of omega grey. Yes,
there was nothing that did not lead somewhere – yet every-

thing also had a built-in trap that at any moment could become an obstacle.

Suddenly the scene changed to a basement in Vienna – he knew it to be Vienna without knowing how he could know; for he had never been there.

A swarm of violins started up somewhere and through half-closed eyes he saw the fiddlers performing their hieratic arabesque – girls combing out their long hair. Bearded candles in the darkness gave them not rose or carmine, but the uniform pork tint of omega grey. A slowly folding line of music from some fugue wrapped them all in a melancholy tenebrousness. There were a dozen or so people there, but he only recognised the faces of Sutcliffe and Pia. There was something startling about their attention and he suddenly realised that they were listening, not to the music which welled from the radio, but to the distant crepitations of musketry and machine-gun fire, punctuated from time to time in the furthest corner of space by the soft thud of a mortar. There was trouble almost every night, they told him, and they were forced to live by a self-imposed curfew, more or less. It had, however, not been going on long, but the persecution of the Jews was beginning.

Then, abruptly, as if the scene had been "cut" like a film sequence, they found themselves walking timorously among deserted squares and startled public statuary, with a light spring snowfall blurring everything and obliterating skylines. They were heading for a quarter of the town which was predominantly inhabited by the intellectual élite of medicine and the arts. Here were the practice rooms where right round the clock one heard pianos playing scales and snatches of classical music, heard sopranos giving tongue, heard the gruff commentary of tubas practising. The nationalists had been busy wrecking this quarter during the earlier part of the evening and had been driven off by police, or else had had their attention diverted by other prey in other quarters where the inhabitants were easier to bait or intimidate. They had, however, left a legacy in the form of two large bonfires burning away – mounds of medical books doused with petrol. All the windows were open and the flats from which these articles had been seized and hurled into the street appeared now to be empty. All the lights burned on, furiously on, as if outraged, but there was no human form to be seen. Then Pia saw the old-fashioned sofa half in and half out of the window on the third floor, and she gave a wild sad cry. These were the old consulting-rooms which the penurious medical crew could hire specially cheaply, for they were subsidised by the university. The sofa! She had recognised one of the old consulting-rooms which an impecunious Freud had shared with Bleuler when they were making their first halting steps towards a theory of the unconscious. It was the same old leather-covered monster of a committee-room sofa upon which the master had (it seemed a century ago now) invited her to recline. On it, writhing to and fro like someone in a high fever, she had embarked on that strange adventure which as yet seemed to be never ending; one promise succeeded another, one remission followed another relapse. Now this fond critical instrument of torture hung there like a maimed crocodile.

In the wild cry of recognition with which Pia greeted this spectacle was mixed all the anguish and reverence she felt for this shabby symbol posed so outrageously upon the window-sill – like a woman too fat to get out or in now, irretrievably stuck, waiting for the fire brigade to rescue her. As a matter of fact they could be heard approaching some streets away, though their customary moaning signals were mixed with the sinister mesh-like sound of caterpillar-tracks upon concrete. A light tank prowled across their line of vision a couple of street corners away. They had been joined by a small group of medical students who were in a high pitch of excitement – they all looked as if they had been drinking.

Now a man had appeared at the window from which the sofa protruded – a sort of janitor it would seem, from his green apron. He had been going round turning off lights and closing open doors. He paused irresolutely for a moment before the sofa, obviously wondering what to do about it. It protruded so far that it was impractical to drag it back, though he seemed at first tempted to try. It was hanging by its back legs above the burning street. The students began to gesticulate and shout in a desultory fashion, though without any clear idea of what might be done to ameliorate the present situation, the smashed lamp standards, the burning books. Suddenly the concierge at the window came to a decision. With a heave he disengaged the back legs of the ugly old crocodile and catapulted the whole thing into the street, where it fell upon one of the burning piles of books. The sirens had come much closer. "Quick!" cried Pia, quite beside herself with anxiety, for the sofa had begun to smoulder at the edges. "Quick!" People gazed at each other wondering what she could mean, but she herself had darted forward and caught the old crock by the shoulders, pulling it with a frantic, almost superhuman force, until it was clear of the flames. "We must save it," she said. "Rob, for Christ's sake ..." Bemused and puzzled as he was he broke into a clumsy run and, without for an instant understanding what their objective might be, helped her tug it clear. Other students now, equally in the dark, came to their aid, and acting like lunatics they picked it up and set off at a trot for the nearest shelter. The whole performance was totally spontaneous and unplanned. It had been sparked by the intensity of her cry and the concentrated passion of her actions – she looked like someone in a trance. Obviously this tattered object was of the utmost value and importance to her. Obligingly the crowd helped her save it and drag it to the relative safety of an air-shelter with a wall where they placed it under a tree. They were all panting and yet somehow exultant. From the other end of the square now burst the police and the fire-engines, dramatic and noise-bearing as a whole opera. It was time to shrink back into the shadows and disappear. They left the old sofa sitting there in the light snowfall.

Events had moved so fast and so dramatically that they themselves were quite out of breath with astonishment at what they had done. "What will you do with it?" cried Sutcliffe now, aware that they could hardly house it in their little hotel, and she thought fiercely for a moment, her pale face bowed. They were already walking fast, almost running, towards their hotel, trying to select untroubled streets where they would not meet patrols. Friends were waiting for them at the hotel – among them the Slav girl – and they ordered coffee in the tiny shabby lounge where they would, as was customary, hear an account of the day's happenings both in the capital and in the world – the outer world which loomed over their daily minds like a storm cloud. "Whatever happens we must keep it," said Pia decisively, in the middle of a conversation about something else; and he knew she meant this stupid old sofa for which he himself felt nothing. Had she gone mad? He asked her, but she was already explaining what they had done to her friend whose face lit up with a triumphant and generous approval. The two women, he thought, were as superstitious as savages. What would they plan next?

The outcome was even more unexpected than he had any reason to suppose. Medical students, friends of the Slav, now arrived upon the scene, and they warmly approved of this absolutely medieval gesture. (They would be selling indulgences next!) They were young and impetuous and determined to rescue the totem. The only problem was to decide what should be done with it. There were several lines of thought. One wished to give it houseroom in his flat, another thought it should be carted to the Faculty and placed in the hall – but of course the medical authorities, who had hardly heard of Freud, would have had a fit at the very suggestion. Suddenly Pia pronounced upon the matter with so much vehemence that everyone knew that she would not be gainsaid. "It is mine," she said, "and I intend to keep it. I shall send it to my brother in Avignon. I have quite decided." There was no more to say; all that was left was to decide upon the details of transport – how the devil could one send a sofa? Obviously by rail. Yes, but what about transport to the station? Here one of the students, who worked part-time with an undertaker, suggested that he borrow the hearse to transport the holy relic. "Yes! Yes!" she cried and clapped her hands exultantly. "That is what we must do. I shall telephone to him tonight."

So it was that, at five in the morning, Mr. Sutcliffe found himself seated with an air of ludicrous amazement in a large black hearse, in front of what to the average passer-by must have seemed something like a very large corpse wrapped up in a brown-paper parcel. They had indeed enveloped the charred old article in several layers of brown paper, the better to label it, and to their surprise there seemed to be no problem about sending it. It would await arrival in Avignon.

Blanford had followed all this hazily, through the heavy meshes of his dream, and he conveyed his approval of the whole initiative through the usual channels – the pulse-beat of the blood. But he had decided that Constance must have the relic, not Pia; and as he carried more weight in everything to do with real reality, he knew that he could override the present decision, and persuade a carter to take charge of the

sofa and ferry it up, not to Verfeuille but to Tu Duc. He said
as much and to his surprise Sutcliffe did not demur – it was a
measure of his indifference to the relic. He had come to hate
the whole science of psychowhatsit, which promised the
moon and came unstuck at every corner.

"Very well, *maître*," he said ironically, "if you say so.
How is Paris treating you?"

"A pleasing priapism rules the waves," said his incoherent and maundering *alter ego* or *summum bonum*. "The
croissants are brown as mahogany. I saw her at dusk, reading
in a public garden, and I longed to approach her and ask
where she had been. She had disappeared for nearly a week.
But I dared not. I sat on an adjacent bench and told myself
that it was not her, it was just someone who resembled her.
She was reading one of my unwritten novels – with pious
intensity. Beside her lay a bag with a half-eaten croissant in it.
She was sunk in profound thought, I could see that, and
would certainly be sulky if approached. I closed my eyes and
waited. When at last she got up to go I saw that indeed it was
not her but someone who resembled her. The discarded
paper bag lay where she had abandoned it. I scattered the
croissant for the birds and went home by the lake in order
not to give her the illusion of spying on her. But of course
when I got back there was, as usual, nobody at the flat."

> Little grains of splendour,
> Little knobs of lust,
> Make a writer tremble,
> Loving is a must
> Nor can he dissemble
> When his heart is bust.

Let all young women bring me their emulsion,
Gods are born thus with every fond convulsion!

THUS SPOKE ZARATHUSTRA!

He went on foundering more and more deeply in these patches of dream-nightmares which stretched away on all sides of him to the horizon, feeling his mind being feverishly ransacked by the combined fevers of medicine and alcohol. The dark streets of Vienna had been replaced by Paris. Night-watchmen everywhere, a tribe of scowling lurkers, loveless as poets whose minds had become viscous with fatigue, waiting for dawn. Broken glasses, club feet, *arthritis deformans*, huge clubbed thumbs. He kept waving his arms and protesting, trying to obliterate these images of menace, but they persisted, they gained on him.

His eventual release from hospital, albeit rather reluctant, was something that he simply had to accept – it would have been malingering to stay comfortably between the sheets with nothing worse than post-alcoholic depression and a touch of shock. The kindly taximan who had knocked him down came to see him and offered him a free ride back into his *quartier*. The young doctor, who was called Bruce, saw no objection. The hospital cashed his cheque without a tremor, leaving him enough change to resume civilian life once more, so to speak. Back then to the empty flat, deposited at the Dôme by his kindly overturner. But once home he became suddenly aware of his weakness, and sat down on the unmade bed with a thump; his desolation continued to manufacture discordant images of loss, but they were more inconsequential now and less forceful. Where could he find some rest – the loneliness in this little box-like flat was intolerable. If he went back to the Coupole or the Sphinx he would be undone. He hid therefore in a local cinema, feeling the fleas jumping about his thighs while he watched the amours of that most congenial of all funny men, W. C. Fields. "Dharling banana, where's your sense of humour? Fragrant yam, you are my dish." Wondering vaguely – the subtitles were hairy with age – how all this would translate. Provide your own version. *"Clafoutis imberbe! Potiron du jour!"*

When at last he struggled to his feet and sought the exit, night had already fallen, the mauve-magenta night which was part street-lamp and part aerial radiation of white light against the blue-black sky of cheap fur. He was hungry; he scuttled to the Dôme and ate bacon and eggs with energy, gazing round with distaste at all the other representatives of the arts and crafts who surrounded him. Pride of lions, skirl of loafers, extravagance of poets. No, he would go far away, he would eat liquid mud on toast in far-away Turkish khans. Far far from the dungy altars of the Nonconformist mind. He would order a clyster for all parish Prousts of the Charing Cross Road. He would . . . On the cusp of a mere nod the waiter replenished his glass. He realised that he was still calamitously drunk in a reactivated sort of way. His blood coursed. He was surrounded by Africans with beautiful fuzzy heads and booming tones. They had all come to Paris to gather culture. Here they were, screaming for worm-powders. What was to be done? Great sweet turbines of black flesh innocently cutting slices of Keats or Rimbaud for their evening meal. A wholesome cannibalism when you thought of it. *O Grand Sphincterie des Romains*! O spice routes of the poetic mind which lead to the infernal regions below the subliminal threshold. Metaphors too big for their boots, literature of the S-bend. Wind in an old chimney – fatherly flatus? He should be more modern, go into business.

> To shit, to codify a business lunch
> A pint of lager and a brunch.

He had ordered various things for which the tally of saucers did not work, so the waiter had issued him with little price slips. It was on one of these that he jotted down a few figures, trying during a coherent patch in his thoughts to mobilise his reason and estimate what his expenses might be when he left Paris on the morrow, as he now intended to do. When it came to pay the waiter tore up these slips as he cleared the table. Then he noticed that they were scribbled over and he turned pale. "*O Monsieur!*" he exclaimed, beside himself with vexation, "*j'ai déchiré vos brouillons!*" He was under the impression that he had inadvertently destroyed the rough notes of some foreign poet of genius. His confusion was touching, his relief when he was reassured on the point, hardly less genuine. Blanford realised that he was madly in love with Paris. He had much to learn from these extraordinary people, for whom the word artist meant so much.

He felt steadier now in wind and limb, and visited the garage where he had left his car, to reassure himself about the servicing, and as to whether he might find it available for him at six in the morning, for he planned to make an early start and perhaps lie for the night at Lyon. All was in order, happily.

He went for one last drink to the Sphinx with the intention of bidding the Martiniquaise goodbye – with the present ambiguous and ill-regulated state of affairs he felt that he should really tell her of his movements, in case Livia reappeared and wished to know where he might be found. But the girl was not there that evening, she had gone to the cinema, though nobody knew which. He wrote her a message and left it with the presiding Mama who regally accepted to see it delivered. Then he drank his drink and departed, making his way back to the sad little flat, so empty now of resonance and tone – as if even its memories of the events which had taken place within its walls had gone dead and stale.

Nor could he sleep – images floated him beyond reach of it. He was hunting down the great rat of the emotions with a heavy stick in a dark house, creeping from staircase to staircase, pausing to listen from time to time. The night was

full of the noise of cats feasting on garbage and each other –
stale cats, the fitting symbol for temple women, all faceless
claws and minds and civet. He threw up the window and
stuck his face against the sky – the whole of space, sick as an
actress, living in a state of permanent and thoughtless manifestation. He would be glad to get away from the Sphinx
where trusting little Benzedrine Papadopoulos opened her
twiggy legs to show a black bushy slit with a red silk lining.
Farewell to Livia and the dry copyists' succinct word for
craving – four letters beginning with L. Avignon radiated the
memory of peace and contentment, and tomorrow he would
be on the road once more.

   In contrast to the affairs of the world, his own were more
or less in order; the little flat would revert to its owner automatically for the rent had not been paid. He had wound up all
household bills, debts to the newsagent, and the like. He was
vacating Paris – it was a hollow enough feeling. He passed by
the Dôme and scanned the letter board which contained as
always a wealth of messages which waited patiently to be
reclaimed. There was nothing from her, and he was a fool to
have expected anything. On an impulse he copied out a
poem from his notebook and placed it in an envelope with her
name on it. It was valedictory enough to suit the occasion;
he felt inexpressibly sad about the whole business, about the
whole failure to connect, to unite. He was also alarmed for
her safety – for he was, unaccountably, still deeply attached
to her.

BURIED ALIVE

for Livia

A poem filling with water,
A woman swimming across it
Believing it a lake,
The words avail so little,

The water has carried them away
Frail as a drypoint the one kiss,
Renovation of a swimmer's loving.

Attach a penny calendar to the moon
And cycle down the highways of the need,
The doll will have nothing under her dress;
With an indolence close to godhead
You remain watching, he remains watching.

When she smiles the wrinkles round her eyes
Are fitting, the royal marks of the tiger,
The royal lines of noble conduct.

Virtuous and cryptic lady, whom
The sorrows of time forever revisit,
Year after year in the same icy nook
With candles brooding or asphodels erect,
Stay close to us within your mind.
These winter loves will not deceive,
Unplanned by seasons or by kin
They feast the eye beneath the skin.

SEVEN

Prince Hassad Returns

N OR WAS HE THE ONLY ONE RETURNING TO AVIGNON, he discovered, for he later found it bruited that Lord Galen and the Prince had already come rumbling and roaring and careening out of Germany together in a high state of emotional and intellectual disarray. It had not taken long for the gimlet eye of the Prince to pierce to the heart of Galen's romantic folly; he could hardly credit what it revealed of the whole catastrophic investment. Among so many miscalculations of the same order, this one stood out as a monument of the purest insanity – and so fearfully expensive to boot. Never in Galen's long career as a "gentleman-adventurer" (he was fond of the phrase) had he committed such a fearful "bloomer" (another he favoured). Indeed the blow appeared to have all but demolished him – at all events temporarily. His sang-froid had turned its back on him. He walked with a stoop, giving the impression that the disaster had actually aged him. You felt he was worn out with the long and humiliating journey back to sweet reason. At all events they drew up at Les Balances in Geneva for an orgy of accounting and numerous vital meetings with paler and paler executives. To tell the truth Prince Hassad was less bruised, less cast down, for he had invested nothing in the scheme. In fact he hovered on the edge of smiles, although his cumbersome coach caused endless annoyance in the parking spaces of the city and his staff much excitement. It was Galen who bore the brunt of it all; try as he might there was no disguising his asininity.

The Prince had, heaven knows, been the soul of tact, but from time to time a mortal chuckle escaped him. He struck

his knee and wrinkled into lizard-like smiles of a private
nature; but Galen could quite well guess why. Though the
little man in his royal green-striped flower-pot actually *said*
nothing his chuckles lodged like barbs in the tender cuckold
flesh of his associate's consciousness. Things had gone so far
that they had actually been threatened with arrest unless they
decamped – and this by the Nazis! Galen rather wished now
they had been arrested – his sadness would have been sub-
limated by an expiation of sorts. "Well," said the Prince, "it
is no use just going on brooding. We have made a ghastly
incoherence. You must save what you can." He was kind
enough to pretend that he had shared the misfortune. "Look
on the brighter side," he said, turning Stoic. "In two or three
months we shall all be dead – you have read about the nerve
gas in the *Tribune?*" Galen obediently thought about his
approaching death and felt quite cheerful of a sudden. Yes,
there was no use brooding. The Prince picked his teeth and
reflected; he had spent all day at the Egyptian Embassy,
telephoning and sending telegrams in cipher. "My dear
friend," he said, "you will go on to Provence and arrange
your affairs. I have things I must attend to. I will follow in
ten days' time and we can decide everything else."

"You aren't leaving me?" said Galen, pulling his under-
lip and pouting. "Only for a while," said Prince Hassad,
"and I think the best thing for you, my friend, is to wind up
things here and then go back south. I will send off the coach
ahead. In ten days we meet again and then there will be big
decisions to make. I fear I must leave all my new friends in
Avignon and return to Egypt for a while, until we see what
form this war takes. There is a big Italian Army on the
frontiers of Egypt, for example, and we don't know . . . well,
anything as yet.* As for you, it is impossible to disguise your

* See Appendix.

incoherences." (His perfect English had nevertheless small and unexpected flaws of usage.) "So why not make the best of them and just be frank. Eh?"

Lord Galen considered being frank, with his head on one side, like a fox-terrier. "Just admit I've been a fool?"

"Exactly."

"I never thought of that," said Galen and looked suddenly relieved. Nevertheless his sorrow and humiliation were not unduly lightened by this decision of the Prince to desert him in Geneva for a few days and take the express for London and just when he needed company and sympathy too! But Hassad insisted that he had a number of things to attend to before returning home, and that these must be despatched before, in the popular phrase of the hour, "the balloon went up". The image of a bright Montgolfière – Europe itself no less – floating up and out into the unknown empyrean of the future was suitably frivolous.

After the comparative calm of Geneva, the cud-chewing capital *par excellence*, it was strange to sit in a first-class carriage of the Golden Arrow as it drew away from frenetic and gossipy Paris where one could secure a laugh at cocktail parties by giving the Nazi salute. (The Prince was terrified when he thought of it.) He sat bolt upright in his corner seat mechanically doing the *Times* crossword puzzle and waiting for the lunch gong to summon him swaying down the corridor towards a hearty but insipid meal.

Yet the quicksand of an international lethargy was still the factor which so mysteriously dominated everything. Time, from being a solution, had become a jelly. On the outer fringe of things everything seemed in a state of violent agitation. There were trumpet-calls, denunciations, sabre-rattlings, government pronouncements . . . but the whole in a sort of void. People scurried about like rats, hoarding food or making testamentary dispositions or booking tickets for

America. But these gestures were somehow shapeless and
without pith because, in fact, nobody could believe that
human beings in this present stage of civilisation could con-
ceive of a war – after the lessons of 1914. The little man said
to himself: "It is because it is quite unthinkable that it must
happen. People want death really, life poses too many
problems." Things proceeded, he had observed, by cruel
paradox. He sighed heavily, for not the least of his concerns
was with the vulnerable and defenceless England towards
which his train was racing, shrieking aloud in tunnels, and
leaving behind it a thick black plume of smuts which always
managed to settle themselves on his grey spats and on the
astrakhan collar of his finely cut overcoat. Everything would
have to be cleaned the instant he got back to: London! The
word made his heart race, for surely there would be a letter
from his little Princess in the diplomatic bag? It was cruel to
have left her for so long alone in the dusty old palace on the
Nile with nothing much to do save to paint and read and
dream about his return. "My partridge!" – the endearment
escaped him involuntarily as he thought of her.

The ceremony of the passport control, followed by the
abrupt change in the scale of things – the new toy landscape
after Dover – set his thoughts wandering in the direction of
his youth as a young secretary of Embassy in an England
which he had loved and hated with all the emotional polarity
of his race. How would she withstand this cataclysm? Would
she just founder? He trembled for her – she seemed so exhausted and done for, with her governments of little yellowing
men, faded to the sepia of socialism, the beige of bureaucracy.
And Egypt, so corrupt, so vulnerable, was at their mercy, in
their hands. . . . Long ago he had made a painstaking analysis
of the national character in order to help in the education of
his Ambassador, dear old Abdel Sami Pasha. But it had been
altogether too literary, and indeed altogether too wise. He

had distinguished three strains in the English character which
came, he was sure, from Saxons, Jutes or Normans – each
Englishman had a predominance of one or other strain in his
make-up. That is why one had to be so careful in one's dealings with them. The Saxon strain made them bullies and
pirates, the Jutish toadies and sanctimonious hypocrites,
while the Norman strain bred a welcome quixotry which was
capable of rising like a north wind and predominating over
the other two. Poor Sami had read the whole memorandum
with attention, but without understanding a word. Then he
said, "But you have not said that they are rich. Without
that . . ."

The long struggle against his English infatuation had
coloured his whole life; it had even imperilled his precious
national sentiment. How would they ever drive them out of
Egypt, how would they ever become free? But then, would it
make sense to replace them with Germans or Italians? His
glance softened as he saw the diminutive dolls' houses
flashing by outside the window, saw the dove-grey land un-
rolling its peaceful surges of arable and crop, like the swaying
of an autumn sea. Yes, this country had marked him, and his
little Princess used often to tease him by saying that he even
dreamed in English. Damn them, the English! He compressed
his lips and wagged his head reproachfully. He lit a slender
gold-tipped cigarette and blew a puny cloud of smoke high
into the air, as if it would dispel these womanish failings of
sentiment! Womanish! The very word reminded him that the
whole of his love-life and his miraculously happy marriage
had been tinged by London. He hoped that Selim had not
forgotten to book the suite at Brown's Hotel – the Princess
loved Brown's and always sent the porter a Christmas card
from Cairo.

But then Egypt was one thing and the Court quite
another; their education had modified fanaticism and turned

them willy-nilly into cosmopolitans who could *almost* laugh
at themselves. It came from languages, from foreign nannies
and those long winterings at Siltz or Baden-Baden or Pau. It
had etiolated their sense of race, their nationalism. The French
distinguish between knowing a language and possessing it;
but they had gone even further, they had become possessed
by English. The other chief European tongues they knew
accurately of course, but for purely social purposes. There
was none of the salt in them that he found in English. . . .
Nor was everyone at the Court like him, for some were more
charmed by French, some surrendered to Italian. But it was
his first firm link with Fawzia, the passion for England. Even
when he was at Oxford, and writing anti-British articles in
Doustour under his own signature! And paradoxically enough
she loved him for it, she was proud of his intellectual stance.

The thought made him stamp his spatted foot on the
floor of the compartment, stamp with delight like a little
Arab horse. He had first met her at the Tate; poor darling, she
was piously copying a Cézanne, pausing for long drowsy
moments to dream – so she afterwards averred – of a Prince
who would suddenly appear from nowhere and ask for her
hand in marriage. This made her copying somewhat haphazard. She was chaperoned by the widow of a Bey whose
son had been at Oxford with him, and this gave him the
excuse to exchange a few words with her, and then to be
presented to the Princess. She curtseyed in an old-fashioned
manner, and he bent over those slender fingers, feeling quite
breathless. Indeed they both paled at the encounter. "It was a
moment of silk," in the Arabic phrase. Her dark eyes were
full of ardour, idealism and intelligence. He put on his gold-
rimmed spectacles in a vain attempt to seem older than he
was. The three human beings – everything had become
dream-like and insubstantial – took a slow turn up and down
the gallery, emitting noises about the paintings displayed. He

could feel the words coming out of his mouth but they were like "damp straw". Inside him a voice was saying, over and over again, "Fawzia, I adore you!" He was terrified lest his thoughts be overheard, but she preserved her demure disposition, though her heartbeat had reached suffocation point. The kind duenna absented herself for a moment and they talked on. He was electrified. *She appreciated Turner!* "We must place him beside Rembrandt," she said firmly, indeed a little school-marmishly. But how right she was! He felt he would start vapouring with devotion if this went on, so he abruptly took his leave with a cold expression on his face which dismayed her for she thought that it was due to disdain for her artistic opinions. She stammered upon the word "Goodbye" in a way that made his heart exult, though he continued to look grim as he stalked out of the gallery. Outside he smacked the back of his hand with his grey gloves, then smelt it to see if any trace of her perfume remained before continuing this reproachful simulacrum of self-punishment. Towards the next religious festival he permitted himself to send her a large and handsome folio of colour reproductions from Turner, expressing the hope that she did not own it already. She did, but she pretended the contrary, and expressed a rapture not the less sincere for being feigned. They met briefly at a number of functions and exchanged quaint fictions of conversation in public, almost suffocating with desire as they spoke. He did not quite know how to advance from this point. He was now a graduate, yes, and though heir to a large fortune in cotton and land, had no precise job. Moreover, their attachment having been launched upon such a high romantic keynote, could not be allowed to sink down the scale and revert to the humdrum. I suppose it was very Shakespearean, but they both believed – privately, secretly, separately, passionately – that nobody had ever loved with such intensity. He was anxious to keep their love free from every taint of Parisian frivolity for he considered French notions about love to be so much straw, vanity and *trompe-l'oeil*. In this period of indecision they made several important discoveries. She found, for example, that his eyes turned violet-green under the stress of aesthetic emotion, as when he spoke of the Turners in the Tate. On his side, he became more and more enraptured by her small vivid hands, so swift in action, and yet folding into her lap like rock-doves. His doctor told him that he was suffering from heightened arterial tension, and gave him a sleeping draught, but he preferred to lie awake and think about her.

Then the way opened before them. His father, after a second heart attack, wrote and told him that he must really consider getting a job and also open negotiations for a wife. He proposed to use (he said) some *piston* in the first instance, (he preferred French culture to English and thought his son's passion unhealthy and indeed unpatriotic): the second contingency he left open, being a wise man. So it was that the Prince found himself a young diplomat *en poste* in his favourite capital; and the young lady received a formal letter which had first been submitted to her aged mother, asking whether he might declare his intentions towards Fawzia. The Arabic he chose was pure though somewhat florid. Afterwards he found that she had been much amused at being referred to as "the person in question" and for a while she signed her love letters with this sweet superscription. Yes, permission was given for them to meet, to speak. The die, as they say in bad novels, was cast.

His good genius, too, must have overheard his prayers, for his choice of a meeting place for the critical encounters with his beloved could not have been more happily chosen. He would call for her, he said, towards the late afternoon and take her for a short drive along the river. She must bring a shawl as the evenings were sometimes chilly and he proposed to show her a sunset before delivering her safely back to her mother's house in Kensington. Call he did, but in one of those smart horse-carriages, with a cockaded and billycocked driver in the Victorian style. There was a whole rank of these smart vehicles, drawn by beautifully groomed horses, which occupied a station near Buckingham Palace – a perfect draw for the sentimental tourists who loved to be photographed in them when visiting London. He was not too formally dressed – just enough for a London sunset. She had put on some finery and had obediently borrowed a shawl from her mother – shawls were old-fashioned articles of a past decade, so this was rather distasteful to her, but it was too early to be disobedient.

She was charmed by his originality and rendered slightly tremulous by his presence. She had practised accepting his offer of marriage in a variety of voices but could not quite decide which to choose. She was going to leave it to fate to decide. For his part he was equally mixed-up but deep down he felt that, in some obscure way, the issue would be decided not by him, but paradoxically enough, by the painter Turner. He began to talk diffusively, discursively, about him, his secret life, the magnitude and simplicity of his vision which ran counter to that of his whole epoch. He quoted, with flashing indignation, the judgement of Constable. ("Paintings only fit to be spit upon.") And she trembled with sympathetic pain and sadness. What pitiable blindness! But his eyes had turned colour again and she felt the deep stirring of her emotions, so deep in fact that she squeezed her thighs hard together in order to allay them. They jaunted out of the Park and took the river at Battersea Bridge from which they could already see the preliminary conflagration of a late spring sunset with all its sultry brutal saffron and carmine. "We shall be just in time," he said. "Do you always do this?" she asked and he nodded with fervour. "Ever since my first

Turner," he said, "years ago now. It is different in each season." He took her hand and pressed it. "It is so very personal," he went on, "and nobody seems to know it. It is his store cupboard, so to speak." Then he broke off to inveigh against the Tate for keeping the vast quantity of the artist's paintings in a cellar and refusing to expose them. And then against Ruskin for exercising censorship. "Shame!" she cried.

How broad it was, and how placidly it flowed, the Thames, under the massive and thickset old bridge. There was little traffic on it at this hour so that they were able to hear the rustle of river traffic, distant hootings, even voices. Spars moved upon the evening sky. All London lay around them in the expiring light. The note of the horse's hooves deepened as they reached land once more, and quite shortly the driver turned sharply to the right, to follow the long sad walls of a factory upon whose river frontage they would later notice the florid legend Silver Belle Flour. On weekdays one could peer through the gates and see flour-whitened figures like snowmen going about their tasks with the air of participating in some medieval rite. But on Sunday all was quiet. Only the children of the poor played their eternal cricket and football upon grass trodden bald by their boots. It was a depressing corner, slummy and down at heel, and she wondered idly where they were going. But it was not far, their destination, for the little church of St. Mary the Virgin still flourished like Martha's Vineyard in the midst of these gaunt deformities of factory and tenement. When they drew to a halt at the slender iron gates which opened upon a green lawn, she saw that there was a great sweep of skyline open to the west with no cumbersome buildings to break it down and arrest the mind. She looked keenly about her with her bird-like grace. "You will see with His eyes!" he cried suddenly, exultantly – and indeed on an almost theological note, so that she wondered for a moment whether there was not to be a touch of religious fanaticism underneath this exuberance. "Whose?" she asked, turning quite white, her pulse a-flutter. "His!" he said sternly and would vouchsafe no more.

So the year 1777 came to meet them across the river water in the form of St. Mary the Virgin, with its four eloquent pillars holding up, caryatid-like, the deep-roofed porch. The spire, the clock, the green belfry – so spare yet so vivacious in execution – set off the whole with unemphatic charm. The whole thing seemed to them a paradisiacal model of what village church architecture should be, should stand for. The growling circumambient toils of London around them faded before the calm of these innocent precincts. The grass was crisp and bright before the church, and was studded with a few tall trees. But it was small in extent and ended in the stout sea-wall against which lay a couple of ships, marooned by the tide and lying on their sides with their spars almost in the garden. She did not dare to exclaim, "How beautiful!" for that might have seemed banal. Instead she murmured the Arabic word "Madness!"

The angle of inclination to the place, too, was inspired and set it at a slight cant towards the curving western corners of the further river, where the dense forest lands gave it a shapely horizon full of screens through which the late sun filtered. The view, so light and airy, could have hardly been any different when the church was first opened to the parish of Battersea five years before Blake elected to marry his Kate there.

Mr. Craggs, the verger, was waiting for them faithfully with the keys, as he always did, for the Prince took the precaution of phoning ahead when the weather promised a fine sunset. Despite the rules, Mr. Craggs had been suborned by the munificence of the Prince's tip. "Never less than an 'ole suffering," he informed the awestruck clients of The Raven, or those equally awestruck in The Jug and Bottle or

The Old Swan, which practically abutted upon the little church. The Prince had once read in a novel by Thackeray that a sovereign was an "adequate recompense" for a special service rendered, and though the coin was no longer in ordinary use he had his bank send him a dozen every month. It worked wonders, he found. But apart from this he and Craggs had become fast friends, and now the verger was enslaved by the Princess; he helped her down ardently if somewhat creakily, for he was a martyr to lumbago. "Well I never, Master Ahmed," he said, "what a nice young lass." The Prince blushed proudly. But today Craggs happily could not stay, for he had a meeting of the Legion – or so he said. "I shall 'ave to 'op it I'm afraid." But he had placed the old oak chair at the strategic place. "I know I can trust you to replace it, sir, and put the key in the 'ole in the wall." It was ancient ritual all this, and the Prince nodded. "Have a nice sunset, then," said Craggs agreeably, winding his woollen scarf round his neck and placing a battered bowler hat on his head. The operation gave him a moment of polite and very tactful hesitation – time to enable the Prince to extract a whole suffering from his waistcoat and press it upon his friend? Craggs gave a false start of surprise as he always did, and then promised to drink Egypt's health and the lady's, before stumping off into the evening. It was so calm. They were alone. The cab withdrew to the pub to wait.

"How kind he is," she said. She had already climbed the two stairs to the deep balcony of the church front. "He has even put a chair out for you. I understand everything now. What a view!" She sat down in the clumsy oaken chair and gazed past the balconies of The Swan to where, on a level horizon and fretted by forest, an unframed Turner sunset burned itself slowly, ruinously away into a fuliginous dusk, touched here and there with life as if from a breath passing over a bed of embers.

"No!" he said, with the same extreme bliss written on his face. "As yet you do not understand. Fawzia, you are sitting in His chair, in Turner's *own* chair which he bequeathed to the church! He sat just here to study the light effects, just where you are sitting, for God knows how many years. . . ." He all but choked with his ardour. To see her there, seated in the Master's own chair – the cockpit, the vantage-point from which he had embarked upon the great intellectual adventure of becoming himself! His fingers touched the expensive engagement-ring in his pocket – he had had it specially made for her in Nubia. He placed it on her finger now and she submitted with bowed head, only giving a small sniff, perhaps a suppressed sob. And suddenly he felt triumphant. "Of course you will, won't you?" he said, sure of his response; and like a rock-dove she replied, "Of course I will. Of course I will."

He sat himself down on the steps at her side, and thus they waited for darkness to fall, hand touching hand, speechless with joy. Even when it came time to replace the holy chair by the pulpit in the dark church and replace the keys in the 'ole, they did not utter a sound for fear of shattering the gorgeous complicity of the moment. She felt as if the ring weighed a ton.

So they clip-clopped home in lazy and loitering fashion, and she was glad of the shawl as they drew near Kensington and her mother. The entire contents of the casket labelled Human Happiness appeared to have been emptied upon their heads from a spring sky. He saw her to her house porch without a word and then, dismissing the cab, set out to walk across London to regain his flat. He felt like a comet, trailing the fire of the painter's inspiration which chance had bestowed on them.

From thenceforward, he reflected now, as the train ground its way towards the capital, everything had borne fruit, and their marriage had become the envy of less lucky friends. She had asked the young Farouk to give her away – her father was dead, she had no male relations, and she had the right to do so, for soon the stripling would be King. This the young man did with grace and style, surprising everyone by his gazelle-like adolescent beauty and his courtier's address. How he had changed now, thought Prince Hassad, stubbing out his cigarette. The caterpillar-like sloth, the sudden rages and fits of weeping . . . What a fate! Yet when he began his reign it was like the début of a Nero, an auspicious entry upon the world of power, full of authority and idealism. He sighed as the new image replaced the old in his memory.

Then followed the good years in London as a young attaché. The wind had set fair for them, London liked them. Their children were beautiful and clever, without problems.

The magnetism held, and here his little wife showed brilliant insight for she adopted more than one role with him. When she was pregnant with their second child they ran away to France and played at being artists in a secluded *mas* near Avignon – two months of bliss. She let herself go, was dishevelled and out of breath as she bent over the cooking pots, while he reverently prepared her vegetables. Her breasts were full of milk from which he drew frequent swigs. They were both of them none too clean, too, like joyous peasants. Her hair smelt divinely of cooking, her body of spices and sweat. He adored her *boeuf en daube;* she admired his wood-cutting and fire-lighting, as well as his fashion of polishing glasses. He snuffled into her wild eatable housewife's hair like a truffle hound on the scent. All this was very good for the gestation of their little son. In the years to come his love-making would profit from all their happy abandonment, their sensuality. "From your way of making love," he said, "one can see that he will print up quite beautifully as a man, little Fouad." They avoided all that was fashionable but they did visit Saint Tropez, a tiny hamlet of scarce a dozen cottages, where already the famous and inebriated Quin-Quin had opened her shop and offered to sell Fawzia a scent which was really vulgar, something from the bazaar. A scent which threw open its arms to you and said "*Me-voici!*" But the Prince was doubtful about its propriety if she wore it in London. "You would excite the whole Embassy unbearably," he said.

Of course there were mishaps as well and shoals to face, as in every marriage, but nothing can withstand devotion. During her third confinement he contracted a vexatious though slight venereal infection from a young lady-in-waiting fresh from Cairo and was very much cast down by the misadventure. But Fawzia took the whole thing in her stride and nursed him with a passionate devotion. She was glad to have an excuse to show the depth of her attachment to him; she almost thanked him for giving her the chance to show how irreplaceable she really was and how magnanimous. He was overwhelmed with wonder and joy. He suddenly realised what a real woman is capable of facing. It was a little frighten-ing. He swallowed his humiliation and submitted to her tender care like a child, glorying in the feeling of security and forgiveness. (The lady-in-waiting was banished back to Cairo, however, in very short order.)

Far from separating them, this little contretemps brought them closer together. He could afford to be weak with her for she scorned to take advantage of his weakness. "Goodness!" he said. "You are extraordinary!" He meant it.

She smiled grimly, almost scientifically.

"I love you," she explained in her somewhat incon-sequential fashion, "not because you are my husband but because you are such a man!" He echoed the word feebly though he did not contradict her. Long may she cherish the illusion, he told himself. She kissed his brow and he fell asleep filled with the density of this loving memory. The other children were told he had gout.

So life led them on in tranquil fashion until it became obvious that he would soon, by pure gravitation, rise to a rank which entailed responsibility as well as hard work – neither was really to his taste. And in the more recent years they had both rediscovered Egypt and found that Cairo had begun to occupy a much larger place in their thoughts than hitherto. It was not to the detriment of London, far from it, it was simply that they both felt the need of a change of scene. They wintered as often as possible in Upper Egypt, and always left it with a pang. Perhaps a new posting? He tried to lobby himself something in Alexandria, but failed. There remained a distasteful choice between the Embassy in Moscow or the one in Pekin – neither tempted him. Then the brilliant notion dawned – why not become a private man again and really take in hand his large property holdings, together with the three or four old palaces which his father had left him, for the most part tumbledown edifices in handsome gardens lying along the Nile? The single one they had done up for themselves largely satisfied their ambitions and their needs. With the others, she had started to play – for her architecture was a game, an eternal improvisation, and he loved to see her haphazard fairy-tale palaces being realised on a more modest scale in mud brick and cement. Business, too, diverted him in such a slippery capital as Cairo. He had a marked aptitude, he discovered, for bluffing and performing confidence-tricks – all business in the Middle East is a variety of poker. It was a relief, too, to finish with protocol and precedence, the ramifications of which he had found so silly. For example, the courtesy rule which forced one to keep a person of superior rank always on one's right, even walking down a street, even in a taxi. One had always to be scuttling

round people or cabs to see that this silly custom was observed – or else your visitor treated you with marked coldness,
or went downright into a diplomat's huff. Phew! All that was
over. He could play cards all night, even cheat if he wanted.
One of his first civil acts was to win a large sum (by cheating)
off Lord Galen who fancied himself as a brilliant courtier and
card-player but who was as innocent of guile as a newly
born child.

The last kilometre or so before they entered Victoria
was taken at a walking pace – why, nobody could tell him,
but it was so. This enabled Selim to walk along the platform
beside his carriage, however, and make agreeable miming
faces. The Embassy had sent a car for old time's sake, and
Selim who was acting as chargé came with it to bring him
his correspondence. He held up three magenta envelopes
which contained letters from the Princess and smiled broadly.
Selim of the quiet studious foxy expression was a Copt and
had all the reserve and resilience of that enigmatic race or
sect. He smiled rarely, and always grimly, for preference at
the discomfiture or defeat of others less wily than he. But
he was an admirable diplomat. They chatted like old friends
in the car on the way to Brown's, and the Prince delivered
his news which Selim was burning to hear. "As I told you in
my telegram from Geneva – not the one *en clair* – Lord Galen
committed an incoherence in Germany, but it was useful to
me. I have it from the highest authority that they will not
move for a while yet. These peace parleys and last-minute
attempts to find a solution will be allowed to fizzle away for a
while. Then . . ." He cut the air with his palm. "As for the
Italians they have orders to do nothing for fear of upsetting
Arab opinion. The build-up is purely a defensive act; even
the British are not unduly alarmed. They know the Italian
capacity for making mud-pies." So the talk went on, and the
gloating Selim was delighted by Hassad's lucidity and the

compactness of his mind. There were at least two long telegrams in the matter.

Meanwhile Abdel Sami Pasha, now long retired, had asked him to lunch at his club, and all that remained was to ask for official permission to send a private telegram *en clair* to his wife. There was nothing to fear about this either, in spite of the dramatic overloading of the wires due to the war situation. "The only thing," said Selim, "is, I did not ring the verger of St. Mary's – it looks like rain today." The Prince said that he would do that himself after lunch with Sami; Selim bowed his head, and after consulting a pocket memorandum said that that was all the business he had for the Prince. "How long will you stay?" he asked. "Just a couple of sunsets! After that I must get back to Provence and get the P. and O. to cart all my affairs back to Egypt. It's all arranged. And Farouk is sending the royal yacht to Marseille. No problems at all, as you see, my dear Selim."

They embraced warmly, with genuine warmth, for had they not been brothers in arms "in the Diplomatic"?

It did not take Hassad long to arrange his possessions in the Hotel and then to take a taxi to the gloomy old reception rooms of Sami's club in Burlington Street. They had not met for quite a time and the older man had become very white and frail. The Prince greeted him tenderly and said: "Excellence, you have venerable-ised and so have I." It was the polite way of dealing with the matter in Arabic. They talked shop for a while and his European news was duly delivered and debated. For his part the old man announced that the British would buy the whole cotton crop for that year – one problem less. "But," he went on sadly, "poor Egypt, so divided! Everyone is on a different side. Everyone hates the English, yes, but who loves the Germans except Maher? Farouk favours the Italians, but only because they are weaker even than us. . . . What a business!" They ate their slow lunch to the tune of a good wine. "As for you, young man," said the old diplomat, "I do not wish to reproach you, but from what I hear your life has become very . . . very *vivid*!" The word was exquisitely apt. Sami prided himself upon the fine apposite Arabic of his despatches. "Vivid is the word," the Prince admitted, and hung his head. "What does Fawzia think?" said Sami – he loved them both like his own children. The Prince said: "She gave me a terrible shock and that started everything off." He sighed heavily. Sami said: "Was she untrue to you?" The Prince reflected deeply and laid down his knife and fork before he answered. Then in a low choked voice he said: "She became a journalist."

Sami was silent – a silence of sympathy and commiseration. "Goodness!" he said at last. "Under her own *name?*" But here the Prince shook his head; at least it had been under a pseudonym. But the basic fact was there. "We drifted apart after that, I don't know why. In Geneva they tell me it is the menopause, that it will last three years, and then go away."

"That is quite different," said Sami with relief. "If it is an illness. Now my prostate . . ."

The conversation prolonged itself over coffee and cigars until it came time to say goodbye which they did with a tender sadness – who knew when they might see each other again in this uncertain world? Rain had begun to fall, a light spring rain, and the whole prospect became blurred like a window-pane. The porter's taxi drew up and the Prince got into it ordering the cabby to drive to Battersea. It was a very unpromising weather for tea-time and he hesitated a moment, wondering if he should not rather go to Simpson's for a crumpet and an Indian Tea. But he wanted to read his beloved's letters at St. Mary's, so that he could tell her so in the long cable Selim would send to her tonight. The place would most likely be locked, but if by luck the key was in the 'ole . . . It was! The creaky lock turned and admitted him to the empty church which smelt of varnish and industrial floor-polish. He tip-toed in, why he did not rightly know; perhaps so that he should not disturb old ghosts? The rain rustled on the roofs and on the water of the river. A wind shook the foliage of the trees. There was only just enough light to see. He sat in the Master's chair to read his precious correspondence which was full, not only of the unwavering affection of this model wife, but also with the delicious small-talk of family life – essential information about children's teeth and examinations and local scandals. The Nile had behaved very capriciously and had risen by fifteen feet in a night, washing away the little turret and hexagonal tower which she had been building for him – somewhere where he could "get away from everything and just sit and think". "Drat!" said the Prince. It was an old-fashioned expression he had picked up from his nanny. "Drat!"

Ruefully he thought of the period when he himself had been just as zealously faithful to her, just as single-minded. For years. Then suddenly in middle life shadows had fallen upon him; irrational fears of impotence, of glandular dis-orders, had been among them – and others less tangible. But he felt that he could not discuss such matters with anyone in any detail – unless it be a psychoanalyst of equal social rank to himself. And where to find such a person? It was a real dilemma! He had even consulted witches: to no purpose. Ordinary doctors gave him ordinary advice, prescribed tonics with unnerving names. But he hoped that they at least would be proved right, and that this period of delightful frenzy would come to an end and leave him in peace once more.

He read on slowly, voluptuously, and as he did so the evening outside suddenly lightened with some rays of un-expected sunlight. Tucking the letters back in their envelopes, which smelt of frangipani, he crossed the church with his light step and threw open the door. The whole sky was a sheet of flame! It was as if Turner himself had come back to welcome him, to give him a last sunset before the end. It might be years yet before he saw another. He did not take the heavy chair but sat upon the steps to inhale the dying light of the sun as it bobbed down to the rim of the horizon. It was like watching a stained-glass window being slowly shattered. And it was for him he felt – for them both. He took the letters out and kissed them for the sake of old memories. A line came into his head, "An Empire upon which the sun never sets." It was setting now over England! And by the same token, towards the north a balloon was going up – lurching heavily, greasily, awkwardly, up above the river. But what nonsense! The real Empire was in the primacy of the human imagination and that must always outlast the other kinds, or so he had believed. The sun was setting, the balloon was going up. He must return to his hotel and make his plans for the end of the week. He replaced the key reverently in the 'ole and walked back to the bridge.

At the hotel he found that Sami had sent his manservant with a bottle of medicine for him – for his "condition", so the visiting card said. It had a terrifying Arabic label and was clearly full of sherbet, the standard Cairo cure for impotence. It was called SFOUM, and that was roughly the noise it made when water was poured on it. One dose was enough. The rest he emptied down the sink. That night he walked a while in the park and then took a cab for half an hour to see the sights, Piccadilly, Oxford Street, the Palace. Who knew how long before he might see them again? But his long cable to his wife went off punctually, as Selim had promised.

EIGHT

Lord Galen's Farewell

DIRECTLY UPON HIS ARRIVAL IN PROVENCE LORD Galen, with a characteristic gesture, invited everyone to dinner – as one might call a committee-meeting to announce a bankruptcy. It was rather fine of him; one saw his essential kindness and innocence. He did not wish to disguise his shame; he stood in front of his own fireplace, empty in the summer save for a basket of blue sea-lavender which gathered dust but withered not, and he allowed a tear to course down his tired cheek as they came into the room, Felix, Constance, Blanford, and Sam resplendent in his "heroics", as he called his service-dress. The old man held out his two hands, asking only that they should be pressed in sympathy after his tragic blunder. Blanford found it moving so to demand the silent commiseration of friendship from them, and his heart went out to Galen. Max blew his violet nose in noisy sympathy and prepared them drinks – whisky mostly, from the ancient cut-glass decanter which had been the gift of a business friend with good taste. The Prince had not yet arrived. Galen hoped he wouldn't suddenly give his eldritch chuckle during dinner.

"I do not need to tell you about my mistake," he said meekly, without theatre, "for you know already! The Prince and I escaped just in time. I have lost a fortune and betrayed my own folk. Nobody will ever speak to me again in Manchester." He hung his head.

He had actually prepared them for this dénouement in the document he had sent Constance by way of a dinner invitation. There was nothing to say; he was most lovable at that moment.

He turned, sighing, to place his glass upon the mantel-shelf; the remains of his old cat Wombat gave a low gasp. It reminded him for a moment of the Prince's chuckle, and he frowned upon the memory. "It has been a calamity," he admitted, "and the whole thing my fault. Crest-fallen is the word. Yes, I am quite crest-fallen!" He bowed his head briefly and in some mysterious way managed to give the impression of an old rooster with bowed crest.

Shyly, from the depths of their youth, they raised their friendly glasses to toast him and to register their concern and affection; and at that moment there came the characteristic rumble of the Prince's coach as it drew up before the house, all its damascened paintwork glittering with high polish, and even its horses burnished and cockaded in the best pantomime tradition. Blanford had last seen this sort of thing at the Old Vic, when Cinderella was carted off to the ball in her transmogrified pumpkin. Quatrefages rode with the little man. He had become very friendly with the Prince, who for his part treated him with affectionate familiarity, often throwing an arm round his shoulder as he talked. ("*Il est redoutable, le Prince*," explained the lean youth to Blanford during the evening; "*il connaît tous les bordels de la région.*") It was not surprising, for the Prince like a good Egyptian had taken the precaution of calling on the Chief of Police during his first week in the city, and of inviting him for a ride in his coach. His knowledge now (compared to the limited knowledge of Quatrefages) was all but encyclopaedic. Lord Galen, however, while full of respect for the blue blood of the Prince, steadfastly refused to share the pursuits of the royal amorist. "He must have his little spree," he might say, cocking his head roguishly, "but I need my eight hours!" Nor did the Prince insist, for he had all the tact of a gentleman of the old school. He went about on his lawful occasions, secure in the knowledge that apart from the factor of diplomatic privilege

accorded him, he also enjoyed the esteem and respect of the
Chief of the Police des Moeurs, who was not above giving
him a ring at the hotel to pass the time of day. But he had, in
a relatively brief delay, accumulated a lot of new acquaintances whose appearance was not somehow altogether reassuring to Lord Galen. There is an indefinable something
which makes a gentleman who belongs to the *milieu*. It
exudes from his person – some of the heavy slothful quality
that emanates from the person of a great banker, or a promoter
of national schemes which collapse in dust, or of an international criminal, a diplomat, a Pope. The Prince's hotel was
now full of sinister silent oracular personages, who spent
hours locked up with him, discussing business or (who
knows?) pleasures as yet to be experienced. There was a
heavy air of mystery which hung about the velvet-lined
double suite of the Prince. The telephone was always going.
They smiled, these dark hirsute people, but the smile was not
full of loving kindness; the smile was like the crêpe on a coffin.

"I wonder who all these new people *are*," said old
Galen in perplexity. "I ask him but he just says they are
associates." He was a little bit put out by the Prince's discre-
tion, and also a tiny bit anxious lest promising business
mergers might be taking place just behind his back. At any
event it was past worrying about, as he had decided that, in
the light of the general war situation, his best move was to
return home and brave the critics. After all, not everyone
might be abreast of his activities; and this fearful mistake
might as yet be hushed up. But he was very sad, he lay awake
at nights and brooded; and in the deepening twilight of peace,
dissolving now all round them, he felt the renewed ache of his
missing daughter. So far all his expensive researches had
yielded nothing concrete, though at times Quatrefages
hinted that fruitful discoveries were just around the corner,
not only on this topic but on the more challenging one of the

Templar treasure – that mouth-watering project which, though he could not foresee it now, was to cause him the unwelcome attentions of the Nazis who were to prove hardly less romantic in their intellectual investments than Lord Galen himself.

But all this lay in the fastnesses of the futurity; tonight was a quiet and sedate affair, imbued with a valedictory atmosphere. He bade them welcome to one of the finest dinners one could command in the region and the amateur gourmets of Tu Duc did ample justice to it. But they were sorry when the old man said: "I have just decided to return to London the day after tomorrow. Things are slowly going from bad to worse and I feel that I must be at my post in the old country if the die is cast and England finds herself at war." It was true, he was moved by a patriotic impulse, but it was mixed with the feeling that it would be more prudent to be nearer his investments. (As a matter of fact, as the Prince explained to Quatrefages, he was not going to London at all, but to Geneva.) He was just naturally secretive, he did not want gossip. And yet, with half his mind, he felt the welling up of warm sentiments for the Old Country. Tonight he talked in a warmly human way of what might be expected to happen after the hypothetical war – for even now the whole thing seemed such madness that one half expected a last-minute compromise or perhaps an assassination to change the trend of things. "We must move steadily towards greater justice and great equality of opportunity," said the old man, appearing to be unaware that such sentiments had been expressed before. He filled them with his own pure and innocent conviction. At such times he would actually inflate his breast, almost levitate, with idealism and emotion. He wished the whole world to have a second helping. Usually this was after dinner over a *fine à l'eau* and with his Juliet drawing smooth as silk.

The Prince also seemed a little sad and withdrawn into himself; he did not like partings and there were partings in the air now – just when he had stumbled upon several very promising lines of activity with his new associates. When Galen first probed him he did not reply directly in order not to shock the old man unduly. It was also a bit from a desire to keep his new friends as far as possible to himself. He had been carefully and conscientiously studying their portraits in the police files which had been placed at his disposal by the head of the Gendarmerie, who had himself been offered a marvellous job in Cairo at an excellent salary, in order to train the Egyptian police. The whole situation was full of promise – only this wretched war threatened to compromise his initiative; if only one could be sure that France would remain free. . . . He thought of the great gallery of photographs of his new friends: Pontia, Merlib, Zogheb, Akkad. . . . Such prognathous jaws, such cuttlefish regards, such jutting forelocks, such rhinoceroid probosces! It was wonderful! Yet they all looked just like great religious figures, like Popes in mufti. He stroked their images mentally like so many imaginary cats. Perhaps he should tease Galen? He gave his dry little clicky chuckle, and saw his host stiffen with pain. "You ask about my new associates?" he said. "I wonder if you would be surprised if I told you they were all bishops and abbots and chaplains and parish priests – all *religious* men?" Galen looked really startled and the Prince released another dry click of a chuckle, though this time he softly struck his knee and followed it up with a laugh, a small laugh, aimed at the ceiling. He looked like a chicken drinking. Quatrefages, who was in the secret, gave a hardly less wounding guffaw. But Galen could now see that his leg was being pulled. "Indeed so?" he said, slightly huffed, slightly pipped.

"My dear," said the Prince, "I was choking. You must allow me my little choke from time to time. *They are all great criminals.*"

"*Criminals?*" echoed Galen with a swishing indrawn breath. "You are associating with criminals?"

"Alas," said the Prince, "I wish it *were* so, for they would be so useful. But the situation does not permit me to risk any Egyptian money on their schemes. This wretched war . . ." It was as if every thought ended in the same *cul de sac*, the brick wall of the war situation. The Prince now explained that in France, when the great criminals became too hot to hold, they were submitted to a sort of exile in one of three great provincial towns, Toulouse, Nîmes, Avignon. They were forbidden to return to Paris. But in these towns they could reside at liberty and cool their ideas. How lucky, he added, that Avignon turned out to be one of these towns. It had provided him with a host of new contacts of the right sort, and had things been different he would by now have initiated several new schemes on behalf of the Egyptian companies he represented. Galen listened with popping eye.

Delighted by his theatrical effect the Prince permitted himself to embroider a little in his almost lapidary English. "Though they are all well bred," he continued surprisingly, "yet there may be one or two who would think nothing of sentencing a rival to *death!*" He paused for a moment and then continued, "They simply have them clubbed insensible and then thrust through the medieval *oubliettes* into the Rhône!" He talked as if the river were choked with corpses. "Goodness me!" said Lord Galen, startled by his obvious relish. "What an idea!" It gave a whole new dimension to business methods.

A few more such sallies followed, but to tell the truth Blanford felt that the evening had begun to lag on in a rather spiritless fashion, as if its back had been broken by the approaching war and the impending separations. Outside the moon was high, and the vines seemed very still, with no breath of wind to stir their loaded fronds. Quatrefages became very thoughtful and sad when Galen told him that he must, in the coming week, close his office and transfer it back to London. "So soon?" he said and Galen nodded decisively. "I know it's hard," he said, "but something tells me it is time to move."

It was, and for once his intuition was correct. But how ironic it seemed that the weather was maturing towards a record harvest – never had the prognostications for the wine been so full of tremulous optimism! "I could, of course, stay until after the *vendanges*, if I wished," said the Prince. "*Après tout* Egypt is to be neutral so I could do as I please. Nevertheless I fear I must go too. The yacht can't wait for ever." He was thinking lustfully of all the up and coming young wines which were raising their proud crests upon the gentle slopes and terraces around them: and not less of all those shaggy old champions once again distilling and renewing their golden weight among the hundreds of square kilometres of vine stretching away on both sides of the swift green Rhône. The very thought made him thirsty. He suddenly became as merry as a cricket. "Must you really go home?" he asked again, and again Galen said he must. "Well, so be it," said the Prince, raising his paws to heaven; and he closed the subject with an invocation to Allah, the Decider of all things.

"But I must not overlook anything," said Lord Galen extracting from his breast pocket a tiny scarlet memorandum book which contained all his engagements written down in a minute spider-scrawl. "I must not forget to go down and play with Imhof once before I leave. It's over two months since I went, and he must get awfully lonely down there in Montfavet surrounded by lunatics and alienists. He loves a game of trains!" Trains – it was the magical draw of the model railway which the authorities had permitted Imhof to construct in the hither end of the asylum garden! Blanford had been invited once to accompany Lord Galen to see his unfortunate ex-associate in his confinement. "Because," he said, "you have a very soothing presence I find. You say little but when you talk it is with a public school accent. Imhof will like that."

It was somehow typical of the essential inconsequentiality of Galen's nature that these arresting things should be said, one after another, as if they were all of the same order of thought; for him, Blanford reflected, nothing was really unusual – it all flowed together with a phenomenological impartiality which carried the colour and tone to Galen's innocent mind. "It must be dreadful," the old man continued while they were bustling down the green lanes leading to Montfavet, nestling in its bowers of roses, "to be condemned to excrete always through a slit in the stomach wall directly into a rubber envelope. Yet he doesn't seem to mind, he is positively *cheery*. He has had a very bad time has Imhof." He went on to describe the slow downfall of his partner's reason in equally colourful terms – terms which startled Blanford out of his ordinary equability and made him glance suspiciously at Galen, wondering if perhaps all this rigmarole did not stem from some secret sense of humour. But no, he was quite serious. It was no leg-pull. He described the first symptom which betokened the overthrow of Imhof's reason. "He went into shops and asked the price of things. Then he would just give a high cracked laugh and leave. It startled people."

Imhof, it turned out, was a massively built, red-headed man who looked like a market-gardener or a station-master with his crumpled black suit and heavy cheap watch-chain. He was rather unshaven as well and smelt strongly of shag. But he gave no sign whatsoever of recognising Lord Galen, and stared at him uncomprehendingly. His model railway was, however, rather an ambitious affair, with several large stations and plenty of engines and rolling stock. But it was obviously too big for one man to enjoy and he grunted with pleasure when Lord Galen started to behave masterfully with switches and points, and make coal and passenger trains perform their various functions. They did not speak but exchanged little grunts of pleasure now as they played like a couple of absorbed children, a perfectly mated couple. They got down on their knees and directed expresses to race in various directions. No words were needed, the railway was in the hands of two experts. Blanford felt deserted. He sat for a while on a bench, and then went for a little walk among the magnificent rose gardens from which the establishment took its name. It was from one of these corners, hedged in by vivid flowers, that he saw emerge a tall frail girl with long and shapely hands. She came towards him, slowly drawing a shawl about her narrow shoulders. Her dark wavy hair framed a face which was beautiful but too thin; her shoes had very high heels. She advanced slowly with a smile and said: "So you are back? O! how was India? I am dying to ask. How calm was India? Nowadays at night I seem to hear Piers walking about in the other room, but he is never there when I run to see. Did you meet him in India? Does the smell of the magnolia still remember me supremely?" Blanford did not know how to react. Though obviously an inmate, her speech was superficially so coherent and her pale beauty so striking.

They stared at each other for a moment in silence while he hunted for a word or a phrase which might suit so strange an occasion. She smiled at him with a tender familiarity and reached out her hand to place it on his elbow, saying: "Of course you did. It is obviously there you met him." Blanford nodded, it seemed to be the right thing to do. They took a few steps and on the other side of the flower-bed he saw an open French window giving on to a room furnished with a certain old-fashioned luxuriousness. There was a tapestry on the wall, and a concert-grand in the corner. Scissors and a bowl of flowers on the terrace explained what she had been doing when the sound of his step on the gravel had disturbed her. "I knew it all the time," she said again, "I knew you would come from him, from Piers." At that moment a flight of birds passed close overhead, and at the whirr of their wings a panic fear seized her. Her face clouded, her eyes became wide and glittered with apprehension. "It is only the birds," he said, hoping to soothe her, but she gazed at him wildly and repeated hoarsely, "*Only* the birds? What are you saying?" Huddling the shawl round her thin shoulders she hurried away towards the terrace and the open window. He stood quite still until he heard the latch click home. Then he made his way thoughtfully to where the two grunting men moved about on the ground like apes, releasing their marvellous models with a high skill and a perfect enjoyment.

It was a full couple of hours before Galen came to himself; it was as if he at last awoke from a deep trance of perfect, transcendent happiness, and sighing, took his leave of Imhof who gazed unfeelingly at him, watched him move away, and then bent down resolutely once more to his trains. Nothing was said about the public school accent. There had been little chance to use it, so mute had been the harmony of the two train-lovers, so deep their concentration. As they drove away Galen said, sighing with repleteness, "Poor old Imhof. I so often think of him. He made just one big miscalculation and pouf! it played on his reason. A fearful bloomer! Shall I tell you? It was during a water shortage in England, a scandal. All the newspapers went on about it, and the Government asked people to save water as much as possible. Then the press said that the Englishman's bath was the reason and gave statistics about the millions of tons of water we waste. It was here that Imhof got the idea of buying all those bidets – hundreds of thousands of them. He said

that if England could be got to accept the bidet we could all
make do with one bath a week. The saving in water would be
immense. I forget the details but he spent millions on advertising his idea, and at the same time, not to be caught short,
in buying up all the bidets he could find. A massive investment
all lined up in warehouses on the coast waiting to invade
across the channel." He gave a sad chuckle. "They are still
there. He seemed not to realise that one of the hardest things
to do is to get a national habit modified. Bidets!"

Remembering this occasion, Blanford reflected com-
passionately upon Imhof and his bidets while the old man
thoughtfully circumcised a cigar and struck a match to light
it. He leaned back now in his chair and smiled round at them;
he had expiated his guilt by his sincerity and now felt calmly
himself again, though of course still saddened by the whole
affair. Constance and Sam said little, and it was assumed that
they were preoccupied with each other and deaf to the
appeals of mere sociability. But she was filled also with a
weight of apathy and weariness which astonished even herself. They were like people living upon the slopes of a volcano,
Vesuvius or Etna, resigned to the knowledge that one day,
nobody knew when, the whole of the world they knew
would be blown apart by forces beyond their imagining. And
yet they continued to respect social forms like automata, like
the Romans of the silver age, when the Goths were already
gnawing at the walls of the civilised world. As if he had
intuited this feeling of remorseful apathy in her, Lord Galen
patted her hand and sighed deeply. "If this goes on," he said,
and everyone knew what he meant by that, "why, money will
become quite worthless." He looked round the table. "And
it's a great pity. It has given us so much pleasure. Indeed
there is something very inspiring about money." The word
was strangely chosen, but one could feel what he meant.
Money, thought poor Felix, working his toes in his dinner

shoes. He had contracted a hammer-toe from his solitary walking about the town. Money – if only he could get his hands on some. Blanford himself had a twinge of panic. "I suppose all investments will collapse?" he said with some alarm. The Prince nodded. "It depends," he said, "some will. But if you have armament shares. . . ." Lord Galen now called to Max to wind up the old horn gramophone and set off the traditional *Merry Widow* waltz which closed all his dinner parties. They took themselves to the quiet terrace where they were supplied with drinks hard and soft and tobacco for Sam's pipe. It was curious that no mention had been made of Livia, and Blanford wondered suddenly if they knew any-thing about her – was it perhaps a tactful silence? But then on the other hand nobody had mentioned Hilary either. The moon shone upon their glasses. There was no wind, but away over the hills there came a tremor of summer lightning like a distant bombardment going on, which must herald one of the thunderstorms which traditionally ushered in the harvest and the autumn. The Prince asked Blanford whether he would not like to visit Egypt. "I would be happy to engage you as a personal private secretary if that were the case. You would live in the Palace and meet the best people, the *top-notch*. It is a very picturesque land."

The proposal was startling and novel and tickled the youth's fancy. He asked for time to consider. As yet his own personal affairs were not sufficiently in order, or so he felt, to embark on what promised to be so exciting and enriching a career as that of social secretary to a prince.

Now, turning aside, the Prince addressed himself to Felix Chatto. They took a turn up and down the balcony and on the lawn, linked arm in arm. Felix was very flattered to be treated with the deference due to a senior diplomat, as if he was in possession of state secrets of the highest importance. The Prince gave a résumé of the political and military state of things and asked him to comment upon it with a becoming modesty and a keen attention. Rising to the occasion Felix did his best to present the balanced analysis so dear to the hearts of diplomats and leader writers. As usual it all depended on If, When and But. The Prince thanked him warmly. "In a few days," he said, "I am going to have a little *spree*. After Lord Galen goes. Do not be offended if I do not send you an invitation, my dear. It will be rather an advanced sort of spree and you have a professional reputation to look after in this beautiful but somewhat sinister little town. But don't take offence. You will understand everything when you talk to your friend Quatrefages." But Felix needed no briefing, he could imagine very well what the little spree would entail. "I must pay back some social debts to my new friends," explained the little man, and the young consul saw in his mind's eye all those faces like crocodiles and ant-eaters and baboons, all dressed in dark suits with improbable ties and fingers with black hair sprouting through their rings. "I shall quite understand," he said seriously, "and I take it as a compliment, sir, that you should bother to explain to me." The Prince squeezed his arm and gave a ghost chuckle.

They broke up relatively early that evening, pervaded by a sense of weariness and loss. Perhaps because he felt that this was probably the last occasion they would meet round his table, old Lord Galen tried to infuse the occasion with a touch of valedictory ceremony. He called for a toast to the Prince and to Egypt which was willingly drunk, and which, by its unexpectedness, pleased the Prince very much indeed. He for his part replied by calling for a toast to His Majesty the King of England. He sprang up as he uttered the words with alacrity and a genuine enthusiasm. He had been received at Court with great kindness, which had seemed to him quite natural and unaffected. Besides, one of the younger members of the Royal Household had elected herself his mentor and

Muse. What he admired so much, he told Chatto, was that in England you could do almost anything without getting into the newspapers. You felt so safe, while in Egypt those dreadful socialist and communist papers were always on the lookout for scandal. "They don't like the upper class to have a little spree. Why are Marxists such spoilsports? I have never been able to understand it, especially when you think of the morals of Engels."

The car came, with a tearful Max at the wheel, and they all said goodbye to the Prince with a genuine pang. When would they all meet again? Nobody could tell, nobody could say.

The inhabitants of Tu Duc took their leave with Max in the old rumble-dusty vehicle of Lord Galen; Quatrefages and Felix, since they were going into the town like the Prince, were offered the trip in his coach. The journey passed in friendly silence; the Prince spent most of it exploring the cavities between his teeth with a silver toothpick of great elegance. He said no more about his spree until the changing tone of the horses' hooves upon the cobbled avenues of the town told them that they were almost home. "The little spree I spoke of," he told Quatrefages, "will be at the end of the week, perhaps when Lord Galen has left the country." Quatrefages asked if he could be of service in the matter and received the reply that everything was going to be arranged at an official level. "It is much safer that way. But I hope you will honour us with your presence. I think the occasion will be a memorable one – in all this fearful war-indecision which prevents us all from thinking or planning. They ring me up all the time from Abdin Palace with rumours and scares, telling me I must return. The palace yacht is already at Marseille waiting with steam up. But I think all this is quite premature."

The others elected to be dropped at Tubain, and to walk

the rest of the way in the deep moonlit dust, under the long avenues of planes and limes. And in silence for a change. Not necessarily the silence of despondency, but a silence which held the whole world of futurity in solution, as it were; the silence in which one waits for an orchestra to strike out its opening statement. Constance linked her little finger to theirs and walked with her face turned upward towards the moon. On the way, flickering among the trees like a firefly, came a bicycle-lamp which fluttered towards them and stopped. It was the son of the post-master of Tubain who had been up to the house to deliver a late telegram, and found nobody in. It was for Sam and they all knew what must be in it. It was only the date of his recall which was in question. He tipped the boy and said goodnight to him before opening the slip of blue paper. Blanford struck a match which gave a yellow hovering splash of light sufficient for him to read the contents. He gave a sigh. "I leave on Sunday," he said, in a tone of elation; it was understandable. It was far better to know for certain – at least one could prepare for the event. Yes, they all felt better armed against the future this way. They would have a few more days together before the parting. Constance was going back to Geneva for her work – she would quit Sam in Paris. Blanford would stay on for a while with his little car (which was at present in a garage, being repaired and serviced), and wait upon events. Never had he felt more useless, more undecided about his direction. The Egyptian project was most tempting; but would a war not qualify it? He presumed he would be called up, and as he could not conscientiously object, he would soon find himself in uniform like Sam.

They crossed the garden in single file, under the cork-oaks with their snowy crests, and turned the creaking key in the tall front door. The familiar smell of the house greeted them in darkness; it smelt of long forgotten meals, of herbs and of garden flowers, it smelt of cobwebs and expired fume of candles. All at once it seemed a pity to go to bed without a nightcap. In the kitchen they lit a paraffin lamp and by its mild unhovering yellow light sat down around the scrubbed and sanded table to brew tea and to play a hand of gin rummy. Blanford opted for a glass of red wine instead, however, despite the lateness of the hour and his general abstemiousness. It was late when they at last bade one another goodnight, and even now with such a fine moonlight outside it seemed a shame to go to bed; so he walked down to the water and took a silent, icy swim, letting the rushing wings of the water pass over him like rain. Closing his eyes he seemed to see in memory all the black magnetism of the dark light which shone out of the earth, whether among these trees and vines or out of the bald stone garrigues and pebbled hills with their crumbling shale valleys. Among these rambling dormitories of shards Van Gogh had hunted the demon of his black noonday sun – and found it in madness. Only when one was here did one realise how truthful to the place was his account of it. He was beginning to realise the difference between the two arts, painting and writing.

Painting persuades by thrilling the mind and the optic nerve simultaneously, whereas words connote, mean something however approximate and are influenced by their associative value. The spell they cast intends to master things – it lacks innocence. They are the instruments of Merlin or Faust. Painting is devoid of this kind of treachery – it is an innocent celebration of things, only seeking to inspirit and not coerce. Pleased with these somewhat rambling evaluations he scampered back to the house and to bed, shivery with cold all of a sudden, so that he was forced to climb between the sheets with his socks on. He would have liked to read for a moment or two, so delicious was the moonlit air outside, but sleep at last insisted. He sank to the pillow as if beheaded.

Down below, in the sleeping town, the pro-consul

paced out his long penitential walk from bastion to dark
bastion; the moonlight only emphasised the shadows, creating
great caves of pure darkness out of which he dreamed that
some brilliant gipsy might emerge and pounce on him; but
more likely it would be a footpad. His fingers tightened upon
the little scout penknife he carried on his person, not so much
for security as for tedious pro-consular uses, such as cutting up
string to make parcels. The prospect of the war filled him,
strangely enough, with elation which was somewhat shame-
making. Naturally he would never have confessed to such a
thing publicly, for he wished nobody harm and was personally too much of a coward to hanker for firearms – he was in
fact rather gun-shy. But the reality of war if it came. . . .

If he had been guilty of imitating the rather pretentious
formulations of Blanford he might have told himself that the
reality of war (death) if it came would render back once more
all the precious precariousness of life which had become stale
with too much safe living. It was not a question of swimmers
into cleanness leaping *à la* Brooke, but simply a breath of
fresh air in a twice-breathed suffocating age. If it came he
would join up at once. He would welcome all the restrictions
which went with the uniform. He would glory in the savage
discipline, for too much freedom gives you vertigo – you
are looking out into nothingness all of a sudden. Nothingness – your own portrait! Much later he would realise that
this feeling was echoed by the whole of the Nazi Youth!

Apart from that, he had started a course of physical
culture with some vague notion of fitting himself for the fray.
He read a cheap pamphlet on yoga and realised that he was
walking in the wrong way, his breathing rhythms were at
odds with his steps. This made him walk in a self-conscious,
rather stilted fashion as he remembered the instructions of
his pamphlet. "Ordinary people breathe eighteen times a
minute but in the best yoga practice you can get down to

less than ten and that will do. But three a minute is really good!" Three a minute? He found himself counting the paving stones and holding in his breath, only to express it in a swish when the strain became too much. Surely this was not right.

But at dawn even he found relief in his weariness, hurrying home along the empty streets now drained even of the moonlight. Time was still there, a slowly discharging wound which the daylight would stanch. But first a little rest. He too climbed into bed and slept, but not before passing in review the sleep of the others which he could picture so clearly. Blanford all tousled, with his head under the pillow, Sam snoring, Constance invisible. Somewhere quite nearby the Prince lay, with a small piece of muslin over his face to defend him against moths – he dwelt in mortal terror of being eaten up by a moth, like an old tapestry. He had wrapped his one false tooth in silver paper, to avoid swallowing it in his sleep. It lay beside him with his beautiful ivory-covered Holy Book. Up there in Balmoral Max snoozed in a sort of cupboard which smelt of dead mice. The poor little secretary preferred a hammock in the garden. Lord Galen lay in his great bed all serene. He wore a night-shirt with frilled white cuffs which he got from Mannering's. It had his monogram on the breast. He slept with his mouth open and from time to time squirmed out a great snore which might be phonetically transcribed as "Gronk-phew"; Felix remembered the Prince saying, "He is such a good man that he is prone to be *spoofed*." And now war was coming.

> Once it was Bread and Circuses,
> Now it is all Dread and Carcases.

Where had he read that?

Yes, Blanford slept, but in his excitement he woke early while the others were still asleep, and tiptoed to the kitchen to make himself coffee. This he took back to bed where, lying luxuriously half asleep, he sent his roving mind as Felix had done, to visit his friends in their several sleeps and to try, by projection, to realise them more fully. Did he know what they felt or was he simply privileged to imagine – the writer's illness? He hardly knew. Yet it was so clear to him that the girl who slept in the afterglow of Sam's embraces was already ahead of them all in a certain domain whose real existence they hardly as yet realised. As for Sam, still drunk on the huge honeycomb of these first kisses, there seemed little beyond death and separation to consider, to evaluate. He had suddenly started to realise that he was now dying, quite softly dying. Mind you it would take time, but it was quite irrevocable. Most people hid their faces and refused to look this moment of realisation in the eyes. He slept on triumphantly in a cone of silence. The realisation itself was a victory, and it had nothing to do with the war. It would have come anyway, simply because of the contact with Constance, she had grown him up, though he would have been hard put to it to describe just how and why.

Even the notion of death offered a sort of hidden glee, it had been mastered! This whole absurd and mysterious business had been sparked off by a simple conversation in which the girl had said, "It will seem to you quite mad but from early on in my adolescence I seemed to have set myself a sort of task. I was trying to want only what happened, and to part with things without regret. It made me sort of on equal terms with death – I realised that it did not exist. I felt I had begun to participate in the inevitable. I knew then what bliss was. I started to live in a marvellous parenthesis. I also knew that it wasn't right to know so much so young. . . ." The effect of these words on Sam was indescribable. He was struck dumb. It was as if he understood exactly what she meant, but that the words had by-passed his reason. Later, much later, she would be able to add to this in a letter to Blanford by saying: "An overwhelming thirst for goodness is a dangerous thing and should be discouraged. I hunted not an ethos but the curve of a perfect licence charged with truth – however disconcerting pure truth might be! I was an alchemist without knowing it. Idiot!"

There they were, sleeping all, quite unaware that their dreams were models and outlets for their future acts. He had fallen asleep again, Blanford, and this time it took Sam an effort to wake him. "No time to lose," said Sam, "these last few days are precious. To horse!"

In some old book of aphorisms he had been surprised by the observation: "A superlative death costs nothing. The lesser ones are the more expensive." Was it Montaigne? He could not remember.

NINE

The Spree

THE PRINCE'S LITTLE SPREE PROMISED TO BE OF SUCH royal magnitude that the excited Quatrefages, when he got wind of the details from the inhabitants of their brothel – their common brothel, so to speak – at once borrowed a bicycle and scorched (the metaphor is an exact one, for it was at noon) out to Tu Duc with news of it. It must somehow be seen, he said, despite protocol considerations; even if only from afar. He himself was, of course, actually invited, but out of considerations of delicacy the Prince had decided to omit their names from his list of matchless crooks – perhaps just as well. But ... he had rented the whole Pont du Gard, and with it the whole of the ancient Auberge des Aubergines which abutted thereon. He was already busy transforming the place to suit his notions of how a spree should work.

The Auberge was a strange, rambling old place, admirably suited to this kind of initiative, with its collection of Swiss chalets hugging the cliffs of the Gardon, buried in plane-shade, leaning practically over the green water. Though it was not a residential hotel it had a series of large interconnecting upper rooms which in summer managed to accommodate tourist groups or clubs devoted to archaeology or Roman history who selected the monument as a point of rendezvous, and sometimes camped out in the neighbouring green glades along the river. The cuisine was what had made it famous, and this was, of course, an important part of the spree. But it was not all, for the Prince, who was a man of the world, knew his France well. He knew that in this spirited Republic any citizen may call upon the *préfet* of any region to floodlight a notable monument at a purely nominal cost, simply to grace his dinner. When he himself had been young and madly in love with his Princess Fawzia he had offered her dinner here, served on the bridge itself by his liveried waiters; just the two of them, quite alone. He always remembered this early part of his married life with emotion. And now the great golden span of the Roman aqueduct was going to hover above their revels, its honey-gold arches fading into the velvet sky of Provence. His heart leaped in his breast when he thought of it. He became absolutely concave with joy. No detail must be left to chance.

Quatrefages had participated in some of the discussions as a friend and helper, and was able to attest to the Prince's thoroughness. He retailed these scenes with amusing irony, even imitating the Prince's accent to perfection. When he had asked, "*Et le gibier?*" the Prince had given him a reply straight from the heart of Cairo: "*Ne t'en fais pas, Bouboule,*" which came from some old musical comedy which time had encrusted in the Cairo soul. His henchmen were already out on their errands. Even the *gibier*, the game, was coming to the party from several different corners of the land, mostly Marseille and Toulouse. The Prince had announced that he liked the girls to be *plantureuses, bien en chair*, which explained the huge collection of cartoons after Rubens which finally arrived at the Pont du Gard. Whenever had one seen so fine a collection of sleepy sugar-dolls in all their finery, and their war-paint, a-jingle with doubtful jewelry and glinting with *toc* – the very perfection of the Arabian imagination? It was clear that the old Prince had been stirred by inherited memories of the Khedival entertainments of Cairo a century ago.

Quatrefages was so engrossed in his exposition that he did not hear the sound of the approaching car in which Felix sat bolt upright in a straw hat looking like a rabbit, and tremulous with indecision. He was still not fully confident of this steel animal. Now everything had to be repeated for his benefit, and he listened with a slight pang of envy, simply because it sounded such a picturesque notion to give a party there, in the heart of the country. Preparations were already advanced; period furniture from all over Avignon, rented at ruinous prices, was being bundled into lorries and trundled out to the Auberge. In actual fact, they would only be about a hundred strong. "But the fifty girls are all *en or massif,*" said Quatrefages, involuntarily licking his lips. "Marseille has outdone itself to provide sumptuous dollies."

"But where do we come in?" said Constance, who was also beginning to feel that they ran the risk of missing a treat, purely by being regarded as too virtuous to participate in it. "Indeed?" said Blanford. Quatrefages chuckled and said, "The roads after eight o'clock will be closed to motor-traffic by the gendarmerie at the request of His Highness. Obviously you won't be able to get in. But I have an idea. You can watch it all from the top of the Pont du Gard – the ballroom windows open on that side and you can see in. I know because once when I was spying on a girl who I thought was doing me down I came there and sat on the top with glasses. She was dining with a man I suspected. I saw them both quite clearly. If you take those little opera glasses you have, you will also see everything from the top."

"Yes, but to get to the top . . . ?"

He gave an impatient shrug of the head and took out a fountain pen. On the local newspaper he swiftly outlined a sketch map of the country immediately surrounding the aqueduct – a drawing which stirred their memories at once for they had walked here. "Do I need to go on?" he asked. "Here is the sunken road near Vers. You climb that slope following the broken arches and the masonry. Then suddenly you turn a corner and . . ."

Yes, you walked out into the sky, and the great crown of the aqueduct with its deep water trench lay beneath you. You walked out, in fact, upon the top of it as if upon a bridge.

"I see," said Blanford thoughtfully. "Yes, it would be possible."

"Of course it would be possible," said the impatient clerk, irritated by these slow English lucubrations, this slow chewing of the cud. "You would have a ringside seat."

"When is it to be?"

"Tomorrow. You will *never* regret it!" His solemnity was amusing.

He went on with his exposé of the details and they could see that indeed this was to be no mean entertainment, but one worthy of such a splendid setting and ... so, well, gallant a company. Yes, they really must go! If nothing else it would take their minds off the perpetual nibbling of thoughts and doubts about the war and about the impending separations. How well such an event would have rounded off a normal summer holiday, how well it would have suited the time too, situated on the cusp of the harvest, with the closing festivals of wine and bullfighting to look forward to! Never mind. Go they must.

So they set off from the house after dinner the next day, by a low and rather famished moon – late in her exaltation and fast in her setting; a deep autumnal haze lay over the land which hereabouts looked so Tuscan in its rounded forms and paint-brush cypresses, its hamlets and villages all to human scale, its rivers small but sturdy and full of trout. Soon the greenery would give place to the more dusty uplands of the garrigue, all stone and shale, and for much of the time regions both parched and waterless. They followed the instruction of Quatrefages carefully so as to avoid the traffic restrictions of the gendarmerie. When they reached Remoulins, for example, they did not cross the bridge – they saw lights and gendarmes on the further side. They turned right, as if for Uzès, and rolled along deserted roads which fringed the river bank, swerving from side to side to follow broad sweeps of the Gardon. The Pont du Gard was already lit up for the feast, its great bronze form lying in the sky like a stranded whale. Underneath it, on a flat mossy glade among the rocks, the Prince had caused a brilliant marquee to be run up, where he sat on one of his pantomime chairs to receive his guests. They were disgorged by their cars among the groves of willow and walked the thrilling fifty yards or so freckled by the light of reflectors, advancing dramatically towards the theatrical hovering aqueduct above.

The Auberge was warmly lighted also, and the whole upper storey had been converted into a sort of harem, with its walls covered with priceless rugs on hire or loan, and cupboards and coffee-tables and filigreed mirrors fitting enough for the Grand Seraglio itself. All the antiquaries of Avignon had contributed their mite to this impressive display. Pinned to a curtain was a beautifully lettered panel which read LADY BOUDOIR POUDRERIE WATER CLOSET. It was comprehensive, it left nothing to chance. On the morrow Quatrefages was to steal it and give it to Blanford who attached it to the outdoor earth closet at Tu Duc, being always glad to point out the felicity of the Cairo French, for "poudrerie" means not "powder-room" so much as "powder-magazine". The great open hearth of the Auberge was ablaze with dry vine-tendrils, crackling and snapping away like the horns of enormous snails. Somewhere in the inner heart of the establishment an orchestra was tuning up softly, suggesting the presence of a dance floor or a ballroom. Everything was in hand.

In order not to over-complicate matters they had elected to travel in one car, despite the crush; this had the further advantage that Felix was able to loan the consular car to his invited friend for the trip. Quatrefages in *tenue de ville* looked splendid, though somewhat nervous. He had actually seen a few of the arrivals from Marseille who were to be accommodated on the morrow at a hotel. He was enthusiastic. "They all look as if their periods were overdue – it gives women a wonderful neurotic magnetism. I saw at least two superb dollies like great caterpillars, covered in pollen." Felix was a bit shocked by the relish of his friend. Quatrefages had drunk a whisky or two with the Prince's major-domo and was in a fine state of exaltation. "Remember the message of the caryatids?" he asked, shaking his finger at the abashed consul into whose car he had now inserted himself. "A girl should always try to look ever so slightly pregnant." It was an old chestnut, invented in the past by Blanford and which had tickled him enough to stay in his memory. "Whatever happens, dear Felix," he said, "don't miss it."

So here they were bowling through the sweet glades of cherries and mulberries; from time to time the brilliant aqueduct emerged upon the blackness to their left, and was then swallowed up by the greenery. They could hear the river grinding its teeth down below to their right. Then came the left turning which normally would carry them right up on to the bridge itself, and here stood a policeman with a pious air and a white barrier which he had placed across the road. But they now pretended they were heading for Uzès and passed him by with a wave, to curl down the long avenue of cool planes until the sunken road by Vers came up and here they drove most carefully on an appalling surface until they came to an olive grove which crowned the slopes. Here it was not possible to continue by car and they started to walk on the shaly slopes among the snatching bristles of holm-oak and thorn. It was harder to navigate in the darkness than by daylight.

The hill was a wilderness of dividing paths and fire breaks; but ahead of them was the furry white light of the reflectors and they navigated upon that until, with the sudden surprise of actors who walk unwittingly out upon a lighted stage, they reached the culvert which marked the first arch. And here began the circumspect descent upon the crown of the aqueduct with its metre-deep gulley – the channel through which the spring water of Vers was conveyed to Nîmes in Roman times. Here they could perch like birds in a high tree and rest their elbows on the side of the trench, to gaze down upon the princely revels below. The idea of the opera glasses was also a brainwave. They had originally been bought for the performances of the Opéra de Marseille, but lately had been much out of use, lying about the house. Now they trained them like sharpshooters upon the Auberge below, and found that, as Quatrefages had said, they had an excellent view of half the great dining-room, one side of which opened into a sort of sun verandah.

The proceedings had already begun with a certain regal formality; the male guests, who were all unaccompanied, had been received in the pavilion and had been offered an aperitif of the Prince's devising – possibly laced with cantharides? Quatrefages indeed wondered about the matter as he gulped down his portion of the fiery colourless brew. The company looked even stranger at night than by daylight. They were all dressed in dark suits which were uncomfortably warm for the time of the year, and they gave the impression of being weighed down by their cravats and heavy rings, and greased hair. At this stage there was no sign of the women. But at last, when the assembly was complete, the Prince beckoned to his guests to follow him, and led them, as if they had been a cricket team, through the glades towards the Auberge, which had stayed all this time in almost complete darkness – just a candle-glimmer here or there which

betokened movement. The Prince held in his hand his little
gilt fly-swash with its length of white mare's tail hanging
from it. It was rather like a conductor's baton. With it he
tapped on the closed doors of the Auberge and they sprang
open at his behest. At the same moment the whole dining-
room was flooded with light and the advancing cohort of
guests gave a collective gasp of pleasure. To the right of each
male guest there was to be a *naked lady of pleasure*! Those
already in place clapped and shouted and vociferated in
ladylike fashion as the dark-suited men advanced with a
thirsty air, each to find his place card with his name upon it.

No phantasy had been spared, it was clear. Constance
chuckled almost continuously at the scene as her glasses
picked up now one corner and now another of the ballroom.
The men, as befitted their superior sex, sat on chairs with
high gilded backs, like thrones; the girls upon velvet piano-
stools. The Prince dominated the table as a good host should.
Behind his chair stood the three dignitaries of high office
clad in the most wonderful service robes of scarlet and gold,
with green facings. One was the official food-taster, who would
not be pressed into service tonight; the other two, one on
each side of his chair, were bearing on their right wrist a
tall hooded falcon. The Prince's rank entitled him to this
dignity, just as a Scottish aristocrat is entitled to his bagpiper.
The dinner began with a swirl of conversation and popping
and waiting . . . a little sticky as yet, despite the fiery aperitif.

The men looked like shy honey-bears at Sunday
school. "But not for long, I don't suppose," said Constance,
who had voiced this thought to the others. The scene was
full of variety and charm. In the bloom of the candles the
women looked as sumptuous and grandiose as the requirements had stipulated. "*J'aime les grands balcons arrondis*,"
the Prince had said, perhaps with his guests in mind. And
here were the great rounded balconies in all their splendour,

covered in fresh violets and jewels and scented in a thousand extravagant ways. The merriment was slow to emerge but it was just as well, for this sort of dinner-party, in which so large a part of the thrill is the marvellous food, should begin on a note of attentive reverence. This fête was no exception. They were, after all, Frenchmen, which meant that they had an innate culture of the table, and also of the human heart and person. Even the most curmudgeonly and bearish of the guests was a born appreciator of *la bonne chère* and turned his eyes to heaven from time to time with ecstasy; some kissed away bunched fingers in the direction of the *cuisine* and the cook. With the tucking of napkins into collars a new ease asserted itself and the conversation flowed in harmony with the excellent wine. Quatrefages, who was not particularly attracted to balconies, found himself with a big shy round dolly with a vulgar laugh, but with all the right instincts for she pressed his knee throbbingly and gave him infinite seafruit to sup. Slightly fuddled as he was, he nevertheless realised that he had never in his experience eaten food so exquisite, yet so simple. The shade of Brillat-Savarin must have turned mumbling in his grave to bless the table of the Prince. So exceptional was it, that he thought for a moment of saving the menu to bestow on Constance, and then he realised that it was useless – it would be like confiding the programme-notes of some superlative performance to a friend. What could they imagine from such a bare recital of the elements of this divine repast?* Where the devil had the old boy found the champagne? Lost in wonder and ecstasy, he allowed himself to be tweaked and tickled and fed like a Strasbourg goose. The watchers on the top of the aqueduct were vastly amused by his beguiling air of helpless content.

It was long, the banquet, but so full of fascinating detail that they were completely absorbed in the watching; towards

* Nevertheless see Appendix.

the end some scattered little sorties took place, to enable couples to dance a stately measure or two on the dark balconies outside. These took place with a slightly absurd formalism, which suggested that the dancers were none too sure of their feet. The orchestra remained invisible, but waltz and tango and "slows" figured on a repertoire which was calculated not to prove too tiring for people after such a mammoth dinner. But to the regret of the watchers the lights progressively became more and more discreet – one last cavernous flare as from the mouth of hell took place with the *crêpes flambées*, that was all, which conferred on each hairy face the kind of dark light which Rembrandt has marked as his own. It was a tremendous success, the snapping of paper favours and even – a stroke of genius – the wearing of paper hats which pushed the scene from the plain picturesque to the absolutely side-splitting. Elderly rats in strange paper hats, waving their cigars at the universe! What a marvellous touch of lunacy was conferred by this simple touch. And the dancing became a trifle more treacly – the ladies swathing themselves more amply, more amorously about their partners, or spreading their arms wide like galleons in full sail – or combine harvesters, to select a metaphor by Felix who found it more appropriate to the approaching *vendanges*.

So things went on in a slightly more sentimental key – even the Prince trod a bird-like measure, but his affections seemed to vary a good deal; several large unplucked-looking girls were competing for his attentions. All that money! All that food! "He has found another lovely word," said Felix. "He says 'spiffing' when he means 'top-hole'."

Their spirits began to droop a little – perhaps because of the notion that the visible part of the revels was finished. Constance thought lovingly of the Thermos of hot wine and the sandwiches which awaited them in the car. Then suddenly the universe was blown out and the whole darkness of the sky came down on them as forcibly, as palpably almost, as a lid. They could not even see each other and the distance between them and the revels seemed suddenly to have lengthened, so that they felt miles high in the sky, seated as if in an aeroplane. Caution also was indicated, for a frolic up here in the darkness could cost a life or a limb. They waited to let their eyes accustom themselves to the dark, but before this happened another kind of light assailed them.

From below there was a succession of bangs and strings of coloured snakes hissed up into the air around them, only to spit out their hot coloured stars and plumes and subside groundward again. They scored their beautiful trails on that dark lambent sky, and their stuttering, pattering trajectory carried them right over the bridge on which they lay. It was relatively short as firework displays go, but the colours and forms were choice, while down below, at water level, fizzed some grand yellow Catherine wheels, and a set piece which looked somewhat like a *santon* of Provence eating olives at the pace of St. Vitus. From afar off they heard the distant clapping and cheering, and now, since the new darkness seemed to be permanent, they crawled back along the stone tunnel and up onto the hill. It was a bit of a scramble, but once on the other side they made better time with the aid of a torch. It had been worth it!

A dense dew had been falling, ripe with the premonitions of the harvest; it dripped from the quiet olive under which they had parked the car. How welcome the wine was. Yet a heavy mist hemmed in the further visibility. As they drank their drink there appeared a sort of secondary cloud, moving up the hill towards them, and they recognised the character-istic clatter of hooves and tonking of bells which betokened a shepherd, who came across to get a light for his cigarette, and was glad of a sip of wine. He spoke in a sing-song southern French. As he puffed and warmed his palms with the cup, his dogs crouched beside him attentively, and the frieze of sheep strung out on the hill behind. Their hooves bruised the sage and set up a dense perfume in the windless orchard. The old man said: "The War has begun," but his tone was one of such incomprehension and unconcern that they could hardly take it seriously. How did he know? He had heard it at the Mairie at midnight. But in a land so poorly equipped with wirelesses rumour makes do for fact to a great extent – and this particular rumour had been often encountered already. And yet . . . It was disturbing. They said goodbye to him, shaking his rough hand, and piled back into their car which took some moments to start.

The heavy ground mist cleared after they had negotiated Remoulins and were safely launched upon the road to Avignon; for about ten minutes there was some disposition to doze, but as they fronted the last hillside before the famous bridge, they all came full awake again and began to debate whether to go home, or whether to go into the town in search of coffee and croissants and some truthful account of what was happening in the outer world. "It's too late to go to bed, and too early to get up," said Blanford, "and Felix is the only one who feels normal at this hour." As a matter of fact Felix was elated – almost the whole night had passed in delightful fashion for once, and here he was, happy and wide awake – only a little disquieted by the peasant's remark about the war having begun.

To town then, but Avignon itself was as dead as a doornail – even the bakers had not started to warm their ovens, while no cafés were open, not even at the Gare. They tried a last chance and crossed Les Balances on foot, skirting its sordid and gipsy-ridden tenements, worthy more of Cairo than of a European city. They dumped the car at the Papal square. But here too, alas, the little Bar de la Navigation was shut fast. They began to feel dispirited.

But in one of the side-streets near the ancient tanneries with their foul network of canals, they heard the throbbing and pulsing note of a powerful engine or turbine. It sounded like the engine of a ship. "It's an old friend," explained Felix, "come and have a look at it! It follows me in my wandering at night, in the first week of the month every six months it 'does' this quartier during the hours of darkness. Then it moves on round the clock." It looked to them like a variety of fire-engine, and it bore the arms of the town painted in gold on its muddy flanks. "What is it?" asked Constance and Felix replied with a knowledgeable air, "It's the *pompe à merde*. You see, there has never been any main drainage, here all the houses have pits, dry pits for their only sanitation. Well, these are sucked out during the night by this old mastodon of a thing. They are all proud of it. They call it 'Marius'."

Mastodon was the word, though it had a long rubber proboscis like that of an elephant which had entered a front door and descended into the cellar where the privies were. The sucking and slobbering were fearful to hear, and the shuddering and drubbing of the pumps fearful to behold – it was like a clumsy animal, sweating and straining at its task, Blanford thought. "It is sucking out the intellectual excrement of the twentieth century in a town which was once Rome. The dry pit of the human imagination perpetually filling up again with the detritus of half-digested hopes and fears, of desires and resolutions." It was a bad sign he thought, frowning, to see metaphors everywhere; though he was not the only one. Constance said softly, "An anal-oral machine most appropriate to our time. Like the Freudian nursery rhyme."

But here afflicted by a sudden modesty she decided not to repeat it aloud; she would whisper it to herself instead.

When the bowel was loaded
The birds began to sing;
Wasn't that a dainty dish
To set before the King?

There was a light in a nearby bistro where the driver of "Marius" was already ordering his coffee and a small marc to drive off the excrementitious odours with which he was forced to live. Well, it was a profession, just like any other.... The others joined him at the *zinc* but Blanford stayed behind, fascinated by the old machine sucking and slobbering its way through the centuries. On one side, the old wrinkled dawn was coming up in coral and nacre, and down here at the same time the stench of excrement was spreading over the whole quartier. Soon it would be time to wind up the rubber hose and drive "Marius" away to its stable, for this kind of sump-cleansing was only done during the night – for the sake of decency, he supposed.

But now he was really tired. A quotation came into his mind. *Inter faesces et urinam nascimur.* Yes, it was appropriate enough. It had been, after all, Augustine's "City of God", transplanted once upon a time to this green and innocent country.

Appendix

* page 18
Full text of the 12 Commandments

1. *Faut pomper la momie allégoriquement.*
2. *Faut situer le cataplasme de l'art chauve.*
3. *Faut analyser le carburant dans les baisers blondes.*
4. *Faut faire faire, faute de mieux et au fur et à mesure faire forger.*
5. *Faut oindre le gorgonzola du Grand Maître.*
6. *Faut respecter le poireau avec son regard déficitaire.*
7. *Faut scander les débiles sentimentales avec leurs décalcomanies.*
8. *Faut sauter le Pont Neuf pour serrer la main d'une asperge qu'on trouve belle.*
9. *Faut caresser inéluctablement la Grande Aubergine de notre jour.*
10. *Faut pondre des lettres gardées en instance, tombées en rebut, Poste Restante, l'Amour O crème renversée.*
11. *Faut dévisager la réalité à force de supposer.*
12. *Faut cracher les tièdes et décendre les incohérents.*

* page 210
Readers who remark a slight divergence between so-called "real" history and the order of events adopted in this novel will, it is hoped, accord the author a novelist's indulgence.

* page 258
MENU POUR LE BANQUET DE PRINCE HASSAD AU PONT DU GARD

Consommé glacé à la tortue
Gratin de crevettes roses en bouquet fait
Darne de saumon sauce Léda
Cailles aux pêches du Pont Romain
Médaillons de veau Sarah Bernhardt
Gigot d'agneau Grand Pétrarque
Aubergines en bohémienne
Champignons truffés Sautebrau
Salade Olympio
Plateau de fromages des douze Césars
Fruits rafraîchis des premières cueilles
Crêpes flambées à la façon de Madame Viala du Pont Romain
de Sommières
Café et Marc du Grand Daudet

❖

Blanc Aligoté 1927
Rosé de Pierre-feu
Morgon 1937
Champagne Mouton Rothschild
Quinze liqueurs

❖